They der

Volume Three

Mark John Maguire

Lightfast Publishing

ISBN 978-1-8384858-6-3

Lightfast Publishing

CONTENTS

1. The Riddle Of Caswell Bay: The Murder Of Mamie Stuart, 1919

In January 1920 Mamie Stuart's family in Sunderland were concerned. She had written to them on 12th November but in spite of being a punctilious correspondent with her family, they had not heard from her since. They supposed she was busy in the Christmas season, and they were relieved to receive a telegram on 24th December from her home in Swansea wishing them a Happy Christmas. They wrote to her in the New Year, but their letters were returned bearing the legend 'House closed.' This seemed odd because Mamie had only provided them with this address recently. They knew from letters she had previously sent to them that her marriage to her husband George was troubled - indeed she had expressed the intention of leaving him on more than one occasion - so it seemed possible that she may have left him. Their anxiety increased, however, when Mamie failed to contact them and her sister Edith wrote to her previous landlady, Mrs Hearn, at 28 Trafalgar Terrace in Swansea asking her if she had heard from Mamie: Mrs Hearn had not.

In March 1920 Swansea Police received a routine call

from the *Grosvenor Hotel*, Swansea, indicating that a portmanteau bag had been left at the hotel in December and had not subsequently been claimed. Upon opening the portmanteau, police found it contained shredded women's clothes, a pair of shoes and a piece of paper with a Sunderland address written on it. The address was that of James and Jane Stuart and on contacting them, police discovered that their daughter Mamie had been missing for three months and that the clothes and shoes belonged to her.

An inquiry was launched to find Mamie, and given the circumstances of her disappearance and the contents of her letters, police were anxious to locate her husband, George Shotton. They found George, but to their astonishment, they discovered he was living with a wife and child at nearby Caswell Bay!

When interviewed, George denied having been bigamously married to Mamie but admitted to knowing her for a time and living with her - but he said they had argued and she had left him. Following this he had left the trunk with her possessions in it at a hotel and had returned to his wife. He had not heard from her again.

Mamie Stuart was born Amy Stuart on the 24th November 1893 to James Stuart, a Master Mariner, and Jane his wife. She was a pretty, bright and vivacious girl with brown hair and blue-grey eyes. At the age of just 15 she left home to go on stage as a dancer and was a member of several touring dance troupes including the 'Three Dancing Glens' and the 'Magnets,' appearing in pantomime throughout the provinces in the years leading up to and during the first World War. Mamie appears to have been a confident, flirtatious girl, always fashionably attired - dressed to attract attention and liked being the centre of it - and she had had a number of lovers. It was on a visit home to Sunderland in July 1917 that she met George Shotton. He was, he later said, surveying a Norwegian ship, the 'Margot,' when he encountered Mamie walking with a friend near the docks and what he termed 'misconduct' occurred between them. She was then 24 years old and he was a 37 year old well-to-do Marine Surveyor from Cardiff, with offices in Mount Stuart Square, in Cardiff's thriving maritime quarter. George was a surveyor of ships, as his father had been before him, and this work inevitably took him to many other major ports throughout Britain - it made him prosperous too. He was a personable and charming man, who took care of his appearance and was described by those who knew him as a 'dandy' and in spite of the fact that he was married, he possessed a keen interest in women.

Besides a mutual attraction, George had something else in common with Mamie as he too hailed from the Sunderland area, his father having moved to South Wales with his family some years before to take advantage of the port's business opportunities. George had met May Leader, whose father owned the *Six Bells Inn* in Newport's St Woolos area, probably whilst staying there on a visit to the port in 1905. They married on 7th September 1905 and afterwards moved to Penarth, a pleasant suburb of Cardiff from which George could easily commute to his offices in the nearby Bay area. They had a child, were quite affluent, and George's business thrived and took him to many ports around Britain which often necessitated him staying away from home.

Then in 1917 he met Mamie Stuart. What had

doubtless begun in the maritime quarters of Sunderland as a dalliance, of which George had probably had many, soon became something more. There is no doubt that George became smitten with Mamie and this was, for a time at least, fully reciprocated by her. On the face of it he must have seemed a good catch to Mamie, who had been on the stage for almost a decade with limited success - hers was a precarious existence. Of course, he was married and in spite of his claims that Mamie had always known this, it is quite clear that she had no idea at all. They married on 25th March 1918 in the Registry office in South Shields, spent a few days in London and from this time on lived in a number of places - often in hotels in Liverpool, Bristol and other places George travelled to with his work. His life was complicated. He was often absent from Mamie due to the requirements of his work and it is apparent that he was attempting to divide his time between his two households.

In February 1919 George and Mamie moved to a lodging with a Mrs Hearn at 28 Trafalgar Terrace, Swansea - another place where George's work often took him. Coincidentally, George moved his wife and son from Penarth to 'Gray House' in Caswell Bay - approximately three miles from Swansea. Here he would spend three or four days each week, whilst being required by 'work' to be elsewhere on the other days. There must have been a great deal of stress on George Shotton during this period of double deception: he had two wives, maintained two homes and had a child who was then three years old - he was living a lie that if discovered would incur the penalty of the law.

And as time passed there was another source of stress for him: Mamie was a young woman of a flighty disposition - she enjoyed the attention of men. In those frequent and necessary absences of his, she sought diversions in the company of other men. She went out with her landlady, and friend, Mrs Hearn. It seems to have rankled with Mrs Hearn because she said later that she had on more than one occasion told Mamie she would not go out with her because she attracted so many men. Mamie was practised in the art of performing for men; she knew very well how to send out the right signals - and she did. It was only a matter of time before such behaviour would lead to further relations with some of them. There were dalliances, and what George knew of these is unclear, but he certainly had suspicions and knowledge of at least one letter she had received from a Canadian officer.

The relationship between Mamie and George inevitably deteriorated; it became strained, quarrelsome, marked by jealousy - and occasionally violent. He accused her of encouraging the attentions of officers. The strain on Shotton was considerable - he had no intention of leaving his wife and child and seems to have been unable to give up Mamie either. It was a conundrum.

For her part, Mamie Stuart seems to have been puzzled by Shotton's behaviour; he was hot and cold with her, often acted bizarrely: he wanted her and he didn't; he was sometimes intense, at other times distant, disinterested. She wrote to her parents describing him as 'odd.' Of course, his behaviour was one of a man caught in an impossible situation: a situation which could not go on forever. It was a fool's paradise he inhabited - there could be no happy ever after.

Mamie wrote to her parents in 1919 saying she was going to leave him; she said he had hit her across the head, left her with bruised arms; he had accused her of stealing £22 from him and threatened to call the police. She also wrote to her sister expressing her fears of her husband and begging her family to inquire of Mrs Hearn if she should disappear...

In July 1919 they split up. George left Trafalgar Terrace on 19th July and Mamie returned to Sunderland on the 22nd July. But he wrote to her and they maintained a correspondence that ultimately led to their reconciliation. He visited her in Sunderland in September 1919, they were reconciled and he returned to Swansea to find them new accommodation. He took a residence called *Bonavista* in Newton, Caswell Bay, near to the family home he had recently taken there. Perhaps he felt that keeping the two homes close together would ease the burden of his commuting between them. Obviously, he was still caught in a double deception of being married to two women. When Mamie returned to Swansea on 5th November 1919, it was the last time she was seen by her family.

The investigation into the disappearance of Mamie Stuart was a complex one; Mamie and George, separately and together, had been associated with many parts of Britain, and Swansea police found it difficult to conduct their inquiries. In June 1920 they called in the assistance of Scotland Yard for this, and Detective Inspector William Draper was dispatched to take charge of the inquiries. He spoke to her friends and acquaintances, to Mrs Hearn, to Shotton and his associates - and an extensive search was launched to find Mamie. A description of her was issued and widely circulated in the press - even in Canada, where Draper believed she might have travelled with a Canadian officer, a paymaster in the army, with whom she had been involved. This latter business muddied the waters somewhat with press and public alike; it led to equivocation in the matter of whether Mamie was alive or not. It was believed that she had been involved with a farmer in the area too, and one letter was addressed to 'My dearest Dulbert.' Sightings around Britain - even as far away as Ireland - at this early stage were reported. Letters were received, and published in newspapers, by people who claimed to know Mamie and to know where she was. But nothing came of these claims. The one consistent suspect was George Shotton.

Inspector Draper established that Mamie had travelled to Swansea on 5th November 1919, with the intention of meeting Shotton at the house he had taken for them at Caswell Bay. She was known to have arrived in Swansea because her ticket had been processed by Great Western Railways. Appeals for information concerning a man driving her from Swansea station on the evening of 5th November produced nothing of significance. George Shotton drove a yellow car and it was hoped that this might have been noticed - but unfortunately it wasn't. Although Mamie had sent a letter home on 12th November, apparently from the house at Newton, in Caswell, no-one had seen her there. It could not be positively proven by any means that she had been at the house, although it seemed fairly certain that she had been there. Her friend, Mrs Hearn, had neither seen nor heard from her during the period after she had returned to Swansea, so it was assumed her disappearance had occurred soon after her return, but after 12th November when she had sent the letter: there was, however, no evidence she had ever left Swansea after 12th November. Mamie was an avid letter-writer and her family became convinced that she was dead. They did not believe that she would not contact them if she was able to do so.

Given the state of the relationship between 'husband' and 'wife,' Mamie's determination to leave Shotton and the fact that Shotton was the last person known (by his own statement) to have seen Mamie; that she feared him, intended to leave him and that George Shotton had married her bigamously, it was becoming increasingly clear that Mamie was dead and that the chief suspect in causing her death was her husband - George Shotton. For his part George Shotton said he had last seen her on 5th or 6th December in Oxford Street in Swansea, the two had argued and it was the last he had seen or heard of her. He had subsequently returned to his wife and child.

This presented police with a problem: the evidence pointed towards Mamie being dead, and to George Shotton being responsible for this, but without a body it was considered impossible to charge him. English law in this respect was established by the *Campden Wonder* case in 1660: a local man, Will Harrison, disappeared and following an investigation it was determined that a woman and her two sons had murdered him. They were tried for this and hanged - then two years later, Will Harrison turned up alive and well with a hazy story concerning his whereabouts. From this time on, the principle was established in English law that if a body could not be found, there could be no certainty that the person was dead - still less, that they had been murdered. This precedent, with rare exceptions, held fast in English Law up until the 1950s, when the Lord Chief Justice Goddard remarked that things had changed considerably since the *Campden Wonder*. In 1919 there would be little prospect of such a precedent being overturned: provided that no body was found, the first stages in the legal process of bringing a murder charge to bear could not be progressed. Even with a body the evidence would be entirely circumstantial: Mamie intended to visit George Shotton, she had travelled to see him; it seems certain that she was at the house in Caswell Bay - but it could not be proved that she was there after 12th November and it could not be disproved that Shotton had not seen her for the last time on 5th or 6th of December. He admitted to leaving the portmanteau at the hotel but said he had left it there because he had found it after she had left the house. He admitted to living with Mamie but not to marrying her. There really was little beyond a reasonable suspicion that George Shotton had murdered Mamie Stuart some time in November or December 1919.

All searches in the Caswell Bay area and of the garden and house *Bonavista*, coming to nothing, the police could not begin to construct a case for submission to the Crown Prosecutor; the only evidence on which they could proceed against him was that of bigamy. Shotton was therefore arrested by Detective Sergeant Arthur Eynon and Inspector Fox as he arrived at Swansea station on 21st May 1920.

But even here, there were difficulties, because a charge of bigamy was almost always instigated by the aggrieved spouse: the proof that bigamy had occurred therefore arose from such a claim by a wife who had believed herself to be married and whose evidence concerning its details would form a major part of the prosecution case. In the case of Mamie Stuart the prosecution had to proceed in the absence of the wife - but the police and prosecution determined that there was sufficient evidence that such a marriage ceremony had taken place to warrant the matter being pursued as a criminal prosecution.

George Shotton was thus charged with bigamously marrying Mamie Stuart on 25th March 1918 at South Shields. He reserved his defence throughout until the trial took place in Swansea on 27th July 1920, saying only that he had a 'complete answer to this.' He was released on bail pending his trial and would go no further than this. The trial began on 27th July 1920 before Justice Avory.

The prosecution case was that George Shotton had bigamously married Mamie Stuart on 25th March 1918, and that there was proof that he was already married at the time to May Leader, who he had married in 1905. The defence countered that George Shotton had lived with Mamie Stuart, but that she had always known him to be married, that she had gone through a marriage ceremony with another man on the 25th March 1918 who was impersonating George Shotton 'to allay her parents' concerns.' They produced letters from Mamie which, they said, demonstrated that she was capable of deceiving her parents. Sir Edward Marley Samson for the defence said Mamie was 'thoroughly immoral and worthless in regard to her relationships with men,' but Sir Ellis Griffith for the Crown said the prisoner's story was 'improbable and incredible.'

There was, however, a wealth of evidence against George:

1. The marriage certificate to his first - his only - wife, was proved in court by the appearance of the Registrar at St Woolos, Newport, the production of the marriage certificate and then a witness in the form of his brother-in-law to confirm the matter.

2. The second marriage certificate was subject to handwriting examination, which suggested he had tried to disguise his handwriting but that it was indeed his.
3. Although witnesses at the marriage in the Registry Office in South Shields were unable to confirm the identity of the groom, various witnesses were called to prove that George Shotton was in South Shields on 25th March, 1918, that he and Mamie Stuart had spent the night of their 'wedding' at the *Golden Lion Hotel* in South Shields and that numerous letters read in court alluded to Mamie as 'My darling wife,' 'my sweet little wife,' and ended 'your loving husband George' etc. He had also introduced himself to her friends and family and other witnesses as her husband and she had shown every indication in her conduct and all transactions that she believed herself to be Mrs Mamie Shotton.

In spite of all this, George seemed confident that he would succeed in persuading the jury that he had not married Mamie and it was reported that he was nonchalantly reading a newspaper on the public benches during an interval in proceedings. But his confidence was misplaced: the jury took little more than five minutes to find him guilty of bigamy. The judge admonished him and indicated that his 'wicked perjury' in court had induced him to hand down a more severe sentence than he would otherwise have done - that of 18 months imprisonment with hard labour at Swansea Prison.

The case of Mamie Stuart thus came to an end. An unsatisfying end for her family and friends. The search for her body was ended and detectives redeployed on other investigations.

But the dead do not always lie easily. In the following years there were sightings of Mamie in India, in South

Africa, Australia and many other places. Some of these sightings led to the case being re-examined and efforts made to establish whether such sightings were genuine - but none of them amounted to anything. They returned her and her case fleetingly to the public's attention, resulting in a brief resume of the case and the circumstances of her disappearance, but little more. A spiritualist stated that Mamie had been buried beneath a tiled floor, fully clothed, and this attracted a great deal of press coverage, but no body was found. Workmen digging in the garden of *Bonavista* some years after her disappearance discovered a woman's shoe, and although this caused a resurgence of interest in the case, the police declined to reopen the investigation: even if the shoe could be linked to Mamie there was little it could add to the matter of her disappearance. Articles written in the 1940s and 1950s on the Mamie Stuart case occasionally appeared focusing on the mystery of 'whatever happened to Mamie Stuart?' There was a consensus in these that she had died, but there was a view that it was a mystery that would never be resolved. But that view was wrong.

One autumn day, 42 years after Mamie had caught a train to Swansea, on Sunday 5th November 1961, three friends - John Gurke, Colin Lloyd MacNamara and Graham Jones - went potholing in Caswell Bay. The area is a rich repository of caves and old abandoned lead mine shafts which offer many opportunities for potholers to explore. It was down a narrow air shaft of such a lead mine in Brandy Cove, Caswell Bay, that the three young men lowered themselves that morning. Some 50 feet down they discovered what appeared to be a tunnel which had been blocked off by stones and rubble. Hoping to find the main tunnel to the mine, they removed the rubble and found a large flat rock the size of a paving stone, which appeared to have been deliberately placed on its edge across the entrance to the tunnel. They removed the stone and found further rubble and soil, under which there was a skull and some bones. The three men took their find to the local police. Police returned to the site of the shaft and using ropes and the slimmest of their officers, they were able to inspect the site, to remove samples of soil, the remaining bones, and fragments of cloth and sacking. A swatch of brown hair attached to a 1920s style hair comb and two rings were amongst the other finds at the site.

Forensic tests quickly revealed that the bones belonged to a woman approximately five feet three inches in height, that they had been sawn through in several places before being deposited in the mineshaft and that the bones had lain in the shaft for some 40 years. Mamie Stuart had disappeared 42 years ago that month. The file on her disappearance was now reopened.

While detailed forensic tests were carried out on the skeleton, which was almost complete, police began to try to trace the relatives and friends of Mamie Stuart. Most of her contemporary relatives were now dead; her father had died soon after the trial of Shotton in 1921 and her mother in 1945, but a woman whom she had known in Bristol and who had once admired her engagement ring was found: she was sure it was Mamie's. The jawbone of the skull had even set teeth with a single peculiarity: one upper tooth, next to the eye tooth on the right-hand side was missing - as Mamie's had been... The search for Mamie Stuart was over. For the first time, and after 42 years, this was now a murder inquiry. The search for George Shotton began.

The investigation was led by Chief Inspector Graham Williams of Glamorgan CID. As there were no organs intact on which to conduct a post-mortem the coroner had to apply to the Home Secretary to conduct an inquest due to the unusual circumstances. The Home Secretary granted permission for this on the basis that there was other evidence to confirm identity, and an inquest was therefore justified.

An inquest was duly scheduled to be held at Gowerton in West Wales under the Gower Coroner Mr D R James; 21 witnesses were called to give evidence and a jury of seven men were appointed to consider the matter. The press meanwhile had dusted off their old coverage from back copies of their newspapers and there was renewed interest in the disappearance of Mamie and in the whereabouts of George Shotton. He was thought by some to have left the country - and a woman, Mrs Ince of Newport, who was a close friend of the first Mrs Shotton, said that she knew that he had died 10 years ago. Then on the 30th November 1961, it was announced by police to a chorus of disappointment, that George Shotton had died three years earlier, in 1958.

The Inquest was opened on 7th December, 1961. The bones and skull lay on the table before the coroner and jury. The coroner spoke to the circumstances of the inquiry and to the procedural formalities relating to identification and called the witnesses.

The circumstances of the discovery of the bones were given by the three men who had found them; a Detective Constable Ken Noakes described how he had enlarged an old photograph of Mamie Stuart and matched it to the skull in terms of its features and the evenness of teeth - and noted the same single missing tooth on the upper left jaw. He said that it made it likely that the skull was that of Mamie Stuart, and the Home Office pathologist Dr W R Lester James confirmed that this was his opinion also. The engagement ring was identified by Mrs Elsie May Evans, now 62, who had known Mamie at Bristol in 1918 as being that which Mamie had shown her decades earlier. All the other features of the skeleton suggested that the skeleton was that of Mamie Stuart. However, Dr James said there was no bullet, knife or other damage to the skeleton to allow the cause of death to be determined.

Her identity settled, the court heard evidence of the letters Mamie had written to her family and had received from George Shotton which alluded to her fear of him, her determination to leave him and the quarrelsome nature of their relationship. These were read out by Inspector Williams.

One letter from George, written to Mamie at Sunderland, during the months of the separation between July 22nd and 5th November, 1919, read:

'You ask to be free. Are you not more free than any other girl? You wander to and fro at your own sweet will, with no-one to question you or prohibit you... I do not quite understand in what manner I can do more... I have no intention of doing such awful things as you suggest. I can only imagine you mean me to go on a wrong path so that you can divorce me...'

Although the letter to which he responds is unseen, this reply suggests that Mamie was seeking a divorce and that she had accused him of threatening her with harm in some way. In another letter to her mother, written in early 1919, she wrote:

'He has been ill-using me in Liverpool and I will be leaving him. The man is not all there.'

The court was told that George Shotton was now dead, had been jailed for bigamy in 1920 but that the absence of Mamie's body had been an obstacle to pursuing a murder inquiry. There was one startling piece of evidence given at the inquest, which deserves mention: an 83 year old retired postman, William Symons, who had been the Caswell Bay postman in 1919, gave evidence that he 'was the last person to see Mamie alive' and that he had come across Shotton in December 1919 putting a heavy sack into his car and offered to help him: 'No! No! No! Oh God!' said George, 'I thought you were the police!' He then drove off in the direction of Brandy Cove.

This story seems to be improbable in the extreme. William Symons claimed that he had not told police of this at the time because he had not thought it relevant. Yet the newspapers were filled with the matter of Mamie's disappearance at this time; police were excavating her garden and scouring the rocks and caves of Caswell Bay - and the suspicions against George Shotton were rife in the press and in the community. It is absurd to imagine that Symons could not have understood the importance of his evidence at the time - or to believe that George Shotton would have been so incautiously stupid as to comment 'Oh God! I thought you were the police!' It is worth remarking on Symons' evidence only in that it is a curious fact that in so many murders an elderly person comes forward decades after the event to claim someone confessed to them or that they witnessed some indisputable proof of guilt. It is simply a curiosity of human nature.

The jury considered the matter and gave its verdict that the bones were those of Mamie Stuart, that she had died between 12th November and 6th December 1919 -

and that she had been killed by George Shotton.

It was a consolation of sorts, that the body of Mamie Stuart had been recovered from the foot of a lead mine shaft on the coast of West Wales; that her end had been settled and the man who was surely responsible for her murder was named, albeit posthumously, as her killer. It gave an assurance, perhaps, to those of her family who remained, that she had not merely disappeared without trace; that she had not abandoned her friends and family or disregarded those duties she owed them. It did something else important also: it assigned the responsibility for her death to its proper quarter, to the man who had bigamously married her and lived with her under false pretences for two years, who had abused her and who had finally taken her life.

It is unsatisfactory to human beings, to society and particularly to those closest to the victim, to see a murderer get away with their crime. Though we know at some level that holding the perpetrator of such a crime to account does not resurrect the victim, that it hardly assuages the grief of those who feel the victim's loss - nevertheless there is a perfunctory satisfaction that a murderer has been brought to justice, by the machinery of the society to which they belong.

There are always other candidates to fill the role of murderer in such cases. In the case of a woman like Mamie Stuart, a flirtatious woman, known as a 'good-time girl,' whose deceits were probably many, there will always be other lovers who may be shoe-horned into the role of her killer. Mamie had an extensive retinue of former lovers on which it is possible to draw. Whilst apparently married to George Shotton she was involved with a Canadian Paymaster, a farmer, and there were doubtless others. In the 1950s a journalist, Bernard O'Donnell, wrote of his being 'one of the last people to see Mamie Stuart alive in Cardiff when she visited a solicitor there seeking a divorce.' He said she had learned here that her husband was already married. The story is dubious at best, and none of this casts doubt on the guilt of George Shotton.

There is no doubt that Shotton killed Mamie Stuart, probably in a fit of jealous rage soon after the 12th November, 1919. He will never be convicted of it and there will always be some who prefer a more convoluted solution to the murder, who may look for one of her elusive lovers, but the evidence is compelling: the circumstances of her life with George Shotton, his bigamy, her relationship with him, the violent nature of their relationship, the mounting antagonism which such toxic relations naturally accrue; the timing of her disappearance, and the place in which she was found - not half a mile from the house at Caswell Bay, down a mineshaft which only a local resident would be sufficiently familiar with - all point to George Shotton's guilt. His claim to have seen her in Oxford Street in Swansea (some three miles away) on 5th or 6th December is exposed as a lie: there would be no reasonable explanation why, if this was so, she would have returned or have been returned by an unknown killer to the place where she was last known to be, if she had already left Shotton. It was a necessary lie to promote the idea that she was still alive on 5th December, and that she had left him and may have absconded with a lover - possibly to Canada.

And Mamie was sufficiently flighty to give the police occasion to consider this initially: Mamie associated with many men; she was not a woman who would be considered, by the yardstick of her time, as being a moral one. She was clearly deceitful, not quite trusted by her friends - one demanded to see her marriage certificate because she thought Mamie capable of lying on such a matter. She was headstrong, independent and she had taken care of herself since she was 15. George Shotton was driven by a jealous passion which by turns shunned and rejected her yet could not quite relinquish her. He moved her to the house in Caswell Bay in November 1919 because he wished to isolate her from the temptations of Trafalgar Terrace in Swansea, from her friends and from demobbed officers seeking transient affairs with a certain kind of woman. Caswell Bay fulfilled this need - but not for her. She was not a woman to be kept in a gilded cage.

The rows continued and so did the threats; what happened sometime after 12th November is unlikely to be discovered, but there must have been an argument - a violent one. Perhaps she finally decided to walk out on him, perhaps reiterating what she had said in one of her letters - that she would go to one who was capable of looking after her. It would have been the final straw for Shotton, whose jealousy was now the dominant emotion governing his relationship with her. Whether she had plans to go to someone else or simply said so as one of the weapons she employed against him is not known - but it is a likely course which the argument between them would take, because arguments between those who are in dying relationships follow a path which is well-trodden, rehearsed many times over, involving the same repetition of the same devices in an ever spiralling descent to the same outcome: either an abrupt severance of the relationship, or a physical end to it. It was the latter outcome, inevitably, which had overtaken George: he had attacked her in the white fury of the moment - perhaps by suffocation, because apart from the saw marks there were no obvious signs of violence to her skeleton. Bruises to flesh leave no tell-tale, but strangulation, blunt force trauma and stabbing almost certainly would. And, of course, poisoning is a weapon of premeditation, rather than one of passion - and this was surely a crime of passion.

When he had killed Mamie, George had the natural relief that the matter had reached its inevitable consequence - but also the shock and fear which accompanies such an act: his own well-being, his very survival was now at stake. He had the advantage that no-one appeared to be aware of Mamie's presence at the Caswell Bay house - there was no evidence that she had been there after 12th November. That gave him time because her disappearance was not in imminent danger of discovery, which might force his hand precipitately and force him into some rash miscalculation - like burying her in the garden. He had time to think of a suitable place for the body: yet still there was a measure of urgency because there was a body in his house, whose discovery would certainly send him to the gallows. He cannot remove the body without dismembering it and this he does, using a saw - he is not a surgeon and he does this inefficiently; the forensic pathologist commented on this at the inquest 40 years later: he has made hard work of the job, cutting through the upper arms and upper thighs to remove the four limbs, removing the head and also cutting the trunk in two - into a total of six or seven parts. There are other abrasions for which the saw is responsible which indicates to the forensic expert that

Mamie had been sawn into parts while the flesh was still on the bones. It must have been a gruesome business and was probably undertaken in the bathroom as this is the commonest place in which such a messy job is usually undertaken.

After he is done, Shotton wraps her in fabric, parts of her clothing and sacking, and he resolves that the best place to dispose of these parts is in one of the many potholes which litter the coast in West Wales. He is acquainted with these from his walks along the clifftop; he knows their remoteness, their inaccessibility. He must also know that there is a risk, because of the proximity to the house.

But he has little choice: the pressure on him to remove the body from the house is enormous - he cannot rest until he has removed it from there - dissociated it from its immediate and natural connection to himself. Yet at the same time the further he travels with the body, the greater the risk to himself. A convergence of these factors lead him to the airhole of a narrow mineshaft. He is a slightly built man; the shaft he chooses is 18 inches across - not many men could negotiate an entry to such a confined space. It is a hazardous trip down 50 feet, not at all for the faint hearted - but then nor is murder. He descended to the bottom of the mineshaft vent and discovered a tunnel at its foot leading to the main mining tunnels. It is here he chooses what he hopes will be Mamie Stuart's last resting place. He must have made at least two journeys down the shaft - one by way of reconnaissance to test its suitability, and another to deposit the body parts there. Of course, it is quite impossible that he should carry all his grisly packages down the shaft at the same time, and the more visits he makes to the shaft, the greater the risk that he may be seen - or that he may leave a visible trail for others to notice, or even follow. It is likely therefore that on his second visit he dropped the packages down the shaft and then followed them, using only an electric flashlight as his guide. At the foot of the shaft he burrowed into the tunnel, clearing away debris, and burying the packages as best he could. Then he covered them with debris, placed a large stone slab across the entrance and blocked up the approach with further debris.

It must have been a relief to him to dispose of the body, but he couldn't rest. He knew that one day someone would come knocking on his door. He delayed the inevitable outcome by sending a telegram from Newton Post Office on 24th December to her family. It was perfunctory but would serve the purpose of effecting a delay to their inquiries. But every time a car drew up or he heard the sound of footsteps in his drive, his heart must have skipped a beat - skipped a beat as it had when he had first seen Mamie in the company of a friend on Sunderland docks during the summer of 1917. The same but different. His world would never be the same again. In some ways he would always be wedded to Mamie - he would never be free from her. As the years passed she must have loomed in his waking moments and in his dreams. He had discovered the burden that all murderers discover: their inability to free themselves of the human imagination: the imagination of the discovery of a corpse, of the dreaded headline alerting them to this, that of apprehension, of capture; the imagination that sometimes takes them 50 feet down a disused lead mine and wonders at the state of decomposition of a woman once loved...

There was a knock on George Shotton's door, but it was not for murder, no body had been found: it related to her disappearance. But as the press focused on the mystery and the police interrogated him and his wife left him, he must have sat in quiet terror of the discovery of the secret he knew to lie in Caswell Bay. When he was finally arrested at Swansea station, his first question was: 'Have you found Mamie?' This was not an innocent deflection of guilt as detectives suspected, it was rather the terror of a man who lived day and night with this fear: a fear that police, who were conducting searches of Caswell Bay, might have discovered her. They hadn't - they were arresting him for bigamy - and strangely that must have been a huge relief.

George Shotton emerged from Swansea prison in the summer of 1922. He was 42 years old. His business as a marine surveyor was finished and prison had taken its toll. His wife had divorced him and remarried to a John C Jones in 1927. His friends and colleagues shunned him. Shotton went to live with his parents at Tintern, where Wordsworth once found peace and inspiration sitting above the 12th Century Cistercian Abbey. There is a peacefulness and tranquillity at Tintern which may have given Shotton succour too, but it was not to last. He seemed unable to settle or to find useful employment in the years that followed. After his father's death in 1929, his mother moved to Surrey and Shotton drifted. He was living in Balham, South London, for a time and when his mother died in 1936, the husband of his sister Gladys, who was a bank manager in Fareham, Hampshire, was granted executor of her estate. It seems that she and two other sisters did rather better from the settlement than Shotton and it led to rancour between brother and sister.

On 23rd May 1938 he travelled to Fareham and confronted his sister. She was afraid of him, of his temper and refused to allow him to enter the house - whereupon he produced a revolver and pointed it at her. He forced her into the house, twisted her arm behind her back and forced her up the stairs. He said he was going to kill her husband, then her and then himself. In the bedroom he held her hostage for two hours, awaiting the arrival home of her husband. He inquired how she would like to die? And warned her that if her husband returned and she called out to him he would 'put a bullet in her' immediately. At around 6 pm her son came home and she spoke in a loud voice to attract his attention. The son entered the room and Shotton ordered him to sit down. 'I'd never have known you!' he said to him, 'Sit down, son.' Gladys asked for a glass of water and when he allowed this she threw it in his face and the three embarked on a vicious struggle on the bed, in a vain attempt to wrest the gun from Shotton. At length Gladys ran from the room and George followed her, but tripped on a loose mat at the foot of the stairs. She and her son Philip went to a neighbour's house and George apparently returned to Balham.

He was arrested some days later, denied that he had threatened her with a revolver and said he had only threatened to kill himself. On 28th July 1938, at the Portsmouth Quarter sessions, he was tried for assault. He was described as a consulting engineer of 'no fixed address' and was sentenced to 12 months imprisonment with hard labour. At his trial a police constable said that he had a previous conviction against him 'for bigamy.' This was widely reported in newspapers at the time, but no-one seemed to make the connection between the case and that concerning Mamie Stuart that had caused such a furore 18 years earlier.

After his release in 1939 Shotton lived in Ledbury in Herefordshire for a time and then in the Bristol area where he had once lived with Mamie Stuart. He was in his late 60s now; he never returned to Caswell Bay. He eventually lived in a care home in Bristol and in the spring of 1958 he had a stroke, was taken to Southmead Hospital in Bristol, where he died on 30th April 1958. He was 77 years old.

*

After the inquest and its verdict upon the death of Mamie Stuart at the hands of the man she believed to be her husband, the case was finally closed - or almost.

Mamie's closest relations were no longer alive, no-one troubled or thought to claim her remains and her bones were forgotten, believed lost. Then in 2020, a great niece of Mamie, Susie Oldhall, studying her family history and becoming engrossed in the sad story of Mamie Stuart, began a search for her great aunt's remains. She found them, locked in a cupboard in Cardiff Forensic Laboratory. Dr Stephen Leadbetter, the Senior Forensic Pathologist at the laboratory travelled to her home in the Midlands and the remains of Mamie Stuart, who had died believing she was Mamie Shotton, were finally buried in Bishopwearmouth Cemetery in Sunderland, besides those of her parents, a century after she had died.

Mamie Stuart.

George Shotton.

Above: *Bonavista* - the house at Caswell Bay.

George and Mamie - newly weds, or so she thought.

Above: Mamie's father.

Above: The three potholers who discovered Mamie's remains.

2. The Madness Of Ronald True, 1922

A little after 9 o'clock on the morning of 6th March 1922, Emily Steel arrived to do her daily cleaning job at 13a Finborough Road in Earl's Court, London. When she arrived and let herself in she noticed a man's coat and scarf lay on the table in the sitting room. This was not a surprise to her since her mistress, Olive Young, was a 25-year-old prostitute whose real name was Gertrude Yates and there were often clients still at the flat when she called in the morning. She went into the kitchen and made herself some breakfast and then proceeded to tidy the sitting room. A man emerged from the direction of the bedroom and she recognised him as being an army major who had stayed overnight previously. He smiled and said to her:

'Don't disturb Miss Young. We were late last night, and she is in a deep sleep. I'll send a car round for her at midday.'

She liked the Major - he was an affable gentleman and she helped him on with his coat and he gave her a half crown saying it was a tip for fetching a taxi for him at his last visit. He left the flat and she saw him hail a taxi cab at the corner of Finborough Road. It was now approximately 9.45 am. A few minutes afterwards

Emily Steel knocked on her mistress's bedroom door and found there was a crack in the glass panel of the door. She entered and called Miss Young and, obtaining no response, went to draw the curtains. She pulled back the eiderdown bed cover and found there were two pillows placed end to end, to give the appearance that there was someone in the bed. The pillows were covered in blood and there was a rolling pin in the bed, which also had blood on it. She saw there were two cups, one of which lay broken on the floor, and the room had clearly been searched as there were drawers still open. She went to a cupboard where Olive Young kept her jewellery and found the jewellery box there, empty. Other small amounts of money, which Olive kept to pay the gas meter and milk bill were missing too. Now very alarmed she went swiftly to the bathroom and, opening the door, she found in the narrow space between the wall and the bath Gertrude Yates, aka Olive Young, lying dead on the bathroom floor.

She rushed out to fetch the landlady, returning with her a few minutes later, and then called the local Chelsea Police Station. Inspector Rouse of 'B' Division got on his bicycle and cycled round there immediately, arriving at about 10.20 am. Soon afterwards, Detective Sergeant Pearce arrived and Dr William Stephen Lee, the divisional police surgeon. He pronounced Olive Young to be dead, and he made arrangements to conduct a post-mortem. Police found that there was blood spattered on the head of the bedstead, also on the wall, over much of the bed and even on the ceiling - in fact most parts of the room and its furnishings had signs of blood spattered on them. There was also a trail of blood leading from the bedroom to the bathroom, where presumably, Olive Young had been dragged by her assailant. There was blood near the bathroom door handle and a violet dressing gown on the floor. The body of Olive was naked apart from a pyjama jacket over one shoulder.

Dr Lee found the body had a temperature of 95 degrees Fahrenheit and, based on the assumption that the normal human body temperature is 98.4 degrees Fahrenheit, he estimated that her time of death was between three and four hours previously. That meant she had died between 7.30 am and 8.30 am that morning.

A post-mortem revealed five major wounds favouring the right side of the head, as if she had been lying on her left side when struck. The broken cup on the floor nearby on that side of the bed suggested that she had been drinking tea, unaware, when she had been attacked. The nature of the wounds and the fact that the rolling pin was found in the bed with blood on it, made it the likely weapon. All five blows had extended down to the bone and would likely have resulted in her death - although in fact they did not. She had died of strangulation. The cord of her dressing gown was found tied very tightly round her neck and a piece of Turkish towelling had been forced down her throat all the way to her larynx, with great violence. There was no sign of a struggle and no other marks which might suggest violence against her apart from her obvious neck, throat and head injuries.

Detective Chief Inspector Brown was on the scene by 11 am and Inspector Albert Burton at 1 pm. They made a careful inspection of the scene: an unopened Daily Mirror lay at the foot of the bed. The maid, Emily Steel, told police of the man who had been at the flat when she had arrived and who had told her not to disturb Olive Young. She said she believed his name was Major True. Police also found a visiting card on the table in the sitting room. It read:

Major Ronald True,
69 South Audley Street
London W1

Inquiries quickly resulted in an ex-Chief Inspector Stockley of Scotland Yard informing them that the family of Ronald True had been trying to locate him for some weeks and he had been engaged as a private investigator to find him. He gave them some known contacts of True and also warned them that True carried a loaded automatic pistol... An extensive and urgent manhunt across London began.

Detectives were able to find the taxi driver who had picked up Ronald True at the corner of Finborough Road. He said he had driven him to *Horne's Tailors* and been asked to wait for him there. He had then taken True to a barbershop for a shave and here he had been paid off. A salesman at *Horne's Mens Outfitters*, James Milne, told detectives that True had bought a new suit and had changed into it in the shop. He had been wearing a bloodstained suit and had told Milne that he had had a flying accident coming back from France that morning and been injured. He was limping at the time and they had packed his old suit up for him and he took it with him. It seems he had left the package with the bloodstained suit in it at the barbershop.

A little while after this, police learned that a driver from a motor garage in Belgrave Square, in Knightsbridge, Luigi Giuseppe Mazzola, had collected True and also a man called Major Armstrong and driven them to Croydon and a number of other places during the day. They had stopped to buy a late edition newspaper but True had tossed it aside having only glanced at the front page. In Mazzola's car detectives found a copy of the Star newspaper, with an account of the dramatic murder prominent on the front page. There were two coats in the car also - and in the pocket of one, a pearl necklace, a platinum and diamond wristwatch and two gold brooches were found. By now it was the evening of the day of the murder. Mazzola told Inspector Burton he had just driven True and his companion, Armstrong, to *Hammersmith Palace of Varieties* in west London. Inspector Burton ordered him to take himself and other detectives to this venue immediately.

Four police inspectors - Hawkins, Brown, Smith and Burton himself - arrived at the Hammersmith Palace at 9 o'clock that evening, greatly concerned that Ronald True was armed, and probably dangerous. But fortunately they discovered he and Armstrong were seated in a private box. With no-one in the theatre apparently aware of the drama being played off-stage, Burton went into the box and seized both of Ronald True's hands firmly and said to him:

'I am a police officer, come out with me.'

Holding both his hands securely until he was outside, the detectives quickly disarmed him of his automatic pistol. They found it was loaded with three bullets, filed across so that they would expand on impact, causing maximum damage. Ronald True was arrested and taken to Wilton Street Police Station and there Burton said:

'This morning I saw the dead body of Gertie Yates, otherwise Young, on the bathroom floor of 13a Finborough Road, Fulham Road, and from inquiries I find that a man answering your description stayed the night with her and left the flat at about 9.30 today.'

True said:

'I can explain how I got possession of it,' but he also said, 'I don't want to say anything tonight; it is no use putting up a defence until the proper time.'

A little later he told police he wished to make a statement. This he did:

'I think it only fair to myself to state that a man, whose description is as follows - age 31, 6 feet 2 inches, dressed in a dark suit, light grey overcoat, and bowler hat - was seen by myself and the chauffeur to run down from Finborough Road to Fulham Road between 10.20 and 10.30 pm on Sunday 5th March. Upon observing me he immediately went faster. This man knew for a fact that I had an appointment with him at Miss Yates' flat, one of several he had already broken. On my calling at the flat at 10.30 on 5th March I was met by Miss Yates, who informed me he was returning at 11 o'clock and requested me to do likewise. This I did and found both there. A stormy scene ensued. I left between 12.30 and 1 am on Monday 6th March. Miss Yates and the man were then in the midst of a violent argument and blows.'

On 7th March Ronald True appeared before magistrates and was remanded in custody and subsequently charged with the murder of Gertrude Yates, aka Olive Young.

Angus Ronald True was born on 17th June 1891 in Chorlton-on-Medlock, Lancashire, to a 16-year-old unwed Scots girl called Annabel Angus. Annabel's stepfather and mother were innkeepers in the town of Rothes, Banffshire in North East Scotland and in this strict, largely presbyterian community there was nothing for it but that Annabel should be sent away after becoming pregnant by a local boy, William Thomas True. She was sent south to Lancashire to a family where her pregnancy would be concealed from the community in Rothes. Ronald was acknowledged by the father on his birth certificate and bore his name, although there is no indication that he played any part in his life thereafter. He was brought up by his grandmother who ran the *Seaford Arms Hotel* until her death in 1899, whereupon he was sent to a governess in Dartford, Kent. By this time his mother, Annabel Angus, was in London. She was a tall attractive girl, spirited and ambitious and she soon met a well-to-do young officer, Lieutenant Henry Lethbridge Alexander, and in spite of the huge social gulf existing between them, they married in 1899. He was soon afterwards posted to India and the young couple travelled there, leaving Ronald at school and in the care of his aunt Grace during holidays.

Annabel returned from India around 1901 apparently due to ill health, and soon embarked on an affair with Arthur Reginald French - the son and heir to Lord de Freyne, scion of a wealthy aristocratic Irish catholic family. They set up home together posing as 'Mr and Mrs Alexander,' were discovered by her husband's family and it led to a scandalous court case in which the then Lieutenant French was cited for adultery. The scandal was such that Lord de Freyne disowned his son. The couple nevertheless married in 1902 - although he apparently deserted her during their honeymoon in Scotland. By 1905, the now Captain French, had resigned his commission and travelled to New York where he disappeared. He was not seen for some years, but in his absence, his substantial £2,500 per year allowance went to his wife Annabel French. That is about £300,000 in 2020 money. She was now a wealthy lady and from this time on Ronald wanted for nothing.

He boarded at Bedford School from 1903, a private school with many illustrious alumni, until he was 17 years of age. He was a poor student who seemed to have no particular aptitude for anything. There was clearly no profession suitable for the rather dim and wholly fatuous Ronald, so he was sent to New Zealand in 1908 to learn farming. It didn't work out and in 1910 he was sent as a farm pupil to a farmer in Yorkshire - but he fared no better here, and he was soon without employment again. In 1911 he was dispatched to Bolivia as something called a 'sub-prefect' and was again returned to England within a year. Next, he was sent to Canada and served briefly with the Northwest Mounted Police, and from here he went to Mexico and then Shanghai. He was unable to settle or make any kind of mark in these places but was sustained in his aimless wanderings by his mother, who gave him an allowance of £300 per year - approximately £40,000 in 2020 terms.

His mother, constantly hoping that her son would mature with the passing years and grow beyond the adolescent mind which seemed to have entrapped him, was to be consistently disappointed. In September 1913, the old Lord de Freyne died and his son Arthur was found - and Ronald True's mother became Lady Annabel de Freyne. The new Lord de Freyne returned to England in 1914 in time for the outbreak of WW1 and he and his younger brother were both killed on the same day on 9th May 1915 at the Battle of Aubers Bridge.

By 1914, Ronald True was back in England too, the First World War now providing a new purpose for him.

In spite of his apparent lack of aptitude for anything, and his obvious mental instability, Ronald was accepted into the newly formed Royal Flying Corps in 1915 as a 2nd lieutenant. His mother must have hoped this would be the making of him. It wasn't.

It was quickly clear that Ronald had no flying ability whatsoever and was lacking in the meanest of skills that might enable him to find a niche in the service. It took him three attempts to pass his flying certificate - whose accomplishment surprised many - but pass it he did in February 1916 and promptly had a set of flying wings made up which were three times regulation size. He was regarded by his brother officers as eccentric, childish and irresponsible - and as a terrible flyer. Soon afterwards he had a flying accident at Farnborough. It was quite a minor accident and he was back in the air within a few days, but a second flying accident at Gosport in March 1916 was serious enough to leave him unconscious in hospital for two days. A further accident resulted in injuries to his hip and leg which hospitalised him for several months - and led to his discharge from the RFC as being 'unfit for service.' By this time it was presumably quite clear to his superiors that such unfittedness was not merely limited to his physical incapacity but to his mental incapacity also.

It was also as a result of the injuries he sustained, which caused him great pain for a long period afterwards, that he became addicted to morphia. This was to be a battle he would struggle with in the ensuing years. He was left with a limp, too, which it has been conjectured, was due to infection with syphilis which he may have picked up on his travels - but it is more likely to have been the result of one of his accidents. Whatever its cause, the long-term pain he suffered certainly led to his increasing use of morphia and possibly to other drugs, which he is known to have injected as well as taken orally. This did nothing to help his mental instability, which was becoming more marked by this time.

Nevertheless, in the spring of 1917 Ronald was employed as a test pilot at Yeovil Government Control, but his shortcomings and general lack of aptitude brought this to an end, before, it might be said, it got off the ground.

Then in May 1917 he travelled to the United States, trading off his image as a broken and wounded British flying ace. It seems to have worked - and it no doubt gave him a latitude to his behaviour and obvious mental deficiencies which would otherwise have been denied him. He met a 17-year-old aspiring actress, Frances Beamer Roberts, in New York and they were quickly married. The status of this marriage is doubtful because he appears to have been married at least twice previously in America in the name of E T Terrell and Arthur Reginald French. He had also served a prison sentence at some time for forging money orders. Soon after this, the US entered the war and True was employed as a flying instructor at Mineola and then Houston, Texas. It was, unsurprisingly, short-lived. In June 1918 he returned to New York and thence within a month and via Cuba and Florida, to England with his wife.

In February 1919 he and his new wife were on the move again, this time to West Africa working as an Assistant Manager for the Tarkwa Mining Company, but in less than two months he had been suspended from this position due to his eccentricity. He was regarded as a fantasist, a teller of tall tales, as being distinctly odd. He challenged one man there to a billiards match and offered him 80 in a hundred shots, claiming to be an 'expert.' The man attempted to laugh it off, but True insisted. The man played him with no shots given and beat True easily. It was an example of this distorted view of reality and of himself he seemed to have. He told people he was going to set up a transport company supplying the Gold Coast and would fly planes across the Sahara and when the impossibility of this was pointed out to him, he said he knew of secret petrol supplies across the desert where he could refuel. The natives regarded him as mad and it was partly on account of the fact that he had become a laughing stock amongst them that he was dismissed.

By August he was back in England with his wife and now with a baby son called Ronald F True and for the next two years he was in and out of nursing homes being treated for morphine addiction. His increasingly erratic behaviour had persuaded his mother and aunt that there was no prospect of him holding any position of employment and from now on he lived off the £300 allowance his mother gave him each year. His existence was aimless, he spent months in nursing homes, and as the unstable structure which formed his world collapsed, his fantasies filled the space it had once occupied.

It should be said that in spite of the trail of negative impressions True left in his wake amongst the many people and places he was acquainted with, he seems to have been capable of occasionally creating a good impression - or at least an impression of a somewhat eccentric man, who possessed a jocular manner and fatuous good humour. But there was also a darker side to True.

The police investigation of the background of Ronald

True revealed a detailed and exhaustive past of minor misdemeanours, lies and petty crime. His tall tales, which some dismissed as the exaggeration of a raconteur, began to assume a distinctly sinister turn: he began to speak of a man impersonating him; a man who was running up debts on his behalf; a man who was calling himself Ronald True.

He had acquired the habit of stealing - generally meaningless thefts, from bookstores and shops - used stamps from a second-hand bookstore, for instance. To feed his morphia habit he would forge prescriptions, create scenes in pharmacies and beg or cajole pharmacists into giving him drugs. He bribed orderlies in the homes and hospitals he was an inpatient at: he became a cunning drug-addict. And at Portsmouth petty sessions in 1920 he was fined 20 shillings for forging a prescription.

By January 1922 his family was despairing of him. He frequently threatened to kill himself; he invented stories in which he was offered employment for large amounts of money and then when these were inevitably discovered to be fiction, he would go out on a drugs binge lasting several days, until his wife Frances would eventually locate him and the cycle of addiction clinics and rehab homes would begin again. His aunt, Grace Angus, said that he had written out a note which was purported to be from the Portuguese government, which offered him employment with a penny stamp on the top, which he had scribbled over. When she told him it was nonsense, he burst into tears and said he would go and kill himself. Those who knew True in 1921 were becoming convinced he was not odd: he was insane.

Then in January 1922, Ronald True disappeared. His

long-suffering wife and mother were unable to find him. He was not to be found at his usual haunts and all enquiries drew a blank. He told his wife in January he wanted nothing more to do with her. His wife and mother contacted Scotland Yard who were unable to help; he had committed no crime; but they put them in touch with an ex-Inspector Stockley, who now worked as a private investigator in London.

Ronald was living at hotels and leaving without paying his bills; he signed bad cheques, which his mother and wife were following in his trail paying off his debts and creditors. He seems to have known this, because he spoke darkly to his associates of a man who was impersonating him, who was running up debts that his mother was having to pay... He told people the man was armed and was going to kill him - but that he was going to kill this man first.

In February he met an out of work motor mechanic called Armstrong and the two became close friends. They were constantly in each other's company. Armstrong sold True his automatic pistol for £2 around 8th February which True told him he needed for self-protection when he sometimes had to ditch his plane in remote and hostile places when flying abroad. True thereafter filed the bullets down to make them lethal expanding bullets. He kept the pistol loaded and in his pocket all the time. He told people it was in preparation for the inevitable day when that meeting would take place with the man who was impersonating him - the other Ronald True.

He met a woman called Mrs Elizabeth Wilson, at a club where he was a member, whom he attached himself to. She was uncomfortable with him - afraid of his oddness, the revolver he showed her, his threats to shoot her and on one occasion telling her he was hoping to meet her husband so he could shoot him. He was joking, of course, but his black humour unsettled her. He told her of the other Ronald True who was going about London impersonating him and he said that they would have to meet one day, and then there would be a 'How d'ye do.' She was sufficiently alarmed to talk to the club management about this and a man named *Ronald Trew* was informed of this in the light of the threats his namesake was making. Ronald True continued to monopolize Mrs Wilson and rang her at 11 pm one evening to tell her that he had returned to his mother's house to find the servants gone and on entering through a window he had discovered his mother battered about the head. She had been taken to a hospital and was to be operated on in the morning by a man named Wilson - but he said he held out little hope for her. Mrs Wilson scanned the newspapers the following day to find an account of this attack but could find none. When she inquired further of him, he said:

'I am keeping it quiet for the time being; there is going to be a big case about it.'

Then suddenly he stopped stalking Mrs Wilson. She was relieved. But someone else was not: because the reason he had stopped pursuing Mrs Wilson was that he had found a new obsession: Olive Young.

The circumstances of his meeting her are not known exactly, but he appears to have known her from around mid-February and his staying at her flat on 18th February might suggest that he met her then as a client. Olive Young was 25 years old, born in 1897 in Warwickshire; she had left school in her mid-teens and become a salesgirl in a fur shop in London. From here she appears to have drifted into prostitution - quite successfully. She was a cut above the average street girl. In a few short years she had acquired a basement flat in Finborough Road, a maid who attended her from 9 until 2 pm each day and some expensive jewellery - she also had a Post Office Savings Account balance of £161.

In spite of his staying over at her flat on 18th February, Olive must have deemed this a mistake, because she did her best thereafter to avoid him. He rang her up each day but to no avail. And in the days before her murder, he began to turn up at the flat each evening, even twice in one day, in the hope of seeing her - but was disappointed each time. She appeared to be avoiding him. But on 5th March he had at last been admitted. He stayed the night, it seems - and in the morning the tragedy unfolded which led to his arrest.

The trial of Ronald True began at the Old Bailey on 1st May 1922 before Justice Henry McCardie. The Crown was represented by Sir Richard Muir and the defence by Sir Henry Curtis-Bennett.

The prosecution had a very strong case against Ronald True. He had been left at the murder house late on the evening of 5th March and on the following morning he had been found at the house by the maid Emily Steel; given that the windows were barred, the back door bolted and the front door locked, only Olive Young could have admitted her killer. Ronald's suit had blood on it on the morning of the murder; his overcoat had her jewellery in one of its pockets and he had pawned both of the rings she had been wearing also.

And there were other circumstances which pointed convincingly to Ronald True's guilt: he had been dropped several times at her address in the days prior to the murder by the chauffeur Mazzola; he had spoken of violence a number of times in the weeks before the murder; he had purchased a gun and declared his intention of shooting the 'other Ronald True.' He had developed, it seems, an unhealthy obsession with homicide, and wanted to kill someone - he told Mrs Wilson to 'watch the papers.' He told another friend of his intention of killing the man who was threatening him and even drew a sketch of the basement flat where he said the man lived - which was clearly a diagram of Olive Young's flat. And on the evening before the murder, he had no money left: he was broke.

Ronald True sat in the dock grinning at police, at witnesses and others in court. He seemed to be enjoying the attention he received enormously. At an earlier hearing he had worn a monocle with no glass in it! He placed a yellow duck on the table before him as a mascot and also a champagne cork for some reason.

The prosecution called numerous witnesses in support of the Crown case. Emily Steel, the maid, identified 'Major True' and gave an account of his actions on the morning of the murder; Mazzolo, the driver, gave evidence of having driven True to 13A Finborough Road on the evening of the murder and on other occasions also. The taxi driver gave evidence he had collected True from the same house on the following morning; of taking him to *Horne's Outfitters* and thence to a barbershop. Milne, of *Horne's* testified that True had blood on his suit when he arrived there, that he purchased a new one and changed into it in the shop; he also gave evidence that he had been shown the victim's jewels by True. Armstrong, his recent companion, testified to Ronald True's movements during the day before and after the murder and to the purchase he had made of the Star newspaper, to his glancing at the front page of this and then dismissing it with the words 'nothing in it.' Mrs Wilson testified to True's odd and frightening obsession with her, to his refusal to allow her to dance with anyone else and the threats he had made towards herself, her husband and to others. A friend, Robert Dare St Aubyn Sach, testified that True had drawn a plan of the flat on the back of a menu saying it was the flat of the man whom he was going to kill. And Inspector Burton and other detectives and police officers gave evidence concerning the crime scene, the circumstances of True's arrest and to the statements made by him.

It was a clear case of murder, surely proved beyond a reasonable doubt.

Sir Henry Curtis-Bennett, retained to defend Ronald True against the charge of wilful murder had an unenviable task in defending his client. The evidence against True was damning and though he pleaded not guilty, this was hardly the basis on which a sensible defence could be mounted. Throughout the trial he was obliged to play a two-handed game: he attempted as best he could to undermine aspects of the Crown case with the one hand, while with the other he began to lay the basis for what would, inevitably, be his chief defence: that of insanity. But he knew that this would be extremely difficult because of the rules and long series of precedents underpinning criminal responsibility in Britain.

The rules governing the use of insanity as a defence in English Law were laid down in the McNaghten rules of 1843. These sprang from the case of Daniel McNaghten, who on the afternoon of 20th January 1843 had shot Prime Minister Sir Robert Peel's private secretary in the mistaken belief that he was the Prime Minister. He was tried and found not guilty by reason of insanity and the concerns over the verdict in his case led to the House of Lords formulating a set of rules as the future basis by which a defence of insanity could be judged.

The McNaghten rules set a high standard for the proof of insanity as a sufficient defence in criminal cases, because it not only placed the burden of proof on the defendant to prove their insanity, but it demanded proof that their insanity was such that they *did not understand that what they had done was wrong.*

Thus a person could be insane but still understand that the act they had committed was wrong, that in the legal sense it was a punishable act. In such circumstances, though they might well be insane, they would still be guilty of wilful murder and subject to the full penalty of the law.

It was on this basis and this basis alone, that Sir Henry Curtis-Bennett could save Ronald True from the gallows. The prosecution expected this defence: Sir Richard Muir had clearly done a great deal of research into the judgements governing insanity defences at trials since the McNaghten case and subsequent appeal rulings. And as a result, one of the most important debates of the 20th Century on the use of the defence of insanity took place between the leading counsel Muir and the Judge, McCardie.

Curtis-Bennett called a succession of witnesses to prove that Ronald True was insane and that his delusions were such that he did not comprehend that what he did was wrong. True's Aunt, Grace Angus, was called and gave an account of Ronald's oddness as a child, of his cruelty to animals and of burying his rabbits with their heads exposed, so 'he could see them.' Of mistreating his pony and at the age of 14, when told his mother was seriously ill, Ronald had simply said:

'Oh well, if she dies all her property will be mine, and I'll give you her two best rings straight away, and you can have anything you like of her things...'

Sir Richard Muir contended that these acts, though unwholesome and undesirable, were not acts which were in themselves insane. Children grow out of such things to become normal functioning adults.

Associates from True's past were called to give accounts of his bizarre behaviour, his boastfulness and fantastical tales - to his fixing a tooter to his wheelchair when in hospital and to his carrying children's toys around with him. An acquaintance from the Gold Coast and Tarkwa Mining Company spoke of the natives there regarding him as being 'not right in the head.' Doctors and nurses and others from various clinics and hospitals and institutions at which he had been treated for addiction to morphine testified that he was regarded as insane.

Two doctors who had watched him while on remand at Brixton Prison declared that True was, without a doubt, insane; and two specialists brought in from the Bethlehem Insane Asylum in London, both averred that Ronald True was certifiably insane.

Ronald True was not placed in the witness box; the prospect of that did not seem to be regarded with favour by anyone involved. The debate was upon the point of whether Ronald True's insanity was sufficient to prevent him from comprehending that the nature of his actions in murdering Olive Young, were wrong and punishable by law.

Sir Richard Muir argued that in placing two pillows in

the bed to give the impression that there was someone in the bed was an act of concealment - that it was the act of a man who knew he had done wrong and wished to evade the consequences of that act. He also argued that when buying a new suit on the morning of the murder he had told Milne, the salesman, that the bloodstains were from a flying accident - that this was clearly an attempt at concealment.

But Sir Henry Curtis-Bennett argued that the attempts he made at such evasion were so risibly inadequate, so utterly ineffective, that they could hardly be thought to constitute serious acts of evasion - and that consequently they did not amount to an understanding on his part of the gravity of the crime he had committed.

It was perhaps a disappointment after such erudite discussion on the principles governing insanity that the defence speech to the jury and that of the prosecution were brief, punctilious and that the judge's summing up was one which left the matter quite open. He made clear that the jury had three possible verdicts before them: guilty of wilful murder; guilty but not responsible by reason of insanity; and not guilty. But, if the verdict of guilty but not responsible by reason of insanity was to be given, then it would be necessary for them to be satisfied that the defendant was insane to a degree that he did not know that what he had done was wrong.

The jury was out for one hour and when it returned the verdict was given to the Clerk of the court: Ronald True was guilty of wilful murder.

Judge McCardie donned the black cap and Ronald True was sentenced to death. He was removed to Pentonville Prison to await execution on what would be his birthday, 16th June.

An appeal was heard and dismissed on 24th May: the sentence of execution was confirmed.

True was not, seemingly, unduly troubled by his impending execution as the following letter to a friend clearly shows, in which he speaks lightly of dying and going to hell:

'Dear Sims,

'Many thanks for your kind letter. If I may say so, life is so short - mine will probably not exceed another 14 days - and as you no doubt know, it's not in my nature. Besides, the weather is so hot. It's unfortunate that I shall probably cash my chips in just prior to my birthday, ie June 16th, and am considering petitioning the King to extend the period to June 17th... Anyway, my motto has always been "kismet."

'I'm feeling fairly fit in myself, but could be better, also worse. As the French used to say, never worry; things are never so bad that they might not be worse, and if they are worse that means you are dead and you couldn't worry then. It was awfully good of you to take the trouble you did over my case, and I can assure you I am grateful for all that you did.

'Naturally there's no news to tell you as owing to circumstances over which I have no control, I don't get much outside information. It may interest you to know that the winner of the Derby is included in this little lot, *Re-Echo*, *Tamar*, *Diligence* and *Lord of Burleigh*, and with a little judicious management you should be able to have them running for you at only a small investment and still be well covered.

'Remember, Sims, keep smiling no matter what happens and no matter what happens you will have done some good in this little old world. A smile is sometimes worth a million dollars. Give my kindest regards to your wife, and again thanking you also. Cheerio, old nut, and if you come to the same place as I'm going to, I'll have a drink of nice cold water ready for you on your arrival.

Yours sincerely

Ronald True'

In early June 1922, just two weeks before his execution, the Home Secretary, Edward Shortt called for reports on Ronald True's state of mind with a view to assessing his general sanity. Three leading doctors led the inquiry into Ronald True's mental condition and declared that he was certifiably 'insane.' As a result of this, on 8th June 1922, the sentence of death was respited and Ronald True was ordered to be detained at His Majesty's Pleasure, at the Broadmoor Asylum for the Criminally Insane. He was taken at 9.30 am the following morning from Pentonville Prison to Broadmoor by train and taxicab. He was in high spirits. A ticket collector recognised him at the station:

'Isn't that True?' he inquired of True's escorts.

'No - he is barmy,' replied one of the warders.

True, delighted to be recognised, said:

'Great chap, what?'

The intervention of the Home Secretary in this matter and his decision to grant clemency in the case of Ronald True caused considerable controversy. The judgement of the jury had been that, according to the application of the McNaghten rules and the directions given, Ronald True understood that what he had done was punishable by law. In effect, regardless of whether or not he was insane, he understood the nature and quality of his actions to the extent that he defied the instruction of the law.

This controversy was intensified by the conduct of the almost contemporaneous case of Henry Jacopy, which to all outward appearances was very similar to the Ronald True case. Jacopy had murdered a Lady Alice White at the *Spencer Hotel* in London. He was sentenced to death. The convicting jury recommended mercy because of his mental weakness and youth; but in spite of this, pleas on his behalf were ignored by the Home Secretary and he was hanged on 5th June 1922. There was considerable public and press anger that a well-connected man of wealthy background should be reprieved for murdering a prostitute; while a working class boy should be hanged for the murder of a titled lady. Both cases were similar in involving brutal murders: the only factors differentiating them appeared to be the relative social backgrounds of the condemned men and those of their victims.

There are three questions arising from the Ronald True case: was Ronald True Guilty of murder? Was his insanity a just defence? And should he have been reprieved?

Angus Ronald True was insane. That he had periods of lucidity and was able to function at some level in society does not affect that judgement. His illness was almost certainly affected by morphine addiction and by the accidents he had suffered. But in February 1922 he was certifiably insane and had become dangerous - his family knew it, the prison doctors knew it and most people who met him knew it.

But there is also little doubt that Ronald True knew

that what he did was wrong and punishable in law - the attempts he made at concealment of his actions indicate that and the inadequacy of such concealment hardly affects that judgement, since it would plainly be absurd to base the measure of a person's sanity on the efficacy of their attempts at concealment of their crime. But with that said, that True knew that what he was doing to some degree was wrong, it has to be considered: what was the quality of that knowledge? The extent of his understanding, his comprehension of the act was in direct proportion to the measures he took to conceal the matter - negligible. By the strict application of the McNaghten rules as they stood in 1922, by precedent and application, Ronald True was guilty of wilful murder.

The defence of insanity was insufficient - and the jury was correct in its verdict, and the appeal court correct in its refusal of the appeal. But it was clear that the use of the McNaghten rules in such cases required updating to suit the complexity of cases, and the advances in medical knowledge, which was apparent in this trial. As it was, Shortt, the Home Secretary, was also correct in applying clemency in the case. In fact, he had no choice in the matter, which was not widely appreciated at the time. This was because under Section two of the *Trial of Lunatics Act, 1883*, the Home Secretary was required by law to appoint medical men to assess the condemned man if insanity was in question, because it was laid down by statute that an insane person could not be hanged. He therefore had no choice in the matter and when the inquiry certified True to be insane, he had no choice but to respite the sentence of death. It was wrong to suggest that Shortt had acted incorrectly in granting clemency in the case of True and denying it in the case of Jacopy because of differences in status. The cases were dissimilar in a very important respect: there had never been and there was no suggestion, that Jacopy was insane. He was undoubtedly a feeble-minded youth; but the law had nothing to say on the matter of low-intelligence in criminal responsibility or in the matter of their punishment. So the Home Secretary had no means at his disposal to respite Jacopy's sentence and no means at his disposal to ignore True's insanity.

It was Olive Young's misfortune that her erring star met with that of Ronald True's on the night of 5th March 1922. Had it not done so it would have been Mrs Wilson, or her husband, or his long-suffering wife or mother whom he killed - not from malice, but prompted by a disordered mind which had confused locations and people and even his personal needs in a distorted idea which had settled upon a determination to murder someone soon. He had become obsessed with killing someone, from delusional paranoia, from the deterioration of his mental faculties due to physical injury, to morphine addiction, out of personal frustration, and from a sense of his own worthlessness. He had a huge ego which conceived of himself - quite genuinely - as the best billiards player, the best golfer, the best pilot - when in fact he was none of these and performed at a very low level in all things. That distorted view of his own capabilities jarred with everyone he met - and it didn't match his own performance in any way. He told tales of his taking on five German planes during the war - when in fact he had seen no service, never left England and succeeded only in crashing three planes before being discharged from the Royal Flying Corps. He told people he had once saved a train full of passengers on the West Coast of the US from robbers, when he shot one of the men and knocked the other down. He told various people that he had once fought a German over a land claim in America - fought him all day and at last killed him...and then he had written out the land claim in the German's blood... He constantly invented jobs which matched his ego - with the Portuguese government for which he drew up a ludicrous contract with a penny stamp affixed. And when brought to earth by the intrusion of reality that he had failed at everything that he had attempted to do, he became frustrated, burst into tears, was conscious in some way of the strange division in himself: the marvellous and successful Ronald True and the one who was undermining him at every point of his life. There would, as he put it so memorably, be a 'how d'ye' do when they met.

Olive Young, like Mrs Wilson and so many others, thought him insane and dangerous - because he was. When she rejected him, repeatedly, and he could not reach her by phone or by visiting her flat at night, that frustration became personified in the form of Olive Young. On the morning of 6th March 1922 Ronald True woke to a brutal reality: he was unemployed, broke and with a prostitute who was completely disinterested in him. The contract he had made with life was not worth the penny stamp he had affixed to it and scribbled over. He got up and fetched the newspaper. He made them cups of tea. Olive, oblivious, wanted this strange man gone. He certainly couldn't pay her - and his admission of this would only complete his humiliation. And here were her jewels lying about her flat.

As she drank her tea he rummaged in the kitchen drawer and brought back a rolling pin, which he concealed from her. He came up silently, smiling even, that inane, fatuous grin he wore so often and hit her; the cup tipped from her hand to the floor, and she collapsed on the bed. And as she did so and as the blood oozed from her wound, he hit her four more times in rapid succession. He rammed a piece of towel into her mouth with great violence and in sudden anger, and pulling the cord from her dressing gown, strangled her. Then he dragged her body to the bathroom. It is difficult to know exactly what his thought process was at this moment. It's difficult too to ascribe all his actions of concealment to rational thought - there is obviously an element of it there - but as in all things with Ronald True it is of low quality, has many blanks in it, is incomplete. He wasn't really firing on all cylinders. He made cursory efforts at concealment - the pillows in the bed, the closed door. And, of course, he asked the maid not to disturb her mistress, leaving unhurriedly - even giving her a half crown of her dead mistress's money by way of a tip. He helpfully left his visiting card, too! He had no hope of escape except in the fantastic world of Ronald True's mind. Because Ronald True was a child, trapped in a man's body, without cognitive or emotional intelligence to inform his actions; or the means of grasping the world outside that he had created for himself.

Ronald True spent the rest of his life in Broadmoor Asylum for the Criminally Insane. He seems to have been popular there and played a major role in its theatre society. He was housed in the 'Gentlemen's ward' there, was known affectionately as 'Ronnie' by staff and inmates alike.

There were many attempts made over the years by his mother to obtain his release, to have him declared sane, but they all failed. She sent him 35 shillings allowance per week, and he lived very well there. He was allowed a garden where he cultivated beautiful roses and was often to be seen strolling up and down the terrace with his mother during her regular visits to him. It seemed in Broadmoor Asylum, Ronald True had found his niche at last. During a patients' dance on New Year's Day, 1951, he collapsed with chest pains and he died of a heart attack six days later, on 7th January 1951. He was 59.

Above: Olive Young.

Above: Emily Steel, Olive's maid (right).

Above: Ronald True.

Above: Lady Annabelle French.

Above: Ronald True as he liked to see himself.

Above: Frances True, his long-suffering American wife.

Above: Sir Richard Muir did his best to prove Ronald True may have been insane, but understood the quality of his actions and therefore should be punished for them.

Above: Ronald True seemed to enjoy the attention he received in court, and it was reported the monocle he wore had no glass in it.

3. Arsenic In Islington: The Murder Of Eliza Barrow, 1911

Ernest Vonderahe had not heard from his cousin, Eliza Barrow, for a few weeks. Although they weren't on the best of terms, owing to the difficult and often mercurial character of Eliza, they nevertheless tried to keep in touch. On 20th September 1911, it being a pleasant evening and Miss Barrow living only about a quarter of a mile from his own house, Ernest Vonderahe decided to stroll over to her lodgings at 63 Tollington Park, Islington, London, and pay his regards. He arrived there at about 8.20 pm and rang the bell. It was answered by a servant called Mary Chater.

'I've come to see how Miss Barrow is getting on,' he told her.

Mary Chater looked astonished.

'Haven't you heard?' she said, 'Miss Barrow is dead and buried.'

Ernest Vonderahe stood and stared, utterly bewildered.

'When did she die?' he asked at last.

'Last Thursday.'

'But this is only Wednesday!' he said incredulously.

'She was buried on Saturday,' said Mary Chater. She told him that the landlord and house owner, Mr Seddon, was presently out but if Mr Vonderahe called later he would be able to explain all.

A shocked Ernest Vonderahe returned to his home at nearby 31 Evershot Road and told his wife the news. After some discussion, the two returned to Tollington Park, arriving at around 9 pm. Frederick Seddon was still absent, but his 15 year old daughter Maggie saw them. She could give them no details of their cousin's death or illness and they left in a state of some disquiet.

It should not be imagined that the Vonderahes were deeply distressed by a much-loved cousin's death, or even that they kept in touch with her periodically out of a sense of familial duty: Miss Barrow was a difficult woman - she had no friends at all to speak of, because she was quick to take offence and fell out with everyone generally sooner rather than later. She had a vituperative temper too, when riled - she had once spat in the face of Mrs Vonderahe, and the latter was said to have described Eliza Barrow later as a 'wicked woman.' Their interest in Miss Barrow was largely pecuniary - she had money and they were her nearest, if not her dearest. They had expectations, and they knew that sooner or later, her worldly possessions would come to them. But Eliza Barrow was only 49 at the time of her death, was in good health and they had little expectation of obtaining her fortune at any time soon. But this turn of events changed things. If she had died without a will - and there was every reason to believe she had - then they stood to inherit a large sum of money.

Eliza Mary Barrow was born in Islington, London,

in 1862. Her father was a licensed victualler and pub landlord who had run the *Mortimer Arms* in Tottenham Court Road, and then later the *Prince of Wales* pub in Kentish Town. After the death of her parents, she inherited property in the form of the *Buck's Head* pub in Camden Town and a barbershop next door; she also inherited a large sum of money, which allowed her to live as a woman of independent means.

For all this, she was an abstemious woman and dressed shabbily according to those who knew her. In fact, Eliza Barrow was a miser - she liked to count her money and keep it close. She rarely spent any and when she did it was only out of necessity. She seemed to move from one set of modest lodgings to another, probably because she quarrelled with her landlords frequently, and was easily provoked. In 1905 she lodged with a Mrs Grant - and when the latter died in 1908, she took responsibility for her daughter Hilda (who was sent away to school), and her son Ernest, whom she informally adopted. She and Ernest - called Ernie - had lodged for about 10 months with her cousins the Vonderahes in 1909 and 1910 for 30 shillings a week, until the inevitable happened: they fell out. After this she and Ernie took rooms at the top of 63 Tollington Park for 12 shillings per week, which was owned by Frederick Seddon and his wife Margaret.

It was a good deal - the 12 shillings rent was very modest and the Seddons seemed ideal landlords - they were very attentive to her, the daughter Maggie cooked her meals and cleaned the four rooms she had taken for one shilling a day - and Frederick Seddon was ever ready to assist and advise with her financial arrangements. He was a man of business, had a bluff attitude, and a quick native grasp of financial matters. She came to trust him, it seems.

Then, at the beginning of September 1911, Eliza Barrow became ill. There was an epidemic of diarrhoea in London, probably due to the hot summer and an infestation of flies which accompanied it. Mrs Seddon called in a Doctor Henry Sworn who had little doubt from the symptoms Eliza Barrow exhibited, that she had succumbed to the malady, which had become so familiar to him in his parish. He prescribed bismuth and morphine and made several visits during the following days, during which Eliza Barrow seemed to improve in symptoms a little, although he had concerns at her general weakness.

Then on the morning of 14th September, Frederick Seddon appeared at his door and informed Dr Sworn that Miss Eliza Barrow had died at 6 am that morning. Having attended her throughout her illness Dr Sworn had no doubt that the cause of her death was due to heart failure as a result of the enteric infection from which she was suffering. He therefore wrote out a death certificate there and then and handed it to Seddon, stating that Miss Barrow's death was caused by 'epidemic diarrhoea.' Although she had only died on the Thursday morning, Seddon visited a funeral parlour and arranged for Eliza's funeral to be held in two days' time - on the Saturday. She was buried in a common grave at Islington Borough cemetery for a knock-down price of £3 seven shillings and sixpence, and Frederick Seddon, ever a man of business, negotiated a commission for himself of 12 shillings and sixpence on this. Thus it was that by the following Wednesday, when Ernest Vonderahe came to call on his cousin, he was astonished to learn that she was dead and buried without any of the family being aware of it.

Mrs Vonderahe and her sister-in-law called at 63 Tollington Park the morning after Ernest Vonderahe's visit and the 15-year-old daughter, Maggie Seddon, answered the door. They were shown into the dining room and, after a long wait, Frederick Seddon and his wife Margaret appeared. Seddon was self-assured, even to the point of brusqueness; his little eyes regarded them with mild disdain - but Mrs Seddon seemed to the two women to be nervous.

Seddon took charge of the situation at once: he informed the two ladies that he was a busy man and could spare them little time - as though to emphasise this, he removed his pocket watch and consulted it. One of the Mrs Vonderahes noticed, with some consternation, that it was remarkably similar to one owned by Miss Eliza Barrow. She also noticed that Mrs Seddon was wearing a pendant which was identical to one belonging to Miss Barrow.

Frederick Seddon seemed to be prepared for this visit. He gave them a carbon copy of a letter addressed to Ernest Vonderahe informing him of Miss Barrow's death, which he told them had been sent on the day of her death. They said they hadn't received it. The letter read:

'Dear Sir,

'I sincerely regret to have to inform you of the death of your cousin, Miss Eliza Mary Barrow, at 6 am this morning from epidemic diarrhoea. The funeral will take place on Saturday next about one to two pm... I must also inform you that she made a will on the 11th inst. leaving what she died possessed of to Hilda and Ernest Grant and appointed myself as sole executor under the will.

Yours respectfully,

FH Seddon.'

With great self-possession and some alacrity he placed the letter, the funeral card and a copy of the will into a large envelope and presented it to the ladies. It was an act of peremptory dismissal. The two ladies, decidedly unhappy, asked if Seddon would see Ernest Vonderahe to discuss the matter further with him? He said:

'I am a businessman, and I think I've wasted quite enough time on this matter. I really can't be bothered answering questions put by inquisitive people.'

This bluff and officious response took them aback - it seemed beyond mere discourtesy - but there was little they could do.

The two ladies left, disappointed. Their conversation as they made their way back to Evershot Road can only be imagined. Suspicions, once rooted, are hard to dislodge. And suspicions there were in the many family meetings which took place in the weeks which followed. They knew something of Miss Barrow's wealth, and the fact that Eliza had made a will - drawn up by Frederick Seddon himself, rather than by a solicitor, and in which he was named as sole executor - seemed suspicious.

Seddon was absent for two weeks following his meeting with the two Vonderahe wives, taking a break in Southend, but on his return to 63 Tollington Park he was visited by Ernest Vonderahe. Seddon at once adopted the same high handed, superior attitude towards him, which seemed to be his stock in trade in dealing with people whom he regarded as being his inferior - which was most people. Vonderahe had to wait 20 minutes in the dining room before Seddon attended to him, briskly. When he appeared in the company of his wife, he was smoking a large cigar:

'Now what is all this about? You are under the impression that some money is due to you from the estate of Miss Barrow? The will is perfectly clear, and I don't see why I should give you any further information. If your solicitor cares to see my solicitor, all very well and good.'

But in spite of this attempt to subdue him, Ernest Vonderahe asked him a direct question, meeting Seddon on his own terms:

'Who is the owner of the *Buck's Head*?' he asked.

'I am,' said Seddon, returning his gaze unfalteringly.

Seddon had clearly decided that a direct challenge was to be met with equal force:

'And the barber shop next door is also mine. I've bought the property - in fact, I am always open to buy property if it shows any chance of a reasonable return.'

Ernest Vonderahe then inquired why Miss Barrow had been buried in a common grave when a family vault existed in Highgate, to which she was entitled?

Seddon said he thought the vault was full up. He refused further discussion of the matter concerning Eliza Barrow's estate, inviting Vonderahe to consult a solicitor, if dissatisfied. Vonderahe's attempts to assert himself into the matter of his cousin's estate had been met with Seddon's bluff dismissal: there seemed to be a stalemate. There was little the Vonderahes could do; Seddon believed, in his own mind at least, that he had put an end to the matter.

But he was mistaken. The Vonderahes nursed their wrath to keep it warm - there were numerous family meetings - and at last they decided to go to the police with their suspicions.

The police received the information from the Vonderahes with courtesy and examined it as a matter of routine - such complaints by relatives bilked of what they regard as being their rightful inheritance are not uncommon and, of course, they rarely amount to anything. But this case was different. It was quickly appreciated by Detective Chief Inspector Alfred Ward, who had charge of the investigation, that this matter warranted further inquiry: the haste with which Miss Barrow had been buried without her relations' knowledge, was unusual; the fact that this had all been managed by her landlord, Frederick Seddon, who was also sole executor of her will and who had seemingly acquired by one means or another, all her wealth, gave cause for concern. Of course, none of this meant that there had been foul play and the police proceeded with the greatest caution.

They looked into the circumstances and made discreet inquiries concerning Frederick Seddon. He was born in 1872 in Liverpool. At the age of 19 he began working for the London and Manchester Industrial Assurance Company. His diligence was quickly rewarded. In 1896 he was made District Superintendent and in 1901 Superintendent for the Islington district. In 1893, at the age of 21, he had married Mary Ann Jones, whose family lived in the same street as the Seddons - Priory Street - in Liverpool. They had five children - the eldest being 16 and the youngest being nine months old at the time of Eliza Barrow's death. Seddon earned about £300 per year in salary and commission (that's approximately £36,000 in 2020) and he had a number of other streams of revenue. The Seddons were a relatively prosperous and hard-working family - a family on the up. Seddon was an eloquent lay preacher and a freemason - he was well on his way to becoming a pillar of the community.

The police inquired into the intricacies of Miss Barrow's financial arrangements; they looked also at those of Frederick Seddon and discovered that Seddon had benefited considerably by Eliza Barrow's death... Miss Barrow had £1,600 (approximately £190,000 in 2020) in three and a half per cent India Stock; she had transferred this to Frederick Seddon in exchange for an annuity of £10 per month - and this would cease on her death. It seems also that she had a large bank balance of £216 and a Post Office account with other funds - all of which had been withdrawn in the past year and had disappeared... A cash box which was known to contain at least £400 in gold and notes had only £4 and 10 shillings in it at the time of her death. All in all, she had been worth at least £4,000, which equates to something like £500,000 in today's terms. And yet at the time of her death it seems she had just £16 remaining. Police interviewed the doctor who had attended Miss Barrow and who had issued her death certificate. After doing so, having regard to all the circumstances, a decision was taken to request of the Home Secretary that he make an order for the exhumation of Eliza Barrow's body, so that further tests could be conducted to ascertain the cause of her death.

The body of Miss Barrow was exhumed in great secrecy from its common grave at Islington Cemetery in the early hours of 15th November, in the presence of toxicologist Sir William Willcox and a young Bernard Spilsbury. It was taken to Finchley mortuary, where a post-mortem was carried out and organs including the stomach, intestines, heart, and liver were removed, and sent to St Mary's Hospital in Paddington for analysis. Here Willcox discovered these contained a large quantity of arsenic: Eliza Barrow had died of acute arsenical poisoning.

Of course, Seddon knew nothing of any of this and must have imagined by early November the matter was long settled. But he was in for a shock.

On the evening of 22nd November Seddon was, as ever, working at his insurance accounts in the basement office at his home in Tollington Place when his daughter Maggie showed a policeman in. He handed Seddon a piece of paper:

'I am the Coroner's Officer,' he said, 'This is a summons for you to attend an inquest on the body of Eliza Barrow, which will be held tomorrow.'

What thoughts must have raced through Seddon's quick and busy mind at this point, are not known, but in the morning he was grey and haggard. The inquest under the Central Middlesex Coroner Dr George Cohen, went poorly for him; the questions for which he had calculated all the answers, and in whose confidence he had upbraided Vonderahe that his solicitor would handle any challenge, did not satisfy the court. The coroner wanted to know what had happened to the considerable sum known to be kept in the cashbox, and to other money Miss Barrow was known to keep. He asked some searching questions of Seddon concerning the property Miss Barrow had owned and which she had exchanged for the annuity with him:

Coroner: How much was she getting from the house in rent?

Seddon: £155 a year.

Coroner: And you promised to give her £52 a year?

Seddon: For life. The lease has only 16 or 17 years to run.

Coroner: It has 18 ½ years to run. Would it bring in £120 clear?

Seddon: I dare say it would.

Coroner: Then for £120 you were going to give her £52?

Seddon: I have brought my own business ability into play.

'Quite so!' said the incredulous coroner.

The fact that Miss Barrow had been poisoned by arsenic, had made a will just three days before her death, placing Seddon in full control of those assets which had not mysteriously disappeared already; his involvement in her financial affairs, the obvious suspicion that he had appropriated her wealth; his conduct and the circumstances of Miss Barrow's sudden and unceremonious burial in the absence of any relations, led to a logical and reasonable suspicion: that Frederick Seddon had murdered Eliza Barrow. But there was no proof of this and the coroner's jury gave its verdict as one of wilful murder against person or persons unknown, just stopping short of naming Seddon.

Nevertheless the police decided to act. At 7 o'clock on the evening of 4th December 1911, Frederick Seddon was approached in the street at Tollington Park by Detective Chief Inspector Ward, accompanied by two detective sergeants, and arrested for the wilful murder of Eliza Mary Barrow.

Seddon replied:

'Absurd - what a terrible charge! Wilful murder...Are you going to arrest my wife as well? Have they found arsenic in her body?'

He was then taken to Hornsey Road Police Station, where he was formally charged.

Detective Chief Inspector Ward searched 63 Tollington Park in the presence of Mrs Seddon - he found a ring, a gold chain and pendant in Seddon's safe, plus gold sovereigns. A gold watch and chain were also found in the bedroom wardrobe and when questioned about these Mrs Seddon said they were hers - but on further questioning said that Miss Barrow had given them to her as a present.

Police inquiries revealed that the 15-year-old daughter, Maggie Seddon, had purchased a packet of six arsenic-laced flypapers from Thorley's chemist, apparently at Mrs Seddon's behest, on 26th August, and Mrs Seddon had purchased more of these from Meacher's chemist on 4th September. In doing so both had specifically requested 'the ones which are soaked in water,' rather than the harmless sticky papers. It was also discovered that Mrs Seddon had cashed in 27 open cheques to the value of £5 each belonging to Miss Barrow, often using a false name and address; and had escorted Miss Barrow to the bank for the purpose of withdrawing £216 in gold sovereigns which had then disappeared. Furthermore, it was noted from the statements made by the doctor, the servant Mary Chater, and by the Seddons themselves, that Mrs Margaret Seddon appeared to have had exclusive care of Eliza Barrow from 1st-14th September - the period covering that of her illness and death.

At 5 pm on 15th January, 1912, Mrs Margaret Seddon was also arrested and charged with wilful murder.

The trial of Frederick and Margaret Seddon began at the Old Bailey on 4th March 1912, before Justice Thomas Bucknill. The Attorney General Sir Rufus Isaacs appeared for the Crown, and Edward Marshall-Hall and Gervais Rentoul appeared for Frederick Seddon and Margaret Seddon respectively.

Seddon was his brusque, confident self at the trial; his wife cut a rather forlorn figure.

The prosecution case was that only the Seddons benefitted from the death of Miss Barrow, that he and his wife had gained full control over Miss Barrow's affairs; they had systematically relieved her of her fortune and had gone to considerable lengths to conceal the matter of her death from her family. They had even sent her ward, Ernest Grant, away to Southend immediately following her death because he attended the same school as the Vonderahe's children, and they feared they might learn of her death by this means. Seddon's guilt, said the Attorney General, was indicated by his attempts to conceal her death and his taking pains to ensure that her family was unable to investigate the circumstances of her illness and death. Seddon was, he said, an unscrupulous operator, obsessed with money and the acquisition of wealth, and he had been assisted by his wife in administering the poison to Miss Barrow. For her part, Mrs Seddon had likewise been responsible for stripping Miss Barrow of her wealth by cashing £5 treasury notes using a false name and address, and by accompanying Miss Barrow to withdraw the £216 in gold from the bank. She had procured some of the flypapers in early September, her daughter procuring the others on her behalf, for the specific purpose of poisoning Miss Barrow. Each flypaper of itself, contained sufficient arsenic to kill an adult and it could be extracted from the flypaper by soaking it in water for 48 hours.

The court heard from various witnesses who testified that the Seddons had sought to estrange Miss Barrow from a couple - Mr and Mrs Hook - for the purpose of isolating her; that Frederick Seddon had been seen counting a large sum of gold in his office in the presence of two employees, Taylor and Smith, of the London and Manchester Assurance Company; and that Seddon had banked an amount of money in his accounts which corresponded to the amount of money Miss Barrow was believed to have had in her cashbox, only days after her death. The undertaker gave evidence of the nature of the arrangements made for the burial of Miss Barrow and, of course, the Vonderahes gave accounts of their conversations with Seddon and his wife.

The defence for Frederick Seddon, conducted by Edward Marshall Hall, averred that all Seddon's money was accounted for; he was a businessman and had a float of cash which he kept in his safe; the annuity arrangement with Miss Barrow was a perfectly legitimate transaction done at Miss Barrow's behest; the will was drawn up at Miss Barrow's request also, because she was ill and had no means of calling a solicitor but was anxious to see that the two children she had assumed responsibility for were left her possessions. In fact, all Seddon's actions had been proper and legal. Furthermore, if arsenic had been administered to Miss Barrow (and there had been an epidemic of diarrhoea in London that summer) then there was no evidence whatsoever to show that Seddon had purchased or administered that. In fact, he had never been alone in Eliza Barrow's company and so had little or no opportunity of doing so. Walter Thorley, the chemist, had been mistaken in identifying Maggie Seddon as being the girl who bought the flypapers on the 26th August. The jewellery and watch were gifts from Miss Barrow, who was an eccentric woman given to bursts of temper and generosity.

Marshall Hall worked hard to introduce uncertainty and sufficient doubt into the matter. If poison was administered, he said, could it not have been anyone in the household? He tried to cast suspicion on the servant Mary Chater, suggesting that her brother was a lunatic, that she, as a nurse, knew a great deal about poisons and might possess a touch of insanity herself. All this was denied by an indignant Mary Chater - and its purpose was simply one of obfuscation: to introduce doubt into every aspect of the evidence heard in court.

Gervais Rentoul associated himself with Marshall Hall's skilful advocacy and pointed out that there was even less evidence against Mrs Seddon.

Marshall Hall advised Frederick Seddon not to take

the witness stand: he had misgivings about allowing the Attorney General, Sir Rufus Isaacs, to probe his actions and motives before a jury - and he was concerned at the abrasive impression which was characteristic of Seddon, and which might turn a jury against his client.

'If the evidence does not convict the man, his conceit will,' he remarked to a colleague.

But Seddon, with characteristic confidence in his own abilities, his vanity flattered at the prospect of being cross-examined by the Attorney General himself, insisted that he appear. It was a grave error.

When Sir Rufus Isaacs rose to cross examine Seddon, he quickly revealed how deadly his style of questioning would prove to be. Speaking quietly, and with unfailing courtesy, the Attorney General opened with a disconcerting line of questioning:

Isaacs: Miss Barrow lived with you from the 26th July 1910 till the morning of the 14th September 1911?

Seddon: Yes

Isaacs: Did you like her?

Seddon: Did I like her?

Isaacs: Yes, that's the question.

Seddon could hardly say yes, because the pauper's burial he had arranged for her would prove him a hypocrite and liar; but if he said no, he might turn the jury against him.

Seddon: She was not a woman that you could be in love with, but I sympathised deeply with her.

Isaacs: During the time she was living with you at your

house did you advise her on her financial affairs?

Seddon: Yes, certainly I did.

The Attorney General then meticulously ran through an account of all the property and wealth Miss Barrow had possessed when she arrived at the Seddons' house in July 1910, to a value of some £4,000 in total, and then asked Seddon to confirm if it was the case that just one year later, on the day she died, everything she possessed including her clothes and furniture, came to a total value of £16 and 14 shillings and sixpence. The effect of this was devastating. It was exposed to all that Frederick Seddon's financial advice to Miss Barrow had been, at the very least, catastrophic to her financial well-being.

Seddon was clever; he did his best to counter the effect of this, but the Attorney General, courteous and relentless in all his questions was clearly getting the better of him. At one point, when disputing the words Chief Inspector Ward had attributed to him on his arrest, Seddon cried, 'I swear before God, that these are the words that took place!'

'All the statements that you are making,' replied the Attorney General, quietly, 'are statements before God.'

Seddon's claims not to know where Miss Barrow's wealth had gone were not at all believable; nor were his frequent claims that he advised Miss Barrow to consult a solicitor, only to have her insist that she would do without one. His suggestion that Miss Barrow may have drunk the water from the saucers which contained the flypapers was, of course, regarded with extreme scepticism.

Mrs Seddon, who also appeared in the witness box, was subdued. She claimed she did not know what had happened to the £216 Miss Barrow had withdrawn; nor to have known why she needed it; she claimed that the £5 cheques she had cashed for Miss Barrow were cashed at Miss Barrow's request and that the pendant, chain and other jewellery had been given by Miss Barrow to herself and her daughter by Miss Barrow as presents. She did, however, elicit considerable sympathy in court due to the subdued manner in which she gave her evidence and her occasional breakdowns. It was in marked contrast to the manner of her husband.

The judge's summing up was notably benign towards Mrs Seddon:

'I know full well you must have sympathetic feelings for the female who stands charged with the wilful murder of another female,' he said, and he intimated that there could be an element of doubt in the case of Mrs Seddon.

The jury retired at 4 pm and was out for one hour and five minutes. Upon its return, it gave its verdict as guilty against Frederick Seddon - but not guilty for Margaret Seddon. Frederick Seddon turned and kissed his wife and she left the dock a free woman. Her sobbing could be heard as she left the side door and the court settled for the next matter in hand: the sentencing of Frederick Seddon.

The Clerk of the Arraigns then put the traditional question to Seddon:

'What have you to say that the court should not give judgement for you to die according to law?' he asked.

It was now that there occurred an extraordinary scene: Seddon made a speech lasting for a quarter of an hour, attacking shortcomings in the prosecution case, criticising the judge's summing up, and even his own counsel's deficiencies. He concluded by turning to the judge and in doing so he raised his hand, taking the freemasons' oath, and said:

'I declare before the Great Architect of the Universe that I am not guilty, my lord.'

It has been said that he then made the First Degree sign - the masonic sign of distress, begging for mercy. This is probably an exaggeration made for dramatic effect.

The act was lost on most of the court - only those who were freemasons would have understood what had occurred in the reference Seddon made to the 'Great Architect' and the sign he made before the judge.

Seddon was a freemason; so was Judge Thomas Bucknill. Bucknill understood the meaning and that Seddon was requesting the urgent help of a brother mason in extremis.

It was an astonishing act. Bucknill was stunned and visibly distressed as he sat at the bench. The court watched in thrilled anticipation. The usher called for complete silence. A chaplain entered quietly and stood to the judge's left side. The doors of the court were locked - no-one could now enter or leave until sentence had been passed. Struggling to recover his composure, Bucknill, wiping his eyes and with great emotion, said:

'It is not for me to harrow your feelings - try to make peace with your maker. We both belong to the same Brotherhood, and though that can have no influence with me, this is painful beyond words to have to say what I am saying, but our brotherhood does not encourage crime, it condemns it.'

The judge's secretary at his side, placed the black cap on the judge's head and, in a faltering voice, Justice Bucknill pronounced the sentence of death upon Frederick Seddon.

Seddon was then removed to Pentonville prison to await execution. His appeal was heard on 1st April 1912 before Mr Justice Darling and was denied; his request for clemency having been denied also, he was informed on 16th April that sentence would be carried out in two days' time. His wife and son visited him at Pentonville prison on Wednesday afternoon, the day prior to his execution, and he took his farewells of them. And it was here that he was hanged at 9 am on the 18th April 1912. The tolling of the bell at 9.05 am and a notice pinned to the door of the prison, signalled to those without, that execution had been carried out in accordance with the law. An inquest was held soon afterwards within the prison walls, at which his 16-year-old son, looking understandably shaken, and his tearful father, identified the body.

There can be little doubt that Frederick Seddon was guilty of the murder of Miss Eliza Barrow in September 1911; nor that this act was the natural consequence of his having systematically defrauded her of around £4,000. There were only four people who could possibly have committed the murder by administering arsenic to Miss Barrow - the 10-year-old son, Ernie Grant, the 15-year-old daughter Maggie Seddon, or Frederick and his wife Margaret Seddon. But of these only Seddon and his wife stood to benefit by her death; only Seddon had displayed in all his actions towards Miss Barrow, a mercenary zeal to divest her of everything she possessed. The course he had embarked on could have only one outcome, because he had swindled her there would be consequences from that, whose avoidance would require the most extreme remedy: her murder.

It was a supreme irony that the will Seddon had drawn up for her leaving all her worldly possessions to the two children, Hilda and Ernie Grant, so framed that it would divert suspicion from the fact of how utterly depleted her wealth was, became one of the most damning documents against him.

The will was an empty document - Miss Barrow had been cleaned out by the Seddons. It was a simple distraction designed to give the impression that she had left her wealth to the two children for whom she had taken responsibility; when in fact there was no wealth left to bequeath. Less than £20 remained, of which £4 had been spent on her funeral - minus Seddon's commission on the transaction. The will was an act of concealment to prevent further inquiry by her relations; to conceal the motive and thereby the fact of her murder.

Seddon had taken the steps necessary to conceal Eliza Barrow's death by visiting the doctor, by expediting the funeral, by carefully depriving the relatives of the possibility of second guessing the cause of death, until after she was buried - at which point, only an order from the Home Secretary could effect her exhumation.

It must also be said that his enormous confidence, which had served him so well in his business and in all the transactions of his life hitherto, was also his undoing. His confidence, that characteristic arrogance - his belief that his assertive, intimidatory manner would win the day - irked the Vonderahes; it irked the police who questioned him - and it produced a disastrous effect on the jury.

Marshall Hall had advised Seddon not to go into the witness box - he feared Seddon's conceit. He was right. All Marshall Hall's eloquence, his skilled advocacy, and the wiles which saved so many innocent people and a good many murderers too in the first quarter of the

20th Century, could not overcome the obvious defects of Seddon's character. His naked avarice, his miserly, obsessive pursuit of wealth not of necessity, but for its own sake, were all laid bare in court. He was a clever man - he has the distinction of being referred to by Marshall Hall as 'The ablest man I ever defended on the capital charge' - but Marshall Hall also found him repugnant:

'This is the blackest case I've ever been in,' he said.

And he had no doubts from start to finish that Seddon was guilty. Frederick Seddon had miscalculated - that precise, neat mind, so adept with columns of figures; which could calculate the risks of a certain investment and allow for a margin of error, had failed him.

Not only did the evidence point convincingly at Seddon, but when 12 men of the jury observed him closely in the No 1 Court of the Old Bailey, they saw that here was a man with sufficient arrogance, meanness, and motivation to carry out such an act. They gave the correct verdict in finding Frederick Seddon guilty of Eliza Barrow's murder. But their verdict was deficient in one notable respect: because they found Margaret Seddon to be innocent. And that, she most certainly was not.

The police had realised in December of 1911, while questioning Seddon and investigating the circumstances of Miss Barrow's murder, that Seddon could not have acted alone. Many of the circumstances relating to the systematic defrauding of Eliza Barrow, and almost all of those relating to her murder, required Margaret Seddon's involvement. Without her assistance the case against Seddon amounted to little more than defrauding Barrow of her savings and property, and seeking to conceal the circumstances and matter of her death from her relations. He had neither purchased arsenic nor could he be shown to have administered it - or even to have been alone in her presence at any time leading up to her death. All of these trails led directly to his wife, Margaret.

But Mrs Seddon gained by comparison with her husband - she was a sorry figure in court, cowed by the circumstances and although her testimony mirrored every aspect of that given by her husband, the manner of its delivery and of her penitent, contrite figure in the dock beside her husband, elicited sympathy, tended to reduce her culpability in the matter; where Seddon's drew only ire and dislike. Perhaps the nature of the evidence - never wholly satisfactory in all respects - seemed too great a burden on which to hang two people for the price of one. And the fact of her being a mother of five children, one only a year old, may well have tilted the judicial scales in her favour. The Attorney General did not go after her with the same vigour as he did Seddon; he alluded to the possibility of her being found not guilty; perhaps there was, consciously or unconsciously, on the part of the prosecutor and the judge and jury, a willingness to contrive an acquittal for her.

Yet the evidence against her, deficient in the matter of concealment and subordinate to that of her husband in swindling Miss Barrow of her property, is nonetheless wholly compelling in the matter of her murder.

1. Mrs Seddon it was who was accused by the Hooks who initially shared Miss Barrow's rooms with her, of turning Eliza Barrow against them, and thus having them expelled from the house, effectively isolating Miss Barrow. Robert Hook said in court that Margaret Seddon was always listening on the stairs, and that he caught her eavesdropping on a conversation he had with Miss Barrow on one occasion.

2. Mrs Seddon it was who had every reason to fear a living Eliza Barrow, because she had drawn 26 or 27 open cheques for £5 notes from her bank account, for the most part at different places using a false name and address. She had even cashed one four days after Miss Barrow's death, claiming most improbably that she had given Miss Barrow cash for it. She had escorted Miss Barrow to the bank to withdraw her £216 in gold sovereigns and change - which had then disappeared. She claimed not to have inquired of Miss Barrow why she was withdrawing such a large sum of money (£25,000 in today's value) to keep in her room, when she clearly had no need of it; she was a frugal woman, who spent very little, dressed shabbily; she received £10 per month from her annuity and Mrs Seddon herself had cashed in the £5 notes regularly for her. Even when they looked in Miss Barrow's room following her death, Mrs Seddon appeared to show no great puzzlement that all the money had disappeared and that they found only £4 and 10 shillings! It was simply not believable.

3. It was almost certainly Mrs Seddon who dispatched Maggie to buy arsenic-laced flypapers from Thorley's chemist on 26th August; Thorley was not mistaken in this, as Marshall Hall claimed - his daughter Mabel was friends with Maggie Seddon and he was quite adamant it was her - and she it was who purchased more flypapers herself from Meacher's the chemist on 4th or 5th September.

4. It was Mrs Seddon who made all Eliza Barrow's meals for her after 1st September in the small kitchen on the top floor provided for Miss Barrow and Ernie Grant. She had complete control of her from that time up until the

morning of her death on 14th September.

5. It was Mrs Seddon who gave her her medicine; Ernie Grant said he had only seen Miss Barrow take her medicine herself on one occasion - she didn't want to take it. On all other occasions, it was given to her by Margaret Seddon. And in this, it must be said, Margaret proved extraordinarily diligent: she took pains to insist a reluctant Miss Barrow take her medicine; so attentive were both Seddons in this that Seddon himself drank some of her effervescent medicine to demonstrate how it should be taken. Was there in either of these two people - who had abused Miss Barrow so thoroughly in the year she had been with them, leaving her with just £4 and 10 shillings - anything at all to suggest they would be concerned for her health? Or that they should care whether she took her medicine? There was not. The only conceivable reason they could have for such assiduous attention to this is that they were poisoning her. The medicine provided a cure not for Miss Barrow's ills, but for theirs. It removed, they thought, the danger she posed to them of the discovery of their fraud. And, of course, Miss Barrow was an eccentric, querulous woman of strange habits, who, having outlived her financial usefulness, now represented a perpetual burden to them.

6. It was Mrs Seddon who claimed that the pendant and chain and other items had been given to her and to her daughter Maggie as Christmas presents and birthday gifts by Eliza Barrow - even the watch treasured by Miss Barrow, because it had belonged to her own mother, had apparently been given to Mrs Seddon. That Miss Barrow, who wore shabby clothes because of her thrift, should have willingly shown such largesse to the Seddon family,

is quite absurd.

In all aspects of the murder, which had begun with Miss Barrow's isolation, had proceeded with the appropriation of her property, through to her illness and death, Mrs Seddon was in absolute lockstep with her husband.

The acts of both husband and wife were inextricably intertwined: if one was to be found guilty, the other by implication and necessity must be also. Marshall Hall's appeal before Justice Darling on 1st April 1912 pointed this out - either both were guilty, or both were innocent. Justice Darling observed, quite tellingly on that occasion, that 'we shall agree that women are treated more leniently...' That was even acknowledged obliquely by Justice Thomas Bucknill in his summing up when he referred to Mrs Seddon's possible involvement in the actions to defraud Miss Barrow. The Attorney General, Sir Rufus Isaacs, hinted that the jury might not find Mrs Seddon guilty. And the police report following the trial, held in the National Archives, states:

'The verdict [is] illogical. Frederick Seddon's wife should, and before a less emotional and sentimental judge, would have been rightly convicted.'

It *was* illogical; Mrs Seddon was as guilty as her husband and, it seems on careful reflection that it is far more likely that she administered the poison in Miss Barrow's medicine, than her husband. He did not give Miss Barrow her medicine; it would have been odd had he done so; the only person who administered this to her was Mrs Seddon.

If Seddon was the avaricious, beady eyed instigator of the crime, she was its chief prosecutor as she procured the poison; she administered it to her food or drink or medicine: she had the means and opportunity, which Seddon did not. Eliza Barrow's death was surely attributable to both of them - but it was Margaret Seddon who tended her patient with such attentive care, and who proved to be her angel of death.

There can be little doubt that Mrs Seddon was guilty of the murder of Eliza Barrow. But she was given the benefit of the small residue of latitude the jury could afford in the case. She gained by comparison to her husband's arrogance: he drew the ire of the judge and jury, by his brazen callousness; his meanness in all his actions, which even Marshall Hall called 'repugnant.' Mrs Seddon benefitted from this; the case against her was given, by a stretch, as not proven. There can have been few who regarded her as innocent - Margaret Seddon, quite certainly, got away with murder.

After Frederick Seddon was hanged at Pentonville Prison on 18th April 1912, Margaret returned with the five children to Liverpool. She sold her story to *The Weekly Dispatch* on 17th November 1912, and to several other newspapers too, in which she made a statement saying she had seen her husband administer the poison from the flypapers and that he had threatened to 'blow her brains out' with a revolver if she breathed a word of it; she kept silent for the sake of the children, she said. The tale is pure fiction; filled with improbabilities. The Seddons were professional liars.

But Mrs Seddon's story is interesting. It is instructive because every lie leaves a trail. And a really good liar beds their lie in as much truth as they dare - that is what makes a good lie work. Mrs Seddon's lies are ones of omission and commission - she says she saw Seddon putting the poison in the medicine, and this seems authentic, but her claim she demurred does not; there was no demurral from her - he was not caught doing it, he never tried to conceal it from her, because he didn't need to. And of course, it was Mrs Seddon who gave Eliza Barrow the medicine she well knew to be poisoned, because she was the only person to give Eliza Barrow her medicine. Nor did her husband threaten to blow her brains out - this was a wholly improbable invention, which she introduced to explain why she did not report the matter to the police. But the story she gives in her account provides a nuanced explanation of what happened - one which naturally expiates herself and ensures the entire blame is shifted onto her dead husband. And she may well have come to believe the greater part of her story; as murderers often do, to try to reconcile their actions with the expectations of society, and even with their own retrospective consciences. In this way, by finding the smallest reason that could support her own actions, she was able to persuade herself that not only Eliza, but that she herself was a victim of her husband's evil. But it won't do at all. Responsibility is a personal thing; not to be devolved to others lightly and never to absolve oneself from guilt or to excuse the terrible acts one does.

Her story had another purpose - the inconsistency of the verdict in finding Seddon guilty and his wife innocent, when all the evidence relating to the murder itself seemed to point irrevocably to her, stalked her. She was booed out of Hyde Park at a meeting designed to gain signatures for a petition for her husband's reprieve on the Sunday before he was hanged. Her being found not guilty, as so often in these cases, did not confer upon her the good will of the general public; or even its consent in the jury's verdict. She was regarded with suspicion; at the very least as a thief and murderer's accomplice; at worst a callous murderer, whose husband had paid the penalty for them both.

Margaret Seddon was not sentimental and her tears dried quickly; she grieved for the loss of her husband for six months and then, on 4th November 1912, she married James Donald Cameron at St Cleopas Church, Toxteth, in Liverpool.

The following month, on 12th December 1912, the family sailed for Boston, Massachusetts, under the name of Budge. They settled in Providence, Rhode Island, where Margaret had three more children, and then retired to Manchester, Connecticut in 1945. The Camerons lived unobtrusive lives of quiet oblivion. None of Margaret Cameron's neighbours seem to have known that she had been tried for murder at the Old Bailey in London in 1912.

Frederick Seddon liked nothing better than to count his money; to add up the figures in the basement office at 63 Tollington Park each evening; to calculate his profits and losses. But there is always a reckoning - as far as we know none of us escape it. Frederick Seddon made his on 18th April 1912. It was to be another 51 years before Margaret Seddon made hers - and that reckoning came to her in Manchester, Connecticut, on 29th December 1963, at the age of 86.

Above: Miss Eliza Barrow.

Above: 63 Tollington Park.

Frederick Seddon.

Frederick Seddon in masonic regalia.

Margaret Seddon.

Seddon family. From left: Maggie, Margaret with 7 month old baby, Seddon 's father, and his son William.

Ernie Grant and his sister Hilda never received Miss Barrow's money. They were separated, though they met again in later life. Ernie was in the RAF and then worked as a fitter until his death in Muswell Hill in 1967.

Frederick and Margaret Seddon in the dock.

Justice Bucknill wearing the traditional 'black cap' sentences Frederick Seddon to death - the only photo of such an occasion in a British court.

4. Murder In The Mews: Elvira Barney, 1932

It was approximately 4.40 am on 31st May 1932 when Dr Thomas Durrant was woken at his home in Westbourne Terrace in West London by the telephone ringing. On answering it, the frantic voice of a woman, which he recognised to be that of a patient of his called Elvira Barney, told him:

'Doctor, come at once. There has been a terrible accident.'

'What is the matter?' he inquired.

'A man has shot himself,' she told him.

He dressed, collected his medical bag and called for a taxi, arriving at 21 William Mews off Lowndes Square in Knightsbridge, where she lived, at about 6 am.

On being admitted to the house by Elvira Barney, Dr Durrant found a young man lying sprawled on the landing and top of the stairs, and a revolver lay close by. It was immediately clear that he was dead, and Durrant quickly ascertained that he had been shot in the chest.

The woman, Elvira Barney, was in a hysterical state. She told him that she and the young man, a friend called Michael Stephen, had quarrelled, that she had threatened to kill herself with the revolver, and he had tried to wrest it from her, during which it had gone off.

'He isn't dead, is he? Do something! Do something!' she implored him. But Michael Stephen was beyond help.

The police were called, and Detective Inspector William Winter arrived at the scene some time before 7 am. He examined the revolver, and surveyed the scene and said to Elvira Barney:

'I want some explanation of this - he has undoubtedly been shot.'

Elvira Barney became angry, and she told him to get out. Miss Barney was clearly the worse for wear, had been drinking and probably taking drugs, which together with recent events may have been responsible for her state of high excitement. Inspector Winter did his best to calm her down.

'We had a quarrel and he got the revolver from a chair,' she told him. 'We struggled and it went off. It is terrible.'

Winter said that he would need her to accompany him to Gerard Road Police Station to make a statement. A colleague, Detective Sergeant Campion, helpfully suggested she could put her fur coat on to keep her warm on the journey to Gerard Road. At this she flew into a rage and struck him in the face.

It was a bit of an impasse for the two rather overly-respectful officers, but at this moment the phone rang. Inspector Winter answered it: it was Lady Evelyne Mullens, Elvira Barney's mother. He dutifully handed over the phone to Elvira. When she had replaced the receiver, she turned to Inspector Winter:

'Now you know who my mother is, you will be a little more careful in how you speak to me. I will teach you to say you will take me to a police station.'

The young woman's parents, Sir John and Lady Evelyne Mullens who arrived at the house a short time afterwards, were a little more tactful than Elvira. They accompanied her to Gerard Road Police Station where she made a statement, taking her afterwards to their home at nearby 6 Belgrave Square.

Neighbours gave police slightly varying accounts of the events of that night, but it was clear that there had been a party at 21 William Mews, with approximately 30 guests arriving there at around 7 pm and leaving at about 9 pm. Soon afterwards, the young man, Michael Stephen, and Elvira Barney, had left in her saloon motor car together. Neighbours had been awoken at around 4 am. There was a violent quarrel in progress between a man and woman at No. 21. Mrs Barney was heard to scream:

'Get out of my house at once. I hate you! Get out! Get out! I will shoot you!'

The man was heard to say -

'I am going.'

A shot followed soon after this and the man cried -

'Good God! What have you done?'

The woman could be heard screaming,

'Michael, come back to me!'

This was followed by silence for 15 minutes. Then Mrs Barney was heard to call the name 'Michael' twice and then - there was a terrible silence.

It seems that rows between the couple were common and that 11 days earlier neighbours in the mews had seen Michael Stephen leave no. 21 following such a row and, as he walked away from the house, Elvira Barney appeared at an upper window with a revolver in her hand and fired a shot at him. She had missed and the couple had reconciled the following morning, Michael Stephen having slept in an empty grocer's van in the mews during the night! Police noted that the revolver had two empty cartridges in its five chambers and examination of the house revealed a bullet hole in a wall. When questioned, one neighbour thought there had been two shots fired that night and another thought it was possibly four or even five - but it may be that doors slamming had confused them.

Elvira Barney confirmed that there had been a party for 30 friends at No. 21 William Mews, which was equipped with a cocktail bar, and that afterwards she and Michael Stephen had left the house at 10 pm in her car. They had arrived at the *Cafe de Paris* at about midnight for a late supper, where they were joined by a friend, Arthur Tilden Jeffress. The three of them went together to the *Blue Angel* club in Dean Street and she and Michael Stephen returned to their mews residence at about 2 am. They had quarrelled and she had told him to leave. She had said she would kill herself and he had taken the revolver from beneath a cushion on the chair in the bedroom. They had struggled over this, and it had gone off. She did not realise he was injured until he called from another room, telling her to fetch a doctor. Michael Stephen had, she said, expressed his impatience several times for the doctor to arrive so he could tell him that this was not Elvira's fault.

But the pathologist Sir Bernard Spilsbury examined the body of Michael Stephen in the house on 31st May before its removal, and later carried out a post-mortem, and as a result of this he considered it unlikely that Michael Stephen had shot himself. Robert Churchill, the expert London gunsmith concurred; he thought that the gun had been pointed directly at the victim and that Michael Stephen could not have fired it himself. Having considered all of the evidence, the police now concluded that Elvira Barney's story was, at best unlikely, at worst impossible.

At 6.40 on the evening of 3rd June 1932, Inspector Winter, together with Detective Sergeant Campion went to 6 Belgrave Square. Here they saw Elvira Barney. Winter said:

'You know that I am Detective Inspector Winter and this other officer is Detective Sergeant Campion. Do you feel capable of understanding anything I may say to you?'

She nodded.

'I am going to charge you with the murder of Michael Scott Stephen on May 31st at 21 William Mews.'

At the police station she was formally charged and said:

'I did not shoot him. I am not guilty.'

Elvira Barney was born Elvira Enid Mullens on 22nd January 1904, the daughter of Sir John Ashley Mullens and his wife Evelyne Maude Mullens. Mullens was a wealthy financier and stockbroker, whose firm, Mullens and Co, were advisers to the Government National Debt Commissioners. The family lived at the prestigious address of 6 Belgrave Square in Knightsbridge, they had more than 20 servants and counted amongst their neighbours King George V's youngest son, Prince George and his wife Princess Marina of Greece and Denmark. Elvira's sister Avril had, at the age of just 16, married a Prince Imeretinsky of Georgia, which had caused a great stir. These were headstrong girls. Elvira liked to be the centre of attention and possessing no academic application which might suit her for one of the professional opportunities opening up to women in the 1920s, she decided to become an actress. She took training at Lady Constance Benson's acting school in London. If she had any talents as an actress, these were of a light, comedic and musical kind. She had a forgettable part in a forgettable play called 'The Blue Kitten' at the *Gaiety Theatre* in 1926, but it was quickly apparent that her greatest role was to be that of Elvira Barney.

The 1920s was a decade of change; there was a

rejection of the values of pre-war society - and the role of women was changing too. The grimness of war, and the terrible toll it had taken on a generation of youth, fostered a hedonistic outlook, which was characterised by drinking, drug-taking and sexual promiscuity - at least amongst that stratum of society which could afford to indulge it. The term 'bright young things' was coined by the press as a phrase to describe a certain type of wealthy young aristocratic person, whose lack of apparent ambition, morals or any great talent was codified and, to an extent, mitigated by this appellation. Elvira Barney was certainly a 'bright young thing' - she had money, or parents who were unstinting in providing her with it, possessed no moral restraint that could be discerned, and had no purpose in life other than to attend parties with like-minded individuals, drinking, experimenting with a variety of drugs and indulging in promiscuous sexual behaviour. Though many of her set consisted of a lesbian, homosexual 1920s sub-culture, she seemed on the whole to prefer men, but she had sexual affairs with women also. For Elvira and her friends, their way of life is immortalised in the words of Cole Porter, 'Anything goes!'

In 1927 she had met John Sterling Barney of a vocal group called *The Three New Yorkers*, who performed at various West End parties and at the *Cafe de Paris*, the epicentre of the louche world of the bright young things. Barney was American and Elvira and he were married on 2nd August 1928 after a brief acquaintance. The marriage didn't last long - within months it was over and by 1929 John Barney had returned to New York. They were still married though.

Elvira, now 25, already known for a lack of restraint in all her conduct, began drinking more and using cocaine heavily. She had a string of lovers, all of whom seemed to be casual, often interchangeable, many indulging in fetishistic sexual activities of one sort or another. The police report into the crime reported that officers found items and literature at the scene which they regarded as being more suitable to a brothel than to a domestic home. In 1931 Elvira met Michael Scott Stephen, who was 23 years old, had been educated at Shrewsbury School, was known as an excellent cricketer there, and whose appetite for partying matched hers. It has been claimed that he was bisexual and whilst there is no proof of this, it is a reasonable assumption, even probable given the circles he moved in and the friendships he cultivated. His family, who were Scottish but lived in Kent, were respectable and well-to-do. His father was a banker and his brother a solicitor. Michael was employed briefly at the Edinburgh Branch of the *Northern Assurance Co*, but he was restless, adventurous. He had travelled to Paris with the ambition, it seems, of becoming a dress designer and it was here he met Elvira, sometime after her separation from John Barney and probably in the autumn of 1931. There seems to have been a brief dalliance between them in Paris, but it was clearly transitory in nature, and it was only when Michael returned to London at the end of 1931 that the two embarked upon a relationship. By December 1931 he had moved into William Mews with Elvira.

They had a volatile relationship from the start. They quarrelled regularly; they partied until the early hours became old and spent their days in bed until noon. Their indolent and purposeless lives were livened periodically by blazing rows, often physical in nature. Michael Stephen appeared to have no source of income except the handouts which Elvira gave him - his family had cut off his financial support two or three years earlier in an attempt to rein him in, though he still occasionally received help from his mother. He was also a prodigious sponger - he borrowed from everyone.

As far as their neighbours in William Mews were concerned, the couple were a nuisance. Most of the residents of the mews were coachmen and chauffeurs for the big houses on Lowndes Square, the mews houses having originally been conceived as stables for the wealthy Square inhabitants' coaches. Elvira Barney, whose mews house was a modern crashpad whimsically converted from a stable coach-house, was regarded as a nuisance - she and her live-in lover Michael Stephen held noisy parties, arrived home at all hours and had rows which disturbed the lives of the working residents of the mews. The shooting of Michael Stephen appeared to them to be the culmination of many months of disturbances.

Proceedings opened against Elvira Barney on 11th June 1932 at Westminster Magistrates Court. The charges against her were of the wilful murder of Michael Stephen on 31st May and intent to cause grievous bodily harm to him on 19th May. The Crown solicitor outlined the case which it proposed should go before the Central Criminal Court for trial. The gist of this was that the two had quarrelled and Elvira Barney had shot Michael Stephen.

There were several important witnesses whose evidence was heard:

Mrs Dorothy Hall, who lived opposite had been witness to many incidents. The mews being narrow, and Mrs Hall being blessed with good hearing, she appeared to have heard a great deal. She said that after the cocktail party between 7 and 9 pm on 30th May, Elvira Barney and Michael Stephen left the mews in Mrs Barney's car at around 10 pm. She was awoken at about 4.30 am by screaming and shouting which also woke her child, and she looked out of the window. At No 21 she heard Barney telling Michael Stephen to get out and then twice heard her say she would shoot him. She said she heard him say he would go, then a shot rang out and Michael shouted, 'Good God - what have you done?' Then Mrs Barney was screaming 'Come back to me.'

This was followed by silence for about 15 minutes. Then Mrs Barney called his name 'Michael' twice and this was the last she heard.

She also told of the terrible row at 3.30 am on 19th May when there had been an altercation with a taxi driver. Michael Stephen was asking Elvira for money, and she refused. At length she had appeared at the window and called out -

'Laugh baby, laugh for the last time!'

And she had then fired a gun at him.

Mrs Kate Stephens, another mews resident, told the court she was awoken by her dog barking and heard pistol shots. She got out of bed and heard two more shots - four in total. Then she heard Mrs Barney imploring:

'Come back, Michael, I love you.'

William Kiff, who lived next door to Elvira Barney and Michael Stephen, gave evidence that he heard a quarrel between the two at around 4.40 am and Mrs Barney called out 'I will shoot you!' making a clear threat, which was followed by the sound of a shot.

Dr Durrant told the court of the phone call in which Elvira had been frantic and told him that 'a man had shot himself.' At 14 minutes past 5 his taxi had arrived and he went to William Mews; Elvira Barney answered the door and ushered him upstairs, following behind him. On the landing, with his legs trailing on the upper stairs lay Michael Stephen, dead. A revolver lay about four inches from his left hand.

Elvira Barney kept saying, 'He is not dead, is he? Do something for him!'

He had said:

'We must send for the police.'

'Oh don't do that; you must not do that!' she had urged him.

'Do be quiet; you must be quiet,' he had replied.

He said that she told him Stephen had said he was going to leave her for another woman; she threatened to kill herself and Michael Stephen picked up a revolver from beneath a cushion on a chair, saying:

'Well, you won't do it with this!'

They fought over it and the gun went off.

Inspector Winter gave evidence concerning his arrival at the scene, the altercation during which she had struck Detective Sergeant Campion, and his examination of the revolver from which two bullets had been discharged. He noticed a bullet hole in a corner wardrobe and a mark in the wall, from which the bullet had clearly ricocheted. On inquiry she told him it was from a previous occasion on which she had fired the revolver at random.

Sir Bernard Spilsbury gave evidence of the scene of the crime, which he had visited on the day of the murder and of the post-mortem he had carried out on the body of Michael Stephen. Death had been caused by haemorrhage due to bleeding from the lungs. The bullet had entered the chest horizontally and narrowly missed the top of the heart. He said death would have occurred no more than 10 minutes after the shot had been fired. He also said that it was 'not impossible, but was extremely unlikely' for the shooting to have been accidental. The absence of singe marks to the sleeves or hands of the deceased, suggested that his hands had not been anywhere near the revolver when it was fired.

Robert Churchill, the foremost gunsmith in London at the time, gave evidence of the 14 pound pull required to activate the trigger of the .32 *Smith and Wesson* revolver, rendering it highly unlikely that it could have been pulled accidentally. He also noted the absence of blackening on the victim's hands which, he concluded, made it improbable he had been in contact with the revolver at the time of its discharge.

As a result of this evidence, on 18th June 1932, Elvira Barney was committed for trial at the Old Bailey.

The trial of Elvira Barney opened on 4th July 1932, before Justice Travers Humphreys. Sir Percival Clarke appeared for the Crown and the former Attorney General, Sir Patrick Hastings, appeared for the defence.

It was an extraordinary affair. For the first time in the Old Bailey's history, the courtroom seats were available by allocation only. A mere 36 seats in the public gallery were available to the public and people who queued often did so in the hope of being able to sell their seats on for an exalted price. Bewigged barristers sat on the floor while celebrities, actors and the noblesse of London society filled the seats of No 1 Court. The Daily Mirror likened it to a theatrical first night: the fashionable and titled were out in force to see the trial of one of their own. Astonishingly, one of the chief prosecution witnesses, with 30 years experience of murder trials behind him, Sir Bernard Spilsbury no less, was unable to find a seat! At length a police Inspector invited him to share his seat, the two alternating. Meanwhile actors like George Arliss and his party sat back to enjoy the show.

The ushers were scarcely heeded when they called for silence, but the audience settled quickly when Justice Travers Humphreys appeared carrying a bouquet of flowers, a holdover from the days when it was believed the scent of flowers could ward off plague. He took his seat and the clerk cried:

'Bring up Elvira Barney!'

Wearing black with a white blouse, demure, puritannical almost, Elvira Barney, accompanied by three warders, made her entrance. Amongst the bewigged clerks, lawyers dressed in the Quaker style of the English courtroom, she seemed perfectly cast for her role. She was holding a pair of white gloves and stared from the dock at the judge as the jurors' names were read out.

Sir Percival Clarke opened for the prosecution with a description of the events of the evening of 30th May leading up to the death of Michael Stephen in the early hours of the 31st. The witnesses gave their evidence very much as they had done at the magistrates' hearing in Westminster police court the previous month.

The prosecution case was based on four compelling pieces of evidence:

1. At least one shot had been heard that night, which was evidenced by the testimony of witnesses in the mews and by the fact that Michael Stephen had been shot.

2. Three witnesses who heard the shot also heard Mrs Barney speak the words, 'I will shoot you!' immediately prior to the shot; all three neighbours separately and independently informing police of a clear intention being

expressed by Elvira Barney prior to the shot being heard.

3. Several inhabitants of the mews spoke of a violent quarrel 11 days prior to the murder, in which they saw Michael Stephen leave the house and walk away, and Mrs Barney open the window and scream 'Laugh, baby, laugh for the last time!' before firing the revolver at him.

4. The expert witnesses, Sir Bernard Spilsbury and Robert Churchill, thought it highly improbable that the victim could have pulled the trigger himself, and that the angle of the bullet wound, its disposition and the resultant wound, as well as the lack of any singe marks or powder residue on the victim's hands or sleeves, strongly suggested that the gun was pointed directly at him, and had been fired by a hand other than his own.

The defence, in the hands of the consummate barrister and former Attorney General Sir Patrick Hastings, countered this by arguing that:

1. There was only one shot fired - the witness testifying initially to two or four shots being fired was mistaken; and, furthermore, the bullet mark in the wall was the result of a shot being fired on a previous occasion - fired 'at no particular person.'

2. The witnesses who heard Mrs Barney shout 'I will shoot you' or words to that effect actually only heard the words 'I will shoot,' because she was, in fact, threatening suicide, not to shoot Michael Stephen, whom she loved.

3. The couple frequently quarrelled, and Elvira Barney freely admitted this; the occasion when she was alleged to

have fired through a window was not reported to police and should be disregarded. No bullet had been found in the mews and the matter was trifling and unsupportable.

4. Sir Bernard Spilsbury and Robert Churchill were wrong in their evidence that the gun could not have been fired by Michael Stephen and there was, in fact, nothing in Elvira Barney's account of events which was inconsistent with any of the evidence. Her account had been given first to the doctor, then to the police and now to the court, unvarying in its detail. Furthermore, Dr Durrant had given it as his opinion that on the fatal morning the defendant's 'condition was hysterical, and she could not have invented the story she told him.'

Sir Patrick Hastings did sterling work in undermining the testimony of the main witnesses, who had testified to the critical points concerning the quarrel - these being the expression of Elvira Barney's intention to shoot Michael Stephen followed by the sound of the shot itself. Dorothy Hall was coaxed into the admission that Michael Stephen was afraid of leaving Elvira Barney alone for fear she'd commit suicide; she mysteriously dropped her insistence on the 'you' part of her statement referring only to 'I will shoot': her claim that Elvira Barney had said 'Chicken, chicken, come back to me' was ridiculed by Hastings and as the witness Mrs Kate Stephens had heard the words 'Michael, Michael, come back to me' and Elvira Barney herself claimed she had said 'Mickey, Mickey, come back to me' - it was clear that she had comically misheard. Of course it was of no substance, but it tended to undermine the credibility of the witness.

'How awful it would be,' said Sir Patrick, 'if the life of

any one of us might depend upon the evidence of women like these...' gesturing towards the 2 women witnesses.

He then called Elvira Barney to give evidence on her own behalf in the witness box.

She proved a good witness; tearful at the right times; fainting (perhaps judiciously) at dramatic moments and even requiring the administration of smelling salts at times. She spoke of her brief marriage to John Barney and her subsequent meeting with Michael Stephen. She wanted to marry him but divorce from Barney was not a simple matter as her husband was American. She said she was sometimes frightened of Mickey and one letter he had written was cited, referring to 'dreadful, horrible things I have done' to support this. On one occasion she was so frightened of him she called the police, she said.

She also said Michael gambled and he did so with a woman. Sir Patrick wound up his questioning of his client by asking:

Hastings: Have you ever in your life desired to shoot Michael Stephen?

Barney: Never.

Hastings: Has there ever been in your life anybody you were fonder of than Michael Stephen?

Barney: No, never.

Hastings: Did you shoot him that night?

Barney: No.

Hastings: Had you a motive for shooting him?

Barney: None.

Sir Percy Clarke's cross-examination now followed. A moment of appreciable anxiety for the defence, because it is here the public prosecutor is expected to break the defendant's composure and expose the inconsistencies and weaknesses of her story. But it was surprisingly moderate. A casual observer might at times have wondered whether Percy Clarke was the prosecuting or the defence counsel:

Clarke: Did you think he was going to leave you for another woman?

Barney: No, I did not think that.

Clarke: You were very much in love with him?

Barney: Yes.

Clarke: Was the cause of your quarrel always money?

Barney: Yes, money and his gambling habits, in which the woman encouraged him.

This somewhat surprising line of questioning, which at first glance appears to be pursuing a motive for her to have murdered Michael Stephen, actually elicits important points for the defence. It allowed Elvira to establish that the relationship with the woman was not sexual, but monetary in nature, and therefore had the effect of diminishing the suspicion of jealousy on her part as a motive; and it affirmed her claim that she loved him and that her concerns for him were selfless, altruistic even - because the other woman was a bad influence on him.

Nevertheless, Sir Percy gave his summary of the prosecution case by stating that the cause of the trouble between the couple was another woman, and the motive was jealousy. There was no blackening on the victim's hand, and he said that it was Elvira Barney's finger which had been on the trigger when it was fired.

Sir Patrick Hastings' final address to the jury was excellent. His opening took a savage swipe at the fashionable and celebrity attendance in court:

'We rather despise some of these people,' he said, 'If they expect to find amusement here, they will not find it in me.'

Turning to the evidence he summarised the inadequacies he had found in the prosecution case and concluded by declaring that there was 'not enough evidence to hang a cat' and that Elvira Barney should never have been put on trial.

The judge summed up calling Sir Patrick Hastings' speech one of 'the finest I have ever heard at the bar.' He told the jury that there was little predisposition to sympathise with either the accused or the victim in the case. But Travers Humphreys made clear his belief that the case against Elvira Barney was not proven by the prosecution. He also gave his direct opinion that had he been asked to rule on the evidence concerning the shooting from a window on 19th May he would have ruled this evidence as being insufficient to go before a jury.

The jury was sent out to consider three possible verdicts - murder, manslaughter and not guilty. They were absent for nearly two hours, which surprised many, and upon their return to the courtroom gave their verdict as not guilty of murder, and not guilty of manslaughter. Sir Percy Clarke promptly withdrew the charge relating to the discharge of the revolver on 19th May - in truth he could hardly do otherwise, as the judge had already determined the matter. A charge of common assault was then formally put to Elvira Barney to which she pleaded not guilty and the judge directed the jury to return a verdict of not guilty in this, which they duly did.

Elvira Barney left the dock a free woman. 'Three cheers for Mrs Barney!' cried a young man with a group of well-heeled people outside the court as news of the verdict became known. Her parents left the court in a large limousine with a young woman, which the crowd assumed was Elvira, but in fact, aided by this subterfuge, the acquitted woman left by a side door unnoticed and walked to the corner of Giltspur Street where a taxi awaited her.

The verdict was greeted by the press with a howl of disapproval. There could be no-one who took any great pride or satisfaction in the conduct of the trial - and the judge, and especially the public prosecutor, were entitled to feel somewhat shame-faced. *Time Magazine* across the Atlantic pilloried the judge's beaming endorsement of Sir Patrick Hasting's great speech. Whatever the merits of his forensic oratory, it had scarcely been an uphill battle for him given the absence of an effective prosecution. Travers Humphrey's praise of the speech merely gave the free-wheeling defence greater momentum.

From the proper but limited perspective of due process, a crime had been apprehended by the police; it had been investigated; the Director of Public Prosecutions had brought charges to bear and the accused had stood their trial before 12 men and women - and had been exonerated of the crime: justice had been satisfied, or at least the process had been. But from the less procedurally sound, yet nonetheless valid perspective of the public, justice had not been done. A woman had shot her lover dead following a row; she had shot at him previously, threatening to kill him; she had been heard to express her intention of shooting the victim before the fatal shot was fired; the relevant medical and firearms experts had declared the victim to have been shot by another person at between three inches and six inches range - yet she had been declared not guilty of any crime. It was treated with some scepticism. Had she been a poor woman from a different background who had shot her lover in the same circumstances would she have been found not guilty? It was a question many felt entitled to ask.

Elvira Barney's claims that she had not at first realised there was anything wrong with Michael Stephen was belied by three facts: first, there was blood spatter on the walls of the room; second, the sound of the revolver heard around the mews, would have been deafening and shocking in the house itself; third his collapse would have occurred quickly as blood filled his lungs. Her claim that he had repeatedly said that he wished to tell the doctor that his wound was not Elvira's fault, bears little credibility in the circumstances: the severity of his wound, which splintered two ribs and had narrowly missed the heart, meant he lost consciousness quickly, and was suffocating on his own blood.

Many years after the trial of Elvira Barney, Judge Travers Humphreys wrote a book in which he devoted a chapter to the case. His account of the trial is fascinating as an insight into his thinking. And it is more than this: it is a careful revisiting and reappraisal of the case with the benefit of hindsight. It is a retrospective justification of his own position, and an explanation by himself, to himself even, of why the prosecution failed: in it, he lays out the conditions for the failure of the case and the positions of the prosecution and defence barristers as well as his own.

There was a glaring error in the conduct of the trial, and Humphreys is aware of it: this relates to the question of the failure of the prosecution to press the charge of manslaughter as a possible option to the jury. A prosecution in respect of murder failing, the charge of manslaughter would surely be the natural alternative. The circumstances were reckless in the extreme, the possession of the gun was illegal, the evidence of what was heard by neighbours, of Elvira Barney shooting the revolver out of the window at the victim on a previous occasion, and of her having either then - or even on a previous occasion - fired the revolver in the house, were surely sufficient, at the very least, to warrant a verdict of manslaughter. Travers Humphreys was not to blame for this failure, but he was not entirely blameless either.

It was a most benign assertion by the judge that had the evidence relating to the incident on 19th May and the discharge of the revolver out of the window been put to him, he would have ruled it out. He effectively dismissed a significant piece of narrative evidence from the prosecution case. There was abundant eyewitness evidence in support of this incident; there was evidence that a bullet had been fired in the apartment and evidence that three bullets had been discharged in total in recent weeks. It was a substantial and reasonable part of the prosecution case that the accused was a highly unstable young woman who illegally possessed a revolver and had on at least one other occasion, shot at Michael Stephen. This act of persistent aggression was supported by other evidence - Elvira had called the police to remove Michael

Stephen from her house on previous occasions; she had done so in respect of a previous lover; and she had assaulted Detective Sergeant Campion on the morning of the murder when he had suggested she put on her fur coat to accompany them to the police station. Michael Stephen had bruises, had received a black eye and swollen lip from Elvira during the altercation on the 19th May.

This evidence was all germane to the case - so would other evidence have been, had it been heard in court: the journalist, Charles Graves, a former lover, had - according to various accounts - been shot at by Elvira outside his flat when she caught him with a male companion there in 1924.

And Humphreys was well aware of this deficiency:

'There remains the question of manslaughter - nothing had been said by Sir Percival Clarke as to manslaughter in his summing up to the jury of the case for the prosecution... I am sure there must have been a good reason for it, though I do not understand it. As a matter of law, the more the theory of attempted suicide was stressed, the more clearly would it appear that the deceased man was killed as the direct result of the unlawful act of the accused.'

Humphreys thus critiques the matter admirably and succinctly. But it was surely incumbent on Humphreys to seek greater clarification for the jury on the manslaughter charge, so that, at the very least, the jury should be aware of what constituted manslaughter. In the event, they were presented with the option of manslaughter as a possible verdict without being given proper guidance as to its application. That meant the jury was presented with a somewhat stark decision: to hang a 27-year-old woman who may indeed have been reckless with a firearm and to have unlawfully killed a man; or to find her not guilty. Given the circumstances it is not surprising they felt obliged to return a verdict of not guilty. Nor is it surprising that the press was unconvinced that due process had served justice in this case - because it hadn't.

In his account, Humphreys, in referring to the jury being presented with a simple choice and effectively denied the possibility of bringing in a lesser verdict of manslaughter, also writes: 'I have known such a thing happen on at least one other occasion.'

The case he undoubtedly referred to here was that of Marguerite Alibert, a woman charged in similar circumstances to Elvira Barney six years earlier. She too had killed her lover - in this case her young husband - in circumstances in which there could be little doubt as to the fact that she shot him and that in doing so she acted unlawfully, due to the position he was found in and the circumstances of the killing. In her case too, there were powerful figures, who sought by all means available to them, to ensure her acquittal. In both cases a set of circumstances were put in place which would offer the best possible chance of securing an acquittal.

All the elements for a successful prosecution in Marguerite Alibert's case were there: a strong police case, evidence of intention, evidence of motive, evidence of means and an outcome which made prosecution quite inevitable. But Marguerite Alibert had been the lover of the Prince of Wales; she had possession of the Prince of Wales' letters and probably a great deal more. The stakes were high. A carefully controlled trial, with an amenable judge, a dilatory prosecutor and a powerful defence barrister would ensure, as far as it is possible to do in such a matter, that the accused was acquitted. The options presented to the jury were stark: the noose or a verdict of not guilty. Manslaughter risked tempting a jury to convict on this lesser charge, which would necessarily result in a lengthy sentence. Therefore, although it was an option, it was never argued in court to give a jury the means to consider it.

It is surely the case of Marguerite Alibert which Travers Humphreys alludes to in this account - and his doing so is all the more remarkable because although he does not allude to this, the public prosecutor, who so inadequately presented the police case on that occasion too, was Sir Percival Clarke... Both trials, heard before a free jury, succeeded in producing verdicts of not guilty against all odds, in the face of common sense, and in spite of considerable evidence of guilt.

Of all the evidence available to him and from which the meanest barrister could have constructed a formidable case, Sir Percy Clarke made a wholly inadequate one for the crown. That he did so was not simply remiss; it was calculated; it was deliberate.

It is not possible to say that the public prosecutor deliberately threw a prosecution case in the manner of a rigged third-rate boxing match. That would be too great a charge to make against essentially decent men, whose lives were spent in seeking to uphold and apply the law. But there can be little doubt that in the case of Elvira Barney the public prosecutor had made a conscious decision to exercise restraint in the pursuit of justice, and that being plainly understood by the principals involved, it was played out to perfection within the constraints placed upon it by the judicial system.

Sir Percival Clarke understood in direct terms that

this was not a case the prosecution wished to pursue with the greatest vigour; but he understood also, as a matter of social class, as a matter of the preservation of the society to which he belonged, that a well-connected young woman like Elvira Barney must not be hanged. He understood it as Detective Sergeant Campion understood it when Elvira Barney called him a 'vile swine' and struck him - struck him as she would one of her father's 20-something servants at 6 Belgrave Square - because police were servants in those days. They were not only servants to society but to those who ran it. And what did Sergeant Campion do when assaulted by Barney? Nothing. Later he says she apologised and said she was 'very very sorry.' Of course, Elvira Barney said nothing of the kind. A woman like Elvira Barney does not apologise to servants. It is not in her social or ancestral DNA. Campion hears his dog call; it amounts to an apology on his part. On hearing of her acquittal in court, Inspector Winter rushes over to congratulate Lady Mullens! She waves him aside dismissively. It is this subservient conduct, the manifestation and assertion of class division which is fascinating in this case and critical to its outcome.

It is the purpose of a court of law to weigh those scales of justice, not to produce a result that is certain. Certainty is not the business of any form of human knowledge and the proof demanded by law is one which is beyond reasonable doubt to the ordinary, intelligent man or woman. It seeks therefore an overwhelming probability in a matter which is sufficient to satisfy the normal intelligent person. In the case of Elvira Barney that probability was surely satisfied in the evidence acquired, though not in its presentation to the court.

Because when the scales of justice were employed to

weigh that evidence, a few counterbalances had been added to ensure the scales produced the desired effect and as a result, in July 1932, Elvira Barney got away with murder.

Elvira Barney was a woman of great arrogance, and she was over-indulged by those who loved her. She was certainly mentally unstable, and she sought out relationships which were mutually abusive. The quarrels, the violence, seemed to have a sexually compulsive charge to them; the risk, the danger, their being on the precipice - was another high. She thrived on the existential thrill of excess.

But the quest for another high is self-limiting, because yesterday's excess becomes today's norm, and it is ever necessary to extend the boundaries of excess to satisfy tomorrow's higher expectations. It is so with addiction.

The relationship with Michael Stephen was going nowhere; from sexual frisson it had pursued its compulsive course of control, demand and insatiable excess. The quarrels and violence could only increase to take up the slack. Disaster was inevitable. Elvira's relationships usually ended when her lover could stand no more; they walked out on her; they left. She dared them to it. Charles Graves had done so and she had pursued him with a revolver. To others she had called the police to have them removed. Michael Stephen seemed extraordinarily resilient - he endured their cycle of fight and make-up. Perhaps that was a measure of his own compulsion, or perhaps of necessity because she held the purse-strings. When they rowed on 19th May in the early hours, he came back twice, then she shot at him - but he apparently still returned to the window to tell her not to make a spectacle of herself. He didn't take her threats with the gun seriously; had he done so he'd have removed it, thrown it away or unloaded it. He didn't fear her shooting him - he regarded it as a gesture. He slept in a grocer's van that night, though, and in the morning, they made up: their passion was requited, again traversing the wide spectrum from hate to love in just a few hours. So would the row in the early hours of 31st May 1932 have probably played out.

But shooting a revolver as an expression of personal frustration, as part of a wild game of increasing stakes is dangerous; Michael Stephen was wise enough to realise her intention in the matter was harmless, but too young to know that her control of the matter was not. His mockery of her, his disbelief that the act of shooting at him, of threatening him, was serious, only hastened the moment at which her judgement would be overtaken by her emotions - with catastrophic result.

When they rowed on 31st May 1932, a row which had been simmering all day, which focused on another woman, a gambit preferred by both apparently, to raise the stakes in this game in which violence seemed always to be the outcome, Elvira seized the gun; she told him to get out, she hated him. He said he would; he would go to his other woman; he dressed. This did not requite the passion of her fury: it was her move.

'I will shoot you!' she threatened. He ignored her, possibly smiled, but would certainly have shown his disregard for her threat - that was his habit - she went to him and he turned to her, possibly holding her arms, as there was evidence he had done so previously and may have done so on this occasion: she fired the gun. It was a perfectly natural consequence of the dialogue running between them.

But his surprise was palpable:

'Good God - what have you done?'

They were probably his last words. The bullet, narrowly missing his heart caused him to cough as his lungs filled with blood and he collapsed very quickly and died within minutes. Of course, Elvira was distraught, remorseful, horrified - and yet here was another extreme emotion savoured. It was a game they had played many times; and this was the perfect game with the most tragic of outcomes. It could never be played again.

After her release from the court, a woman acquitted of the worst of crimes, her conduct was such that Justice Travers Humphreys remarked:

'Most extraordinary! Apparently, we should have given her a pat on the back!'

But people like to see justice served. And in a Britain, where the differences between the social classes were being slowly but surely eroded, where a Labour party had eclipsed the liberal party as the voice of the mainstream left, and where women had achieved universal suffrage only four years previously, there was a demand for an equality before the law also. It seemed to many that the invisible yet indelible social contract upon which the lord and servant were treated with equal regard before the law, had not been observed that day.

Elvira Barney returned to her parents' house in Belgrave Square after the trial. It was remarked that she looked much older than her 27 years. She had a distinctly middle aged, almost maternal appearance for one so young. The following day, a beaming Elvira Barney was out in her car, a blue *Delage*, which had been fetched by a chauffeur from 21 William Mews on the previous afternoon, valeted and washed and wax-polished. There was a stream of bouquets of flowers delivered to 6 Belgrave Square throughout the day and it was reported that she received hundreds of letters and many telegrams congratulating her. She drove off to visit her friends and reportedly to visit her hairdresser. Five weeks in prison can wreak havoc with your hair. In fact, it was reported that during the trial for her life, she had been occupied making such appointments, so certain was she of her acquittal. In any case, whether that was true or not, within a short time she had returned to her old haunts, and to drinking and drugs. She visited the *Cafe de Paris*, for the first time since that night when she had shot her lover dead. And according to the press, who followed her and her every indiscretion, she called from the dance floor there:

'I am the woman who shot her lover! Take a good look at me!'

It was hardly calculated to endear her to the press and the public to whom it was eagerly reported; nor to the authorities who had done all in their power to contrive an acquittal for her. And if it did not prove her guilt, being something in the nature of a taunt, a fatuous witticism rather than a confession, then it hardly showed remorse or regret for taking the life of her young lover, whether by accident or design.

It is likely, of course, that her exuberant indiscretion owed something to alcohol and cocaine. But this was 1932, bright young things were no longer regarded as bright and were not particularly young anymore either. The hedonism of the post war 20s, conceived of as a reaction to a war which had visited such horror upon a generation, had given way to a more sober 30s, a rapprochement of old values, re-couched in new fashions.

Elvira Barney found herself unfashionable; a byword for excess; mildly shunned; a somewhat unstable woman; whispered about wherever she went; unsuitable company, except for those who sought the fleeting and undiscriminating attention notoriety brings.

She moved to France within weeks of the trial, where her alcohol-fuelled, drug-dependent and sexually driven lifestyle continued remorselessly; in the end she was fined a mere £50 for the illegal possession of the gun which killed Michael Stephen; she had a much publicised car accident in Cannes in which a Countess Karolyi was severely injured for which Elvira was arrested and which cost her, or her parents, £800 in damages when it was settled.

She was somewhat estranged from her parents; the suicide of a woman called Gertrude Gamble in a Mayfair street some weeks after the trial, who had sent Lady Mullens a letter concerning her daughter's lesbian indulgences, may have been the last straw.

There was a certain self-destructive impulse in Elvira Barney now; the joy of living a life of excess seemed to have become a compulsive, and tawdry one, made arduous by its very predictability. And whatever her indulgence, it was blunted by the terrible inescapable memory of a man she undoubtedly loved, choking to death on his own blood, as she knelt beside him promising him the world.

Just four years after her trial for murder, in the early hours of 25th December 1936, Elvira Barney returned from a party to her hotel off the Champs Elysees, the *Hotel Le Colisee*. She had drunk far too much and snorted copious quantities of cocaine that evening, and had to be assisted by the hall porter to her room, where she collapsed on her bed. Here she was found dead later that Christmas Day when her door was forced by hotel staff. She was lying half on the bed and half off, wearing her jewels and furs, and all her finery. She had died of some form of haemorrhage during the night, possibly as a result of taking a cocktail of alcohol and drugs the previous evening. Her father and mother went over to Paris the following day to see their daughter for the last time. Elvira Barney was cremated in Paris on 29th December 1936. She was 32 years old.

Elvira Barney.

Michael Stephen.

Dr Durrant.

21 William Mews.

The bedroom.

Sir Patrick Hastings.

Sir Percival Clarke KC.

Acquitted: Elvira looked distinctly older than her 28 years.

5. The Suspicious Death Of Mrs Rosse: Arthur Maundy Gregory, 1932

On 19th of August 1932 Mrs Edith Marion Rosse became ill just after lunch, which she ate alone in her home at 10 Hyde Park Terrace in West London. She had been quite well before lunch but within minutes of her meal she became very sick with vomiting and diarrhoea. Her housekeeper, Mrs Lottie Eyres, sent for a doctor and also, at Mrs Rosse's request, for Mrs Rosse's friend Arthur Maundy Gregory, with whom she shared the house but who was presently at his office in Whitehall.

'I feel so ill I don't know if he will arrive in time,' she said.

In fact, Mr Gregory arrived at Hyde Park Terrace at the same time as the doctor, a little after 3 pm, and the two hastened to Edith Rosse's bedside. Dr Plummer examined Mrs Rosse, who was 59, and he concluded that as 19th August was a very hot day she was suffering from heat stroke. He prescribed complete bed rest, aspirin and ice. It seems that although very sick - or perhaps because of this - Edith Marion Rosse wished to make a will. Indeed, so urgent was the matter to her that Maundy Gregory, the friend, fetched a discarded Mayfair restaurant menu card and pencil, and Mrs Rosse dictated her last will and testament to him, which he duly transcribed on the back of this menu. This was signed by Mrs Rosse with some effort, and witnessed by Dr Plummer and Mrs Eyres.

Mrs Rosse's belief as to her dire condition turned out to be wrong, because in the next few days, she recovered. The following week she went out driving and by early September her health and spirits had returned to their former condition.

Then on Saturday evening 3rd September, Mrs Rosse, who dined in the evening with her friend Maundy Gregory in the upper floor apartment at Hyde Park Terrace, was once again struck down by the same terrible illness.

It was just after midnight when Dr Plummer was sent for. This time he thought some form of blood poisoning was responsible for her illness - possibly a dysfunction of her kidneys. Mrs Rosse regained consciousness only fitfully in the ensuing days, was confused, she was seen by two specialists who gave various opinions on the cause of her illness, and at 12:45 in the early hours of 14th September, she died. Dr Plummer gave her cause of death as being 1. cerebral haemorrhage and 2. chronic Bright's disease - a generic term for kidney disease. Arthur Maundy Gregory, her friend in the apartment above hers, made the arrangements for her funeral at a small graveyard at Bisham near Marlow on the banks of the River Thames, and it was here that Edith Marion Rosse was laid to rest on 19th September 1932. The familiar adjunct, 'Requiescat in Pace' was carved onto the foot of her marble crossed tombstone - may she Rest in Peace. And for a little time, she did.

Edith Marion Rosse was born Edith Davis in Edmonton, London in 1873. She was an attractive woman and being in possession of a good singing voice she went on stage and made a good living as an actress in musical comedies. She appeared in 'Dorothy,' the 'Duchess of Danzig,' and also in Gilbert and Sullivan operettas, under the stage name Vivian Pierpont. In the early 1900s she met the composer Frederick Rosse, and they married in 1908, informally adopting her brother's daughter Ethel Davis, after he was widowed, around 1911. Husband and wife became very friendly with an actor-cum-impresario called Arthur Maundy Gregory, and the three lived together at a wooden bungalow called *Vanity Fair*, at Ditton Island on the Thames, from around 1919 on. Later they lived at number 3 Abbey Road, in St. John's Wood - the house which 40 years later became a recording studio, and outside of which, John, Paul, George, and Ringo, famously walked across the zebra crossing in the summer of 1969.

In 1923 Edith and Frederick Rosse separated, Edith and her niece Ethel remaining with Maundy Gregory at Abbey Road. Arthur Maundy Gregory and Edith were close in a platonic sense; he was probably a latent homosexual, and they told people they were brother and sister for the sake of appearances. Edith spent much of the money she received from her estranged husband on property - she owned four houses and seven flats by 1932. She also had substantial savings. Her niece Ethel was periodically with them, but the two women had a stormy relationship; Edith was demanding, and Ethel had a rebellious disposition. Edith had made a will out favouring Ethel but following a row over a ring she had given to Ethel, and Ethel had pawned, she tore the will up, saying, 'Now you've burnt your boats!' But privately she made another will favouring Ethel and she nevertheless supported her with a weekly allowance.

Sometime in the 3rd week of September, 1932, Ethel Davis visited her aunt at Hyde Park Terrace. She was shocked to learn from the housekeeper that Mrs Rosse was dead and had been buried. It had all been arranged by her aunt's friend, Arthur Maundy Gregory, without the family's knowledge. Ethel Davis telephoned Maundy Gregory; he was uncommunicative, and he told her he was unable to discuss her aunt's illness as it was a matter of 'professional secrecy.'

Inquiries of Dr Plummer concerning these matters drew a similarly short, unhelpful response; he too cited 'professional secrecy.' Ethel's brother, Fred Davis, visited Maundy Gregory's office at 38 Parliament Street, but his secretary Mr Pratley, said he was too ill to see anyone. He then rang Dr Plummer's surgery and requested an appointment to see the doctor, but the following day he received a letter from Dr Plummer curtly refusing this, again citing professional secrecy. Fred Davis went to the Coroner's Court in Paddington, but was simply advised to contact a solicitor.

He decided to write to Maundy Gregory inquiring about his sister's grave and also about her will, which he said his sister had led him to believe he would benefit from. He received a reply from Gregory's secretary:

'Dear Sir,

Mr Gregory has asked me to thank you for your letter... He would like a little later to consider personally making you some little gift from himself as a memento.

Believe me,

Yours faithfully,

G Pratley
Private Secretary'

It was all very frustrating. Fred Davis then visited Somerset House, the public records office, and asked to see Edith Rosse's will. Here he discovered that on the reverse side of a menu card, written in pencil and in a hand not familiar to him, was a will. It read:

'Everything I have, if anything happens to me, to be left to Mr J Maundy Gregory, to be disposed of as he thinks best and in accordance with what I desire.'

It was a shock. Fred Davis thought the will must be a forgery. He wrote to Edith Rosse's estranged husband, Frederick Rosse, who lived in Torquay, telling him of his suspicions. Rosse passed the matter to his solicitors for advice. He was himself somewhat concerned, because as part of their separation agreement, he had paid Edith half of his yearly earnings for the past 10 years - a sum not less than £4,000, all told (that's at least £250,000 in 2020). He also realised - as he pointed out to Fred Davis - that as he was still technically married to Edith at the time of her death, he was legally her next of kin.

By the New Year 1933, Ethel Davis was living on charity at a convent and Fred Davis was broke. There had been no progress for them in the matter. Then on 7th February Ethel Davis saw a newspaper headline which astonished her: Arthur Maundy Gregory had been charged with trying to sell a knighthood to a wealthy man for £10,000. The newspapers were filled with the story. And Ethel Davis knew she now had a bigger story to tell, because she believed that Maundy Gregory was more than a conman, he was a murderer.

Emboldened by this knowledge she went straight to Scotland Yard and spoke to Detective Inspector Arthur Askew, who was in charge of the matter. She soon convinced him she had a lot to tell about Maundy Gregory and indeed she did: it took Detective Sergeant Percy Ruffett and Detective Constable Hodge three days to take down Ethel's statement, which ran to 60 pages.

Detective Inspector Askew read this and pondered the matter. On the face of it a 59-year-old wealthy woman had died; she was in the care of a doctor, and he had signed a death certificate giving her cause of death as a natural one. But Arthur Maundy Gregory, the man who had been present when she died, and who was the sole beneficiary of her will, was not only a man who had been charged with attempting to sell a title, he was someone suspected of a bewildering number of crimes, including fraud, receiving stolen goods and blackmail. He was also a man with friends in high places - and Arthur Maundy Gregory had proved astonishingly adept at avoiding prosecution until now.

Arthur Maundy Gregory was born at Southampton in 1877, the son of the vicar of St Michael's Church. He attended Banister Court School, and for a time attended Oxford University studying divinity intending to take holy orders. At school he had discovered an affinity for the theatre and befriended another boy, Harold Davidson, who was to become a lifelong acquaintance, and who was himself to become well known as the infamous Rector of Stiffkey. It is worth mentioning this because there are extraordinary parallels in the two friends' careers and fortunes, and it seems rather curious that two bad apples should be contemporaries and friends, alumni of the same school - but friends they were, and both shared the same interests in religion and the theatre. Harold Davidson, like Maundy Gregory, began as an actor, and then took holy orders, both were religious men with a dark side barely concealed beneath the surface - and Davidson's fall from grace as Rector of Stiffkey was to be every bit as spectacular as that of his friend Maundy Gregory.

Having initially started out as an actor, Maundy Gregory established a touring company and in 1908, with the assistance of his friend Harold Davidson and others, he mounted a West End production of *Dorothy*. It was here he met Edith Rosse. The two became platonic friends. The Rosses shared Maundy Gregory's homes and vice versa, until Frederick and Edith separated. Maundy Gregory was unsuccessful as an impresario - his talent lay in his bonhomie, his avuncular air of geniality. It provided him with the perfect role - one which he was to play for the rest of his life. He was acquainted with a large number of people in the theatrical world and beyond and in 1914 he set himself up as a private detective of sorts. He had a talent for weaselling out the private indiscretions of people and he soon found he could use the information he obtained on people to blackmail them.

He began to supply information to MI5 too. He was probably responsible for the acquisition of Sir Roger Casement's so-called Black Diaries, whose wide dissemination revealing explicit homosexual activities led to a collapse in public sympathy for Casement after he had been sentenced to death for treason in 1916. Calls for a reprieve for Casement were loud; he had done notable work in his earlier years for humanitarian causes. The US senate was vocal in seeking Casement's reprieve, and in 1916 Britain was assiduously courting the US in the hopes of persuading her to enter WW1. The sharing of Casement's diaries with the US Ambassador led to a swift collapse in support for Casement - and he was executed.

But the Secret Service did not trust Maundy Gregory. A report written in March 1926 began:

'We know him, and we don't trust him.'

He became editor of a society magazine called *Mayfair* and of the *Whitehall Gazette* too. But it was in 1918 that he became involved in the scandal for which he is best remembered. Prime Minister Lloyd George needed to raise funds for the Liberal party, to fight the forthcoming general election and he decided to do so by selling titles for cash. Maundy Gregory was just the man for this: he used his knowledge of those on the fringe of society; his knowledge of their lives and aspirations - and most of all their vanity, to sell honours to them. The going rate for a knighthood was about £10,000 (approximately £700,000 in 2020 terms) and for a peerage £40,000 (approximately £2.8 million). Maundy Gregory approached people with this tariff, and as a result, a great many peerages and knighthoods were dispensed after 1918.

The coffers of the Liberal Party filled with lucre - and so did Maundy Gregory's pockets. He became a very wealthy man. It should also be said that he was a generous man also - he gave money to those he knew, freely - he funded an author to write a book on the eccentric Baron Corvo, whom he admired; he funded gilding work at Westminster Abbey for £5,000 - and he was careful to ensure everyone knew of this. He acquired the *Ambassador's Club* in Conduit Street, which he used as a front for much of his business, and the 90-bedroom *Deepdene Hotel* in Surrey, with the aid of a rascally second-generation Italian called Peter Mazzina. Most of his shady enterprises were loss-makers, but the titles brokerage was very lucrative.

By 1922 the matter of titles sales was becoming a national scandal: four notorious businessmen, war profiteers, were ennobled and took their seats in the House of Lords, angering King George V. It became known that they had purchased their titles. Amidst a public outcry parliament resolved to act. The practice was curtailed by the Honours Commission of 1922 - and in 1925 the *Honours (Prevention of Abuses) Act* explicitly forbade the sale of honours, making it a criminal offence for anyone to seek to sell an honour or title of the United Kingdom or to pay for one. It was a blow to Maundy Gregory, but Maundy Gregory was nothing if not adaptable. He continued to offer honours for sale by stealth to those unaware that he had no titles to dispense. When he sold titles to people which failed to be delivered, they were left in the invidious position of not being able to report Maundy Gregory to the police, since they would themselves be liable to prosecution for having attempted to purchase one!

Maundy Gregory was now a fully-fledged conman. His approach was comical, incredible even: he would have a likely dupe ushered into his plush office at 38 Parliament Square, a whisper away from 10 Downing Street, where he sat behind a large desk, equipped with a phalanx of telephones and signed photographs of various royal persons. He would greet his intended mark with an outstretched heavily ringed hand; they would notice his diamond encrusted cufflinks, a black pearl tie pin, and he would offer them a cigarette from a gold cigarette case, which he would contrive to mention was a gift from the King of Greece. Perhaps they would care to meet him? The phone would ring and he would have a nondescript conversation, which would involve him saying, at some point, 'Certainly your Majesty,' or 'of course, your Royal Highness.' At some point in this act he would inevitably be interrupted by a private secretary to inform him in hushed tones that No 10 was on the phone. He would excuse himself apologetically, while turning over in his fingers a large rose diamond he kept in his waistcoat pocket, which had once belonged to the Czar. He was also known to drive to Buckingham Palace with a potential dupe, stop off, excusing himself, and appear to enter the palace by a side entrance; after a while he would reappear, apologising to his would-be victim and inform them how important it was for him not to be seen to enter by the front gate! 'His majesty would not like it,' he would tell them solemnly. In this at least, he was probably correct.

But Maundy Gregory's fortunes were in terminal decline - the new laws and other measures had a serious impact on his activities, and when a wealthy man died having paid him for a title and not received it, his family sued - and Maundy Gregory was forced to repay the money - £30,000 (£2.1 million in 2020). He didn't have this sum of money and he took greater risks to recoup his losses, like a gambler doubling down. He diversified too: he converted to Roman Catholicism and proceeded to offer papal knighthoods for sale - he awarded one to himself. The Roman Catholic father of Mia Farrow was sold an annulment to his marriage by Maundy Gregory so that he could marry the actress Maureen

O'Sullivan - he didn't get it. Gregory became involved in the Anglo-Ukrainian committee, which was set up to fight bolshevism, but which Maundy Gregory used to sell Ukrainian titles - and pocketed the money himself until he was scuppered.

Even so his debts were mounting. His sources of revenue were shrinking. Taking ever increasing risks, in December 1932 he attempted to sell a baronetcy to Lieutenant Commander Billyard-Leake - it was a mistake. Billyard-Leake was a wealthy landed man, old money, not a new industrialist jockeying for acceptance on the fringes of society. Billyard-Leake went to the authorities. It was this that led to Maundy Gregory's being charged for offences against the Honours Act.

If his own career had taken a nosedive, perhaps he could take comfort in the fact that his old school friend Harold Davidson, who had always had a passion for pretty young women, an obsession with them even, had come to grief also. The good Vicar Davidson spent too much of his time in London rather than in his parish, rescuing and rehabilitating prostitutes, until it was discovered that he was doing rather more than merely saving their souls. He was tried by an ecclesiastical court and defrocked, which was perhaps ironic because his downfall owed much to a photograph taken of his reverence with a woman who was at the time, herself, defrocked.

By the summer of 1932 Maundy Gregory was in severe financial difficulties. It was at this point he turned to his friend Edith Marion Rosse for a loan. She refused him. It was just a few weeks after her refusal of a loan that Mrs Rosse became violently ill and soon afterwards died.

Inspector Askew knew that Maundy Gregory was

thoroughly dishonest, a man without scruple, a conman, an accomplished liar: was he also a murderer?

Askew took statements from the doctor, the undertaker, and from the dead woman's brother and her niece. Fred Davis told Askew that three days after her first illness, on 22nd August, Edith met him at Baker Street Tube station at 7.30 pm - there was a witness to this. He said that on that occasion she seemed quite well.

Askew had amassed a large amount of indicative evidence, but he knew that really this did little more than suggest that Maundy Gregory had the motive to commit the act of murder - nothing existed in the way of actual proof. The prosecution in respect of the sale of honours was difficult enough - and fraught with political sensitivities. An ill-supported charge of murder risked upsetting this finely balanced matter.

Inquiries with medical men produced the unequivocal opinion that the symptoms described by those who had been with Mrs Rosse during her illness were those of acute poisoning, and nothing that could possibly be attributed to cerebral haemorrhage or Bright's disease. But the opinion of an entire medical community based on reported symptoms alone was of little value against the stubborn fact of the death certificate issued by the doctor who treated her.

Askew interviewed Mr Benjamin Pengelly, Maundy Gregory's and Mrs Rosse's accountant, who told him that a second will had been made by Mrs Rosse after she had torn up the original one - Ethel was still the chief beneficiary and still nothing had been left to Maundy Gregory. He also told him that Mrs Rosse's cash books and a diary of accounts book which he had requested from Maundy Gregory, had been duly sent to him, with sections having been removed. *29 pages in all were missing.* Pengelly said Mrs Rosse had told him Maundy Gregory was very bad-tempered recently and said she thought he was financially worried. She expressed her surprise at this because she had thought him to be wealthy. She also inquired, he said, whether Mr Pengelly had told Maundy Gregory of her financial deposits, which appeared to show a concern on her part for Maundy Gregory's interest in her finances. In addition, Frederick Rosse, the estranged husband, flatly denied his wife would have made such a will and certainly not whilst in her right mind.

The investigation was slow. Then on 6th April, 1933, the solicitors acting for Mr Rosse requested an exhumation of the body of Edith Marion Rosse: they wanted a second opinion on her cause of death. Six days later, on advice from Scotland Yard, this was granted.

Meanwhile, Maundy Gregory, who appeared before magistrates for attempting to sell a baronetcy to Lt Commander Billyard-Leake, on the advice of his counsel Norman Birkett KC, pleaded guilty. He was also counselled by others, and may have obtained the promise that if he pleaded guilty it would spare much embarrassment to many people in public life and avoid a terrific scandal - and in doing so, he would be taken care of afterwards. As a result of this, the matter did not go to trial; and he received a two-month prison sentence and £50 fine. As far as the police were concerned Maundy Gregory was now safely in prison while the matter of Mrs Rosse's death could be investigated.

On the morning of 28th April 1933 Askew received the order authorising exhumation of the body of Mrs Rosse, and he moved quickly. By nightfall he and Dr

Roche Lynch, the Home Office analyst, along with other detectives stood at the graveside in Bisham Cemetery, on the banks of the River Thames. A derrick was erected over the grave and the marble cross headstone weighing half a ton was raised and then the men began to shovel away the clogged heavy riverbank clay.

It didn't take long as the coffin was discovered to be buried a mere 18 inches beneath the surface. Canvas straps were placed under it and the men lifted it to the surface. Water streamed from it as it tilted slightly. It was an ill-omen and Roche Lynch cursed and attempted to catch some of the water draining from it in a beaker. The undertaker peered at its brass nameplate and confirmed that this was the coffin of Edith Marion Rosse. It was then sealed with red bands and the ends of the coffin sealed too, and then it was trundled some 20 yards to a van which awaited it. From here it was taken under police guard to Paddington mortuary, arriving there at 10:45 pm, where it remained overnight.

In the morning at 10 am the press, having learned that an inquest was to be opened, were out in force at the Coroner's Court in Paddington, which was situated in the same building as the mortuary. Askew was first to arrive, with other detectives, then Roche Lynch carrying a large square box in which empty sample jars could be seen - and then the pathologist Sir Bernard Spilsbury arrived at a little after 10 am. With the coffin on the bench Spilsbury cut the sealing tapes under the watchful eyes of Askew and Roche Lynch.

The lid was lifted and Spilsbury at once tutted. The coffin, which was lead-lined because the graveyard was on the Thames floodplain, had not been sealed. The usual practice was to seal the coffin by soldering the lid, but this had not been done and consequently it was filled with water.

It had lain underground for some months - the state of preservation of the corpse was not good. It was a great disappointment.

After Frederick Rosse had confirmed the identity of his wife's body, the corpse was lifted from the coffin and Spilsbury commenced his grim work with his customary matter-of-factness, punctuated only by his clipped observations. Various organs, including the stomach, liver, kidneys, brain and heart were removed, and placed in glass jars by Roche Lynch.

As the post-mortem was in progress, just a few yards away Samuel Ingleby Oddie, the Paddington coroner, opened the inquest into the death of Edith Marion Rosse. Her husband, Frederick Rosse, confirmed the identity of the woman as seen in the coffin, as being his wife Edith. The formalities of identification completed, Ingleby Oddie adjourned the inquest to permit the pathologist, analyst, and police to complete their enquiries. It had all lasted for less than 10 minutes.

Later that same day, in the early evening of 29th April, the coffin of Edith Marion Rosse was reinterred in its grave at Bisham Cemetery, while a fascinated crowd assembled on the opposite bank of the Thames to watch the procedure.

In the weeks that followed, speculation was rife - the *Daily Herald* confidently asserted that poison had been found; it was widely known that this was a murder investigation; Maundy Gregory featured prominently in newspaper reports, and the attention on him was intense. He had not been seen. Where was he? He had been released from prison.

Askew was hoping to arrest Maundy Gregory and subject him to the pressures of interrogation. But he had disappointing news: Gregory had been released early from Wormwood Scrubs for good behaviour, on the morning of 12th April. He had been collected at the prison gates by a friend of JCC Davidson, the Chairman of the Conservative Party; he was driven directly to Newhaven, where he took the ferry for Dieppe. Within 12 hours of his release from prison, Arthur Maundy Gregory was in Paris. DCI Arthur Askew knew nothing of this development until it was too late. His only hope now was for the coroner to order the return of Maundy Gregory.

The inquest was finally reconvened on 19th July. The Coroner's Court was packed. The family was present, and the detectives, the expert witnesses, and an army of reporters - but there was no sign of the principal character, Maundy Gregory. The coroner opened the proceedings with an account of the events which had led to Mrs Rosse's death and to her exhumation. This account clearly followed the official narrative and police view of the matter.

'In August 1932 Maundy Gregory was in financial difficulties, owing £1,000 and creditors were in pursuit,' he said. He spoke of Mrs Rosse's sudden illness after lunch on 19th August and Dr Plummer's improbable diagnosis of heat stroke. He referred to the arrival of Maundy Gregory from Whitehall and the hasty dictation of the will to him, in pencil on the reverse side of a menu card. He referred to Mrs Rosse's recovery under her own doctor, and of her being taken seriously ill a second time on the night of the 3rd/4th September after dinner with Maundy Gregory, which led to her death on 14th September. He said that Maundy Gregory had thereafter obtained probate of the will and had set about its disbursement immediately. Mr Gregory had arranged for her burial, and the enquiries of relatives had led to a police investigation and to the exhumation of her body.

Frederick Rosse, her ex-husband, was again the first witness; he gave evidence of his separation from his wife in December 1923, and said he had not seen her since that time. He said he had heard of her death in a letter sent by Maundy Gregory. This read:

'Dear Fred,

Poor Edith passed away peacefully early this morning at 10 to 1. She had a heat stroke nearly a month ago and a relapse last Saturday week. We did everything we could for her, three specialists and two nurses. She did not suffer at all towards the end.

Yours

JMG'

Lottie Eyres, Mrs Rosse's housekeeper, said she had believed that her mistress and Maundy Gregory were brother and sister. Mrs Rosse's lunch on 19th August had been of sandwiches and half a bottle of champagne. She had heard Mrs Rosse call out -

'Come quickly Eyres! I am so ill!'

She collapsed on the bed and Lottie Eyres and the other housekeeper, Mrs Wells, put her to bed.

Mrs Kate Wells, who was Maundy Gregory's housekeeper in the upper floors, told the court Maundy Gregory had taken care of the drinks on the evening of 3rd September.

Hilda May Howard, Mrs Rosse's former housekeeper,

said that when she visited her on 4th September she found her ill and nursed her. She said all Mrs Rosse's food was prepared by Mrs Eyres. The coroner's line of questioning was indicative of suspicions in the matter:

Coroner: Was Mr Maundy Gregory frequently in her room?

Hilda Howard: Very frequently.

Coroner: Did he ever give her food?

Hilda Howard: None at all.

Dr F Curnow Plummer said he had never attended Mrs Rosse until called on to do so on 19th August. The will was genuine, he said, and was dictated in his hearing.

Coroner: Did you at any time suspect that anything had been administered to your patient in the way of poison?

Dr Plummer: No.

Mr Benjamin George Pengelly, accountant, said Mrs Rosse had left an estate of about £18,800 (approximately £1.3 million in 2020). He said that Mrs Rosse had told him Maundy Gregory had pressed her for financial assistance before July 1932. She had refused him. She had made a will in 1923 naming Miss Ethel Davis, her niece, as the chief beneficiary of this, and Maundy Gregory did not benefit at all from it. He said that Gregory persuaded her to tear up the will and destroy it on account of the niece giving so much trouble. However, she had made another will reinstating her niece as main beneficiary of her estate, and still leaving nothing to Maundy Gregory. He spoke of large chunks from her accounts books having been removed when he received them from Maundy

Gregory.

Walter William Mann, undertaker, said he had asked Maundy Gregory whether he wished for the coffin lid to be sealed and he had declined.

Sir Bernard Spilsbury told the court he could not ascertain the cause of death. He said there had been no haemorrhage of the brain and there were no signs of Bright's disease - he agreed with the coroner that the death certificate was 'quite wrong.'

Dr Roche Lynch said he had been unable to find any trace of poison or noxious substances in the samples he had taken. He said this may have been due to the waterlogged condition of the body as it had been under water for some months due to the site of the grave being on the banks of the Thames.

Dr George M Blair, Mrs Rosse's usual doctor, said he had been very surprised when he heard Mrs Rosse had died. There had been nothing in her health to suggest she had serious illness.

Detective Inspector Askew said that he had subpoenaed Maundy Gregory to appear at the inquest but that he had not done so and that he was believed to be in Paris. The solicitor for the family of Mrs Rosse, Mr Vine, probed Askew, pointedly:

Mr Vine: You have not had an opportunity of having an interview with him?

Askew: That is so.

Mr Vine: He would be a very important witness?

Askew: I take that view.

He then followed this by requesting that Maundy

Gregory appear before the court for questioning. But the coroner rejected this. He said that in view of the fact that no cause of death had been discovered, the only possible verdict the jury could give was an open one. He also said there could be no purpose in subjecting Maundy Gregory to cross examination because it would lead nowhere.

'The result is a negative one,' he said, 'No poison has been found and no poison will ever be found in the body. Therefore, no possible charge could arise out of this inquiry.'

He recorded:

'There is not sufficient evidence to show the cause of Mrs Rosse's death, which is therefore unascertained.' And there the matter ended.

It was a great pity that the coroner rejected the opportunity of some searching questions being put to Maundy Gregory - he was the principal witness, against whom the whole court narrative was directed. Detective Inspector Askew had hoped that in spite of the negative result of Roche Lynch's poison tests, he could effect Maundy Gregory's return through a Coroner's order, which might enable him to arrest him. It was most unsatisfactory. The coroner may have felt he had little choice in the matter because the inability to establish a cause of death meant that it could only be an unexplained death. If death could not be proved to be due to wilful murder, then there could be no murderer. It was an unhappy end to the police inquiry and entirely unsatisfactory for the relations of Mrs Rosse.

The narrative pursued in court by the coroner left little doubt that he suspected Maundy Gregory of being the murderer. His entire mode of questioning was directed to this end, constantly probing at the motive and opportunity Maundy Gregory may have had. And of course he did this in the full knowledge (and having known personally for some weeks) that no poison had been found in the organs by Roche Lynch, and that Spilsbury had been unable to ascertain the cause of death. His intention here was therefore plain: to indicate that the death was highly suspicious, that it remained so, and that only Maundy Gregory could be linked to that death by motive and opportunity. But he was also clear that, however great such suspicions might be, no further action was possible in law because no proof existed or could ever exist. Ingleby Oddie was a barrister as well as a doctor - he had in fact played a part in the prosecution of Dr Crippen 20 years earlier. He knew the inquiry could lead nowhere. This may account for his pointing so deliberately at Maundy Gregory's actions in his conduct of the hearing and his suggestive line of questioning – it was the best he could do. It would still, however, have been acting within the scope of his authority, for him to issue a summons for Maundy Gregory to appear to give a full account of his actions in the matter. It is unlikely that it would have resulted in a different verdict at inquest, but it would have permitted searching questions to be put to him. It would also have given Askew the opportunity of arresting Gregory and obtaining a detailed statement from him.

Spilsbury himself was in no doubt in the matter: there was no sign of chronic illness which could account for Edith Rosse's death, and her symptoms were highly suggestive of poisoning. He believed that the burial had deliberately taken place on the Thames floodplain to ensure the dissipation of evidence. Roche Lynch too was dismayed that the body and coffin had proved to be so waterlogged owing to the lead lid being left unsealed. Furthermore, he remarked in court that he had never seen a coffin buried so near to the surface. And, of course, the police were quite certain that Maundy Gregory had murdered Mrs Rosse and that he had done so to acquire her money. Years later, Detective Inspector Askew said:

'I'm convinced Gregory murdered Mrs Rosse. Furthermore, if he had not skipped out of the country on his release from Wormwood Scrubs, I would have re-arrested Gregory on a murder charge.'

What subterfuges Maundy Gregory employed to persuade Mrs Rosse to disinherit her niece in favour of himself we cannot know - but he was a man schooled in the art of persuading people to hand over money for a fistful of beans. It is probable that the will she made was written with a wording devised by Maundy Gregory - it's not at all believable that the words appearing in the will were those she spoke. In her confused state it is likely he asked her a series of carefully phrased, leading questions, such as, 'would you like me to take care of things in accordance with your wishes, dear?' She would naturally assent and an inattentive doctor and housekeeper would believe that they had heard her dictate her will. Had Edith said anything not to Maundy Gregory's liking he would simply have omitted it from the will. The use of pencil in the transcription was also peculiar: both Maundy Gregory and the doctor signed their names in pen - it was the suspicion of the police that it had been transcribed in pencil to enable it to be revised subsequently if necessary... When Edith began meeting Ethel in the park in the spring of 1932, she kept these meetings secret from Maundy Gregory, knowing he would disapprove; nor did she tell him about the new will she had made in Ethel's favour.

But none of this was enough to charge, still less to convict Maundy Gregory. The most persuasive circumstances were nothing if it could not be proved that there had been a murder in the first place. The public prosecutor does not waste time pursuing cases which cannot be won, or which do not have a good prospect of being successful.

It is possible that Maundy Gregory used the fortuitous circumstances of Mrs Rosse's natural death to his own advantage, but it is improbable. Too many circumstances tell against this: the timing of her death, the suddenness of her illness, the onset of her final illness after dinner with Maundy Gregory on 3rd September; the will made in his favour only two weeks before this, made by him, dictated to him, leaving all to him; the circumstances of his financial difficulties and her refusal of a loan to him; the choice of burial site and the shallowness of the grave and the unsealed coffin. All offer an overwhelming suspicion that he did indeed kill Edith Rosse - but this is not the same thing as a legal proof. However, as a matter not of satisfying the high standard of legal proof, but that of historical judgement, whose requirements are not constrained by considerations affecting the life and liberty of an individual, it may reasonably be judged, that in September 1932, Arthur Maundy Gregory probably got away with the murder of Edith Marion Rosse.

She was said to be Maundy Gregory's friend - but Maundy Gregory had no friends; he was a strange, sociable, yet solitary man, somewhat insulated against the world. He had many acquaintances - but if the 1920s had begun with Maundy Gregory at the height of his powers and wealth; they closed with him out of favour and broke. He had creditors snapping at his heels; he had debts and no means of clearing them. The net was closing on him. *Deepdene Hotel* was closed; the *Ambassador's Club* too. He could no longer pay the rent on his Whitehall Office: his Empire was shrinking. His urgent request to Edith Rosse was denied. He resented her refusal to lend him money; she paid him a peppercorn rent of £1 per week and he had paid for holidays for her in Monte Carlo - he was a very generous man. It was the first time he had asked her for anything - and she refused. He believed he had done much for her and he lived by the principle of quid-pro-quo. For every action he undertook he expected an equal and opposite reaction in his favour. He knew no other kind of transaction.

Edith Rosse was a 59-year-old woman whose value to him was diminishing, both as a friend and as a future resource. But she had property, she had wealth; she probably knew things about Maundy Gregory too. And Maundy Gregory weighed such factors and in doing so he found that Edith Rosse was worth a great deal more to him dead than living. The idea of the loan he had sought from her was replaced by a new plan; his creditors had become more insistent and more threatening; his needs more urgent. Her trust in him as a friend remained intact, of course. He had seen to that. He knew that a conman must never lose that... His smile, his kindly avuncular demeanour was undiminished, did not disclose what lay within; his manner never betrayed him. Edith Rosse didn't see the glint in his eye, that had her measure, that sought the means and moment of converting his acquaintance with her into cash to offset his financial difficulties.

Maundy Gregory knew how to acquire the trust of

someone for his own purpose or use, and the right moment to turn that trust into a subtle threat. It was what he did best. He persuaded her, provoked her even, into destroying the earlier will in favour of her niece at a propitious moment of anger at one of the niece's many transgressions. The destruction of the will left a vacuum; a problem for the woman who had now disinherited her only relative of the succeeding generation - this would inevitably play on her mind, especially in times of sickness. Perhaps she and her niece would be reconciled; they always were - she had taken care of her niece since she was a child; such bonds, even when anger strikes at them, are hard to break. She made another will but did not tell Maundy Gregory. Oblivious to this, he continued to supply her with the ideas to suggest with great subtlety how she might proceed, to imbue her with trust in him and faith in his good will to carry out her wishes. And when the moment came, in crisis, and through the fog of illness enveloping her, Edith Rosse was prepared to place all in the hands of her oldest friend, and though she didn't know it, as she was signing the will in his favour, she was signing her own death warrant. The con worked; and the murder was a necessary part of the con. He was never questioned by police or obliged to appear before the inquest, but the reasonable suspicion which attached to him has remained ever since.

As soon as Ethel was dead, he lost no time; he took possession of all her papers from the bureau in her apartment; doubtless Gregory found the second will amongst her papers - and destroyed it. Pengelly, Ethel and Fred Davis, were all quite certain she had made a second will, but it was not found. The menu card written in pencil by Maundy Gregory on 19th August, was to be the sole determinant of her wishes.

The matter was closed, but it should be mentioned that this may not have been the only occasion Maundy Gregory had been involved in murder. Because 12 years earlier there was another occasion, whose outcome remains one of the most enduring mysteries of the 20th Century in Britain - and at the heart of this mystery is Arthur Maundy Gregory.

In 1920 Maundy Gregory was making a fortune from his highly successful honours broking business. But the more successful such a scheme, the more widely it becomes known, and people were becoming aware of it. In 1920 this situation came to the attention of a man called Victor Grayson. He was an ex-MP and maverick firebrand socialist, who had come to public attention by winning a sensational by-election in Colne Valley in 1907. Grayson and Gregory became friends, possibly even lovers, and when Victor Grayson discovered that Maundy Gregory was relaying information on him to MI5, he felt betrayed. Maundy Gregory now had a mortal enemy.

Grayson knew of Maundy Gregory's role in the honours business and he also discovered that Maundy Gregory had been responsible for the discovery of Sir Roger Casement's Black Diaries, which had destroyed Casement's public reputation, paving the way for his execution on charges of treason. He believed - erroneously, as it happened - that Gregory had forged the Casement diaries himself. He was determined to expose him. In a public speech in Liverpool, Grayson spoke of Lloyd George selling honours:

'The sale of honours is a national scandal. It can be traced right down to 10 Downing Street and to *a monocled dandy with offices in Whitehall*. I know this man and one day I will name him.'

It was clear to Maundy Gregory and to others that the 'monocled dandy' referred to was himself. Maundy Gregory knew he was in danger. He was a man who operated by having something on everyone; knowledge was the lever he believed could move the world. But now someone had something on him: something that would bring his intricate Empire of Cards down, and with it all his connections and influences; the network he had built up over many years. Victor Grayson had something on him which would mean his ruin.

Grayson lived rather well in 1920, for someone without an income. He was almost certainly blackmailing Maundy Gregory - which would explain why he had only referred to a *monocled dandy*, but didn't name him. The release of the name would remove the power of blackmail - blackmail exists as a threat of exposing someone - not of actually doing so because that deprives it of its force. But blackmail is only ever a temporary solution: it must be resolved by another means sooner or later. It was: Victor Grayson vanished.

Accounts of his disappearance vary greatly. One account tells of Grayson drinking with some friends when he received a telephone message; after which he left assuring his friends he would return in a few minutes - but didn't. It has been claimed that Grayson was seen entering Maundy Gregory's house that evening at Thames Ditton, where he lived at the time - coincidentally with Edith Marion Rosse and her husband Frederick - but the evidence for this is unsatisfactory. It has also been claimed more recently that Grayson was paid off and lived in France under an assumed name until the 1950s. There were, of course, numerous sightings of him, but the Grayson family dismissed these, and said the last definite sighting of him was leaving on the train from Liverpool to Hull - his luggage arrived there without him. Whatever the details, on or around 28th September 1920, Victor Grayson disappeared. Grayson's family searched for him and made subsequent public appeals in 1927, 1934 and 1942 - without success. An MI5 inquiry failed to elicit any positive result either. He was never seen again. The likelihood, once again based only on the weight of motive and other circumstantial features, which are nevertheless substantial, is that Maundy Gregory arranged for the disappearance of Victor Grayson. It can never be proved. Grayson had other enemies, but the greatest of these and the one to whom he posed an urgent threat, was Maundy Gregory.

After leaving Britain in great haste that April night in 1933, Maundy Gregory lived at No 8 Rue d'Anjou, which had been the Paris home of the Marquis de Lafayette at the time of his death in 1834 - suitably grand for an Emperor in exile. He must have felt a little like Napoleon on Elba; remote from the world he knew; hopeful of a return one day. There was an understanding that he would only be arrested if he returned to Britain. He received money from Britain from different sources - many illicit. It was said he received a pension of £2,000 per year, paid to him each quarter, by the Liquor lobby in Westminster. Like most things about Maundy Gregory, it is hard to pin down the extent to which this is true.

He lived well. His apartment was grand but he was not proficient in French and he liked to buy English newspapers. He will have read here of the fate of his old school friend, Harold Davidson, disgraced ex-Rector of Stiffkey, still seeking the limelight, appearing in a sideshow in Blackpool, sitting in a barrel, with Diogenes-like resolve; and in 1937 of his entering a lion's cage like Daniel, but unlike Daniel, being seized by a lion and shaken like a rag doll - and dying from his injuries. Maundy Gregory no longer sought the limelight. He was somewhat isolated. He had a small dog called Monsieur Le Beau and he spent most of his days drinking whisky.

Maundy Gregory had in him both the seeds of his success and of his destruction. Those qualities which had brought him success made his ruin a certainty. He was a vain man: the monocle, the jewels, the finger rings, the emerald in his waistcoat pocket, the gold cigarette case; the signed photographs of royalty on his desk at 38 Parliament Street, Whitehall. All were used to engender the confidence of those he wished to profit from; and to flatter his huge personal vanity. That was a deep failing. But his vanity was also his strength. He recognised it in others and knew how to work it to his own advantage better than almost anyone. It was vanity that caused the wealthy northern cotton manufacturer or industrialist to pay him £10,000 for a knighthood, or £40,000 for a peerage and by so doing attempt to raise themselves above their fellow men. It was a vanity which overturned their sense and natural prudence.

It was a confidence trick on the grandest of scales; since nothing material was given in exchange for the large sums of money paid - because a title has no substance - he sold them thin air; fine clothes for the foolish emperor to adorn and flatter him alone.

We are all susceptible to flattery and vanity, and no one knew this better than Maundy Gregory. It made him a fortune and it lost it for him too. Maundy Gregory remains today the only person ever convicted of selling titles under the 1925 Act. If there is a lesson to be learnt from Maundy Gregory's life, it is that the gods care nothing for those who seek to elevate themselves above their fellows; and make fools of those who try. Maundy Gregory was a busted flush after 1933. MI6 was still concerned Maundy Gregory might assist the Nazis and as late as March 1940 asked the French authorities to keep an eye on him. But the war had no place for monocled mountebanks.

In May 1940 the German assault on Western Europe began, sweeping all before it: France had fallen within six weeks and Maundy Gregory, now 68 years old, was detained in Paris in October 1940 by the German authorities and interned at Drancy Camp. He was ill, spent most of his time in the camp infirmary and was then transferred to Val de Grace hospital on the Left Bank, where he died of heart failure on 28 September 1941, which was, curiously enough, the same day Victor Grayson is said to have disappeared two decades earlier.

Death is a great leveller. Maundy Gregory was buried anonymously and years later disinterred, his bones finding their way to one of Paris's great ossuaries, along with those of 1000s of others - tens of thousands. Here there is nothing to tell the bones of prince or pauper apart - or even those of an emperor. At the entrance to the great Paris ossuary, the catacombs, which houses the skeletons of some seven million people - where the love and laughter, hopes and fears and vanities of all are stilled, the words 'Stop. This is the Empire of the dead,' is inscribed. Perhaps Arthur Maundy Gregory, in common with those who sought titles from him, and to whom he sold the invisible fine raiments which he himself wore, had found his empire at last.

Arthur Maundy Gregory.

Edith Rosse.

Dr Plummer and Mr Pengelly.

Ethel, the niece.

Mrs Rosse and Maundy Gregory.

Kate Wells, housekeeper.

Inspector Askew.

Grayson - his disappearance one night has never been solved.

6. An Anatomy Of Murder: Burke & Hare, 1828

It was something of an inconvenience to William Hare and his wife Margaret when a resident of their lodging house in Tanners Close in Edinburgh died on 29th November 1827. He had not paid his rent and had no money, possessions, or family for that matter to offset his hosts' losses. The local parish was responsible for the burial of the man, whose name was Donald, but the matter of the unpaid rent could only be written off by Mr Hare. A rough deal coffin was knocked together by a local carpenter and delivered to the Tanners Close lodging house, where the body of Donald was placed in the coffin by the parish undertaker, and it was nailed down. The undertaker said he would call to collect the coffin later that day for burial in the local cemetery.

William Hare lamented the matter of the lost rent over a drink with his friend, William Burke, and one or the other or both, came up with an ingenious plan, which would cover the dead man's unpaid rent and also turn a handsome profit for them: they would sell the corpse to one of the medical men up at Surgeon's Square.

Hare prised open the coffin and the two men removed the corpse, placing it under the bed in the room where Donald had died; they then fetched a quantity of wood bark from the local leather tanner's yard to the rear of the property, and filled the coffin to a point at which its weight was similar to that of a corpse-laden coffin. Then they resealed the coffin, which was duly collected and buried with minimal ceremony in a pauper's grave in the local churchyard.

The evening of 1st December was a moonlit night in Edinburgh and the two men, Burke and Hare, took the body of Donald from beneath the bed, placed it in a sack and carried this with some nervousness to Surgeon's Square, where they were directed to the home of one of Edinburgh's great surgeon anatomists, a man whose name was Dr Robert Knox. This man, disfigured from smallpox and blinded in one eye from the same cause, was only too delighted to pay them £7 and 10 shillings, which they divided between them, after making allowance for Hare's unpaid rent. It was made known to them at Dr Knox's house that they would be similarly remunerated when they had another corpse to sell...

For the two men it was a good night's work; it was also

a fateful day, because it marked the beginning of one of the most notorious episodes in British criminal history: the reign of Burke & Hare had begun.

William Burke was born in 1792 in the parish of Orrey in County Tyrone in Northern Ireland. His parents were tenant farmers there, and as a youth he spent time with a Presbyterian minister, where he learned to read and write. After this, he joined the Donegal Militia, and spent seven years as an officer's servant. While stationed at Ballina, in County Mayo, he married and had two children. But when the militia disbanded at the end of the Napoleonic Wars, he was unable to find work in the West of Ireland and so he travelled to Scotland for work. Later he said he had written to his wife in Ireland several times but never received a reply; it has also been claimed that he simply deserted his family, possibly following a row - but whatever its cause, he lost touch with them, and was soon working as a navvy on the Union Canal between Edinburgh and Glasgow, amongst the many thousands of other Irishmen who made a living in exchange for gruelling work with a pick and shovel.

He met a Scots woman called Helen McDougal in about 1819. She adopted his surname as a matter of convenience, although no marriage ceremony was held to confirm this. William Burke thereafter spent time as a labourer, 18 months as a weaver, and five months as a baker, before learning the art of cobbling from a man he lodged with at Leith.

In the autumn of 1827, Burke and his common law wife were working on the harvest near Edinburgh, and in November he met Margaret Laird, whom he already knew, possibly from Ireland. She was living with William

Hare - and although she had adopted his surname calling herself Mrs Hare, there is no evidence that a marriage ceremony took place here either. Nevertheless, the two couples became friends and the Hares invited the Burkes to stay at their lodging house in Tanners Close in West Port, Edinburgh. Here they established a life of more or less constant drunkenness, whose sessions would frequently conclude with the two men quarrelling and coming to blows. During the daytime, Burke initially attempted to ply his trade as a cobbler, repairing the shoes of the poor in Edinburgh. He was a cheerful and companionable man, literate, and he was also known as a religious man, well-versed in scripture, always ready with a quote from the good book. Hare, by comparison, was a thick set, ferocious and brutal man of quieter disposition; he could neither read nor write and had also come to Scotland from Ireland to work on the Union Canal. Here he had met Margaret Laird, who ran a lodging house with her husband, until his death in 1826 when the two had established a conjugal partnership in a common-law fashion.

The Hares' lodging house is more aptly described as a kind of doss house for the transient and itinerant population of Edinburgh - it comprised of a large dormitory, which contained eight rough pallet-beds, which slept two or three people a bed for which accommodation they paid three pence apiece. There was a rear room also, which looked out onto the blank wall of a pigsty behind the house where Hare kept pigs and stabling for his horse. On the outside front of the dwelling was a sign proclaiming, 'Beds to Let.'

William Burke can have spent little time in his employment as a cobbler before the sale of the corpse to Dr Robert Knox relieved him of the need to work at the beginning of December 1827. It is a salutary fact that although Messrs Burke and Hare had committed a crime in selling the body of Hare's lodger, in Edinburgh in 1928, the laws applying to the theft of bodies were more honoured in the breach than their observance: the demand for corpses for Edinburgh's thriving anatomy lectures scene was such that there was no real appetite to legislate or apply existing laws against this practise with any degree of rigour. This led to the thriving trade of the so-called 'resurrectionists,' men who would raid graveyards of freshly interred bodies and sell them to the anatomists.

Strictly speaking, the only corpses used by the anatomy schools should have been those of ex-prisoners, people who died in the workhouse, orphans and suicide victims. But demand was such that it was quite impossible for famous anatomists like Dr Robert Knox to be supplied with sufficient corpses from these sources. The resurrectionists therefore filled a gap in the market and the authorities turned the proverbial blind eye to this - although the poor, whose deceased relatives were chiefly affected, greatly resented this. No sooner had a body been buried, than watchful 'resurrectionists,' body-snatchers, often gangs of medical students, would dig up the grave. Working in relays of diggers it took about one hour to uncover the coffin; the lid would be prised free and the corpse pulled out and removed to the anatomist's rooms in the famous Surgeons's Square in Edinburgh - where there would be a ready buyer.

Families too often visited their loved ones' graves, only to find they had been dug up and removed - and delivered into the hands of the anatomists, who would dissect their nearest and dearest before large audiences. Dr Robert Knox commanded huge fees from his audiences of up to 300 students to his daily lectures and often ran three lectures per day to satisfy demand. It was a macabre and unwholesome practice, that did nevertheless place Edinburgh at the forefront of anatomical studies in Europe. Meanwhile those who could afford it paid for 'mortsafes' to be installed over their loved ones' graves to ensure that they could rest in peace. A visitor to an Edinburgh graveyard at this time would have been astonished to see the steel cages erected over the graves not to imprison the dead, but to keep the living out. Some graveyards erected watchtowers to guard the graves and relatives often kept vigil over their late departed family members.

Dr Robert Knox was a revered man in the medical world; his anatomical lectures promised the freshest cadavers would be dissected for those willing to pay a fee. And there was competition between the anatomists for the best and freshest bodies to dissect. It was perhaps inevitable that these anatomists would ask few questions of those who brought them corpses, because such corpses were seldom obtained by legal means. In fact, they encouraged their assistants and students to procure bodies for them.

It was the widespread knowledge of the thriving trade in bodies which had given William Burke and William Hare the idea of selling the deceased lodger's corpse to the anatomists in Surgeon's Square. The ease with which it was accomplished both surprised and delighted the pair. It was clear to them that far from being a misfortune that a lodger had dropped dead owing the week's rent, it had turned out rather well - indeed they reflected that it was a pity that more did not do so. And they had been told at No 10 Surgeon's Square that they would be happy to see them again when they had another corpse to sell...

For Burke and Hare, it quickly became apparent that their success was more than good fortune - it suggested the model for a business: they had an established buyer, with a seemingly unending need for their product; there remained only the difficulty of procuring sufficient products to satisfy this demand. They undoubtedly discussed the prospect of procuring more cadavers and various sources for these - and in this way they became slowly accustomed to the un-expiated horror of what would follow.

It was perhaps a little over a month later, but no more than six weeks after their transaction with Dr Knox, a man named Joseph, a miller by trade, was staying at William and Mary's lodging house in Tanners Close. He had a fever and was something of a nuisance. It was bad for business that a man with an infectious disease should be staying at Hare's lodging house, and it vexed the Hares; William Hare discussed the matter with his friend Burke. Of course, they both knew what they were about to do. Joseph was given whisky, ostensibly to ease his condition, and then, by their mutual agreement William Hare placed a pillow across Joseph's face, while Burke lay on the victim's body and held his arms to prevent him from struggling. Within a very short time, he was suffocated. The two men then stripped his body and placed it in a tea chest, employing a porter to carry this for them on their morbid journey to Surgeon's Square, a journey which would become so familiar to them. The delighted Dr Knox paid the men £10 for this surprisingly fresh corpse. That is approximately £1,000 in 2020 terms.

The murder of Joseph had now put the two in business and they negotiated a contract with Dr Knox - £10 for a corpse in winter when it would keep well; and £8 for a corpse in summer, when conditions were too warm for storing corpses. While Dr Knox had a voracious appetite for fresh cadavers, Burke and Hare had only to source a ready supply. With the murder of Joseph the miller, they seemed to have resolved this supply problem and for the next nine months they plied a grisly, merciless, and harrowing trade of murder on anyone unfortunate enough to cross their path be they friend or foe, relative or stranger. There was no malice involved whatsoever. It was merely business.

Their next subject for the good Doctor Knox was an unnamed English male lodger, a tall man about 40 years of age, a match seller from Cheshire, who stayed at Hare's lodging house a week or two later - he had jaundice; it was, of course, bad for business for the lodging house, but the perfect treatment for jaundice was readily supplied by Messrs Burke and Hare. They were £10 wealthier after their arduous journey to Surgeon's Square. Although the division of the profits was 50/50 Mrs Hare had to be recompensed for the use of her property: she was paid £1 by Burke. So Hare's take was effectively £6 and Burke's £4.

The two entrepreneurs were now constantly on the look-out for possible subjects - 'a shot for the doctor' was their way of describing a person whom they intended to murder to meet the demands of the anatomist. It didn't take long to find another victim. Hare and his wife met an elderly pensioner and salt seller, called Abigail Simpson, on 11th February 1828. They plied her with whisky at their lodging house; and the Burkes joined them in a convivial gathering. Abigail said she had a daughter:

Hare told her he was a single man and would marry her daughter - she seemed enamoured at this prospect, though presumably she'd have been less so if she'd known his trade and his intentions towards his prospective mother-in-law. In the morning the two killed her by their now established method in which Hare suffocated her by holding her nose and mouth while Burke lay upon her to restrict her movement and held her hands and feet. The following day they packed her up in a tea chest and went to Dr Knox's to inform him they had another subject for him - he sent a porter to collect the body - they met him clandestinely at the rear of the castle after nightfall and then accompanied him to Dr Knox's who inspected the goods, declaring his satisfaction at its freshness - and paid them the agreed price of £10.

Sometime in the spring of 1828 Mrs Hare lured a woman to her lodgings, where she was first given whisky and then put to bed - three times apparently, as the unhelpful woman kept getting up. When he came home for his meal, Hare stuffed a rough blanket in her mouth and nose and suffocated her. She was then packed in a tea chest and taken to Surgeon's Square, where Dr Knox gave the two men £10.

On 9th April Burke lured Mary Paterson and her friend Janet Brown, two Edinburgh prostitutes of 18 years of age, to his brother Constantine's house in Canongate; he pretended - with his brother's acquiescence - that he owned the house, to impress the girls. Janet Brown was somewhat cautious, but 18-year-old Mary Paterson, who was apparently very attractive with a much-admired figure, became very drunk and in due course passed out on a bed. Burke then made a play for Janet Brown; it may be he was seeking to do a double, but he was interrupted by the return of his wife Helen McDougal, who flew into a jealous rage, which caused a row and led to Janet Brown's leaving the premises hurriedly. Mary Paterson remained unconscious with drink throughout this altercation, and presently Burke and his confederate Hare killed her with little effort. Janet Brown returned with a servant girl on the instructions of her landlady to retrieve her friend - but she was told that Mary had gone off with a man to Glasgow. Within four hours of her death, Mary Paterson was lying naked on Dr Knox's dissecting table, still warm. One of his assistants recognised her, and Dr Knox ordered that her hair be cut off. Knox brought an artist in and a small crowd assembled to marvel at the naked beauty of Mary Paterson. Knox decided to preserve her corpse in whisky for a while, in which state she remained for three months before proving to be a popular and lucrative dissection subject. She was well worth the £8 he paid for her.

Mrs Mary Haldane, also a prostitute, was lured to Tanners Close in early to mid-1828, where Burke killed her alone by suffocating her face down in the stable where she had fallen asleep. She was delivered to Dr Knox's, Cash on Delivery the next day.

Peggy Haldane, her daughter, began to make inquiries about her mother's whereabouts - as luck would have it, a grocer's shop owner had seen her enter Hare's place and so she went to inquire there. The two wives were indignant - Hare emerged from the rear room and quietened the two women, inviting Peggy to take a seat. She was offered whisky... within three hours, Peggy Haldane had joined her mother at 10 Surgeon's Square. Price £8.

Around this time also, Burke, acting on behalf of the

firm, killed a woman alone and the two partners happily obliged a delighted Dr Knox, who paid them the agreed tariff.

Next came Effy, a cinder gatherer, a woman who scavenged for scraps amongst the garbage of Edinburgh. She was induced by Burke to enter Hare's stable, where he plied her with drink, then killed her. 'She was then carried to Dr Knox's at Surgeon's Square and sold for £10,' he later said.

One morning, Burke, out looking for business, saw two policemen dragging a drunk woman to West Port watch-house to sleep off her condition - he interceded, saying he knew her lodging place and would take her there. The policemen relinquished her to his care - which proved to be worth £10 to him and his colleague Mr Hare.

In June, Burke encountered a frail old man whom he invited to have a drink with him at Hare's lodging house; when with the greatest of fortune for one, equalled only by the misfortune of the other, an old Irish woman, who had walked from Glasgow with her 12 year old grandson who was dumb, to seek kinsmen who might help her stopped him and asked for his help in finding her relative... The frail old man was released, though he can hardly have realised his good fortune to be deprived of Burke's hospitality. Burke took the woman and her grandson to Hare's where they were greeted with warmth by Mrs Hare. Soon Hare had appeared in the doorway and whisky was being liberally given to the delighted old woman. In due course, she was taken into the rear room to rest, while the grandson sat by the fire. She was dispatched in the usual fashion by Burke and Hare, while the women occupied the grandson. The boy became anxious for his grandmother and a hurried discussion took place over his fate between the four - it was not decided in his favour. He was carried by Burke into the back room, and he too was killed. The terror and piteous look in the boy's eyes, Burke said later, haunted him. After this killing Burke said he always slept with a candle burning at his bedside and took refuge in drink increasingly. The two victims were forced into a cleaned-out herring barrel, because they could not be fitted into a tea chest, and the two men loaded this onto Hare's cart which they then accompanied to Surgeon's Square. The horse would not or could not pull its cargo the whole way; and in spite of the imprecations and blows rained upon it by Hare, it could not be persuaded to complete the journey. A crowd was assembling. A nervous Burke and Hare employed a porter to take the herring barrel to Dr Knox's, where 'The students had hard work to get them out of the barrel, their being so stiff and cold.' They received £16 for the two - £1,600 in 2020 terms. A good day's work.

On their return home, Hare, enraged with his horse, shot it twice, and they plugged the bullet holes with cotton and horse hide to conceal the cause of the horse's death.

In the summer Burke and McDougal made a visit to Falkirk to relatives; it was late June because Burke recalled it was on the anniversary of Bannockburn (which is 24th June). When they returned, he found Hare and his wife had money - suspecting that he had been trading without him, he challenged him. Hare denied it, so he went to Dr Knox who confirmed that Hare had brought him a body recently for which he had paid him £8. This caused a major rift between the two partners and Burke and his wife moved out of Tanners Close and into John Broggan's lodging house two streets away. But the estrangement did not last long. A relative of McDougal's, presumably as a result of their recent visit to Falkirk, arrived to stay with them: her name was Ann McDougal. Hare was happy to reunite with his colleague for this latest enterprise. She was made drunk, and Burke told Hare, showing extraordinary delicacy, he would have to do most of the work as 'he did not like to begin first on her as they were friends.'

'It was in the afternoon when she was done,' he recalled, 'at John Broggan's house.'

A trunk was provided by one of Dr Knox's assistants and the body was placed in this. When Broggan returned home he found the trunk and seems to have discovered what was in it - Burke and Hare had to pay him money and he left Edinburgh for this. They received £10 from Dr Knox.

A stout charwoman, engaged to do the Broggans' laundry, Mrs Hostler, was invited to take a drink with the four when she was finished with her work; she did; that same afternoon she was on Dr Knox's dissecting table. Price £8.

James Wilson, known as Daft Jamie, a mentally challenged boy, was next. He was 18 years old, barefoot and with deformed feet, and was a familiar sight begging on Edinburgh streets; he lived with his mother and sister. Mrs Hare lured him to Tanners Close and then went in search of Burke, whom she found in *Rymer's Tavern*, drank a dram of whisky and she then stamped on his foot to indicate he was wanted. When he got to the lodging house, he found Hare entertaining Daft Jamie. Jamie would not drink much, in spite of the inducements, but he was coaxed into the rear bedroom to lie down for a rest, beside William Hare. On his other side was Burke; the two men like watchful cats, poised to spring. Mrs Hare discreetly left, locking the door and pushing the key underneath. When Jamie closed his eyes and seemed to be asleep, Hare threw himself on him and attempted to hold his mouth and nose, but Jamie surprised them; he put up a tremendous struggle. Hare and he both fell off the bed, and Burke joined the fray, holding Jamie's hands and feet until they succeeded in subduing and suffocating him. He was dead at noon and was then stripped and sold to Dr Knox that day for £10.

They were becoming a little careless - Jamie was distinctive, not only because of his deformed feet, but he was a well-known and somewhat popular figure in Edinburgh. He was known to be a harmless, good-natured boy. Some of the medical students recognised him - and Dr Knox sharply rejected this. But when it became known in the city that Jamie was missing, Dr Knox brought forward his dissection, removing the head and deformed feet first...

On the morning of 31st October 1828, eight and a half months after their first murder, William Burke was sitting in *Rymer's Tavern*, having a dram of whisky, when a middle-aged Irish woman entered, begging for alms. Burke struck up a conversation with her: her name was Margaret Docherty, which led him to believe that as she came from the same part of Ireland as himself, and had the maiden surname of his own mother, they must be related. She must have thought this fortuitous indeed, because she had come searching for her son, and Burke invited her to Broggan's lodging house to stay. His wife, Helen McDougal was equally pleased to meet her husband's kinfolk and she entertained her - while Mr

Burke went out in search of Mr Hare. He said he was going to buy more whisky for them. He found Hare at *Rymer's* and quickly informed him he 'had a shot for the doctor.' Hare returned with him to Broggan's lodging house. But there was a problem: staying at the lodging house at this time was an ex-soldier named James Gray and his wife Ann and their young daughter. They were asked by Burke to leave on some pretext, and had their lodgings paid for at Burke's expense to which place they were led personally by Mrs Hare.

It was Halloween, and soon the party from hell had commenced. Margaret Docherty, as with Burke, Hare and their two wives, became very drunk that evening. Neighbours Mr and Mrs Conaway and Mrs Law came to join the celebration: the Grays returned at around 9 pm to collect some clothes from Broggan's and they saw Mrs Docherty dancing with Burke and Hare and their wives, all very drunk, and singing Irish songs.

At 11 pm Mrs Conaway last saw Margaret Docherty; at 11.30 pm a man named Hugh Alston was passing in Tanners Close and heard banging from within and a cry of 'murder!' He went to fetch a policeman but could find none and returned to Broggan's lodging house: but all was now quiet, and so, reassured, he went home.

The Grays returned at 9 am in the morning to a subdued household to that of the night before - but there was no sign of Margaret Docherty. The atmosphere in the house was watchful and Ann Gray noticed that when she tried to retrieve some stockings she had left near the foot of the bed, where there was a large pile of straw, William Burke shepherded her away hastily. He was also acting strangely - he began to throw whisky up at the ceiling and sprinkled some under the bed and on the bed near the pile of straw. When Ann asked why he was throwing whisky around, he said 'it was to make room in the bottle!'

Her suspicions were roused, and she awaited her opportunity. In the early evening Burke left the house to get drink, but ordered young John Broggan to sit in a chair at the foot of the bed and not to move. Helen McDougall lay sleeping on a bed. Broggan went out, in spite of Burke's orders, and McDougall went out to see what was keeping her husband - Ann Gray and her husband went to the straw and cleared some away. Here they found Margaret Docherty's dead and naked body. They ran from the house in a state of terror to raise the alarm - outside they met Helen McDougall, who realised at once that they had discovered the dead woman. She offered them £10 per week not to inform the police, which very wisely, the Grays refused - not only could this offer not be paid, nor was intended to be paid, but its acceptance would quite certainly have resulted in two extra £10 payments being made by Dr Knox for the Grays' corpses. She followed them down the road imploring them not to inform the police - and here they met Mrs Hare, who inquired what all the noise was about. The four retired to a tavern to discuss the matter at Mrs Hare's urging - but the Grays would not listen: they went to the police and told them of the woman whom they had seen in Broggan's lodging house on the previous evening, and whom they had just discovered beneath straw there dead.

This sudden and very unwelcome turn of events to Burke and Hare and their wives resulted in the two men removing Margaret Docherty's body hurriedly to Dr Knox's rooms, for which Dr Knox paid them £5, with the promise of another £5 on Monday when he had inspected the body.

As a result of the information supplied by the Grays, a Sergeant Major Fisher of Edinburgh Police turned up at Broggan's lodging house along with James Gray at 8 pm that night. They found Burke leaving the house and obliged him to go inside. He was truculent with them and said he had thrown the Grays out. Here they searched the premises but found no corpse. But they did find bloodstained women's clothing under the bed. They questioned Burke and his wife about Docherty. They both claimed she had left - although there were inconsistencies between them, sufficient to persuade the police that the Grays' story had substance - and William Burke and his wife were arrested.

The following morning at 7 o'clock the police visited Dr Knox's rooms in Surgeon's Square and here they found the body of Margaret Docherty in the cellar. She was positively identified by James Gray as being the woman whom he had seen with Burke and Hare and their wives at Broggan's lodging house on the evening of 31st October; and also that she was the woman they had found dead beneath straw the following day. Securing the body and placing it under guard, the police went to Tanners Close, where they arrested William Hare and his wife Margaret.

The four were kept in separate cells and all gave statements at variance with each other. None of the four owned to recognising the woman Docherty, whose body was now being kept at the police lock-up. We have little more than an indication of the statements made by Hare and his wife because of subsequent developments, but Burke originally told police that he had never seen the woman before; that a man in a great coat, whom he met in the street, the collars concealing much of his face, had asked where he could get his shoes mended. Burke, being a cobbler, offered to do this for him and loaned him a pair of shoes while his own were being mended. The man examined the room and noted that it was a quiet place - and asked if he could leave a package there, which Burke assented to. He soon returned and deposited something in the corner near the foot of the bed, where the straw lay. When the man had left, Burke - who had been too preoccupied mending the man's shoes to notice - found there was a dead body there. The man returned in a while and Burke told him it was not right, and he must move it - which he did, on Saturday evening. He had neither seen the man before or since and had no notion of his name.

A few days later Burke made a further statement, amending his earlier account, to the effect that the old woman had indeed been there on Friday and had drunk a great deal during the evening, eventually falling asleep on the floor and crawling in amongst the straw, where they later found her to be dead. He had then got in touch with Dr Knox for the disposal of the body.

The body of Mrs Docherty was initially examined by Alexander Black, the police surgeon. He found numerous contusions on her limbs and body, none of which were sufficient to account for her death. The livid colouring of her face and suffusion of the eyes led him to conclude that it was probable she had died of suffocation.

A full post-mortem was conducted by Dr Robert Christison and Dr William Newbigging on Sunday and Monday 2nd and 3rd November, at which her organs and body were found to be in excellent condition, and free from disease; the various minor cuts she had received - some prior to and some after death - were such that they could not have caused the woman's death. But the darkening of the face and suffusion of the eyes, together with ruffling to the skin of the throat, led them to conclude she had probably been throttled - but there was no certainty that this had caused her death.

Dr Knox and his assistants agreed they had taken a number of bodies from Burke and Hare in the previous months, but as all were past examination now, still less identifiable, this was of little value.

Nevertheless, Burke and Hare, and their common law wives Margaret and Helen, were charged with murder.

The newspapers had a sensation on their hands. It was quickly learned that four people had been arrested for the murder of a body which they had sold to the anatomist Dr Knox. It was also known that there were believed to be many other victims.. How many people had been lured to Hare's home to be murdered and sold still warm to Dr Knox? A great many people went missing in Edinburgh each year - were these to be accounted for amongst the corpses sold to the anatomists of Edinburgh?

The public prosecutor, Sir William Rae, Lord Advocate, had a problem. There was no real doubt that Burke and Hare and their wives had murdered Margaret Docherty; indeed, it seemed to be a certainty that they had murdered a great many more given the number of bodies taken in by Dr Knox. Statements taken separately from the four principals were contradictory, but he concluded that there was insufficient evidence to secure a conviction. There was a substantial risk, even a probability, that all four suspects would be found not guilty, and at best *not proven*, because the crown had failed to prove its case. The evidence was deficient.

Rae knew there was only one way forward. He needed a confession from one of the four: in other words, he needed one of them to turn King's evidence. In effect this meant a confession from one implicating the others, and this would, of course, mean granting immunity from prosecution for one of the four. He realised too, that neither of the women knew all of the details, and in any case could not give evidence against their purported husbands. There was nothing for it but to offer either William Burke or William Hare immunity in exchange for turning King's evidence. It would not be a popular or satisfactory solution, but it seemed to be the only way forward. The two miscreants and their wives were now reviled throughout the land - speculation had become rife as to how many people they had murdered. There was a huge public demand for the four and others widely believed to be implicated to be held fully accountable for their actions. But this was simply not possible. Rae had to take a decision - and he did so: in late November he offered William Hare immunity from prosecution if he would turn King's evidence and provide a full account of the murders to the authorities. Hare agreed and on 1st December made a full statement on the murders of Margaret Docherty, James Wilson and Mary Paterson to the Procurator Fiscal.

It was on this basis that William Burke and Helen McDougal were committed for trial on three counts of murder.

The trial of William Burke and Helen McDougal opened at the Edinburgh High Court of Justiciary at 10 am on 24th December 1828, before Lord Justice-Clerk David Boyle, sitting with Lords Meadowbank, Mackenzie and Pitmilly. James Moncrieff, the Dean of the Faculty, appeared for the defence of Burke, and Henry Cockburn for the defence of Helen MacDougal. The Lord Advocate, Sir William Rae, was the chief prosecutor.

300 special constables were deployed in the city, infantry from Edinburgh Castle and cavalry from Piershill were placed on alert to restore order if required: the city was baying for blood. Early on 24th December William Burke was brought from Calton Jail to the cells below the Court of Justiciary.

It was to be a marathon session. The court would sit without an adjournment until the case had been heard and the jury had delivered its verdict. In fact, the court sat throughout the day and through the night until the following morning - almost 24 unbroken hours.

As the trial opened a significant delay was caused by preliminary legal discussion over the conduct of the trial and over which case should be heard. Moncrieff, for Burke, argued that there were 'three unconnected murders, committed each at a different time, and at a different place' and that the co-defendant, MacDougal was not even alleged to have been present at two of those. It took until the early afternoon for this matter to be settled; the outcome being that Sir William Rae would prosecute the charge relating to the murder of Margaret Docherty first. This was the logical course to pursue since the strongest evidence related to this case - and of course, it was the only instance in which there was a body found. If this charge failed, then the others would likely have been dismissed. But it meant in effect that no other case of murder would be tried.

The court began to hear evidence in the early afternoon of 24th December. The Crown case was that Burke had murdered Docherty and that his wife had assisted in this. They had been seen in her company on the evening of 31st October at 11 pm; on that occasion all were drunk, and efforts had been made to ensure that other residents at the lodging house were absent for the night; a man had heard a disturbance and a cry of 'murder' at 11.30 pm and in the morning Mrs Docherty was nowhere to be seen, but Burke and his wife acted in a manner which aroused the suspicions of the lodgers James and Anna Gray. They had subsequently discovered the body of Margaret Docherty in the lodging house concealed beneath straw and reported the matter. The police had found the clothes of the woman underneath the bed and on visiting Dr Knox's premises had discovered the body of Mrs Docherty in the dissecting room, which Dr Knox confirmed had been sold to him by Burke and Hare. Burke had informed Knox's assistants that he would have a body for the doctor at 10 pm - which indicated that as Margaret Docherty was still alive at that point, she had not long to live; and at 12 midnight, Burke had escorted Knox's assistant to his lodging to view the body. Hare had, in exchange for immunity, agreed to give evidence against Burke and his wife.

The Crown had named 55 witnesses and called 18 of these at the trial.

William Noble from *Rymer's Tavern* described Burke and Docherty meeting on the morning of 31st October and the purchase of a tea chest that same day. Mrs Conoway, a neighbour, saw Burke bring the woman whom she later was introduced to as Docherty. Next morning at 9 am, Burke was throwing whisky around and the woman had gone. Mrs Law, who had also been present during the Halloween celebrations, confirmed Mrs Conoway's evidence. Hugh Alston spoke of hearing noise and a cry of 'murder' from Tanners Close lodging house at 11.30. Elizabeth Paterson told the court of Burke calling at her brother David Paterson's house at 10 pm on the evening of 31st October to inform him he had a 'subject' for him. David Paterson said he arrived at his home at midnight to discover Burke rapping on his door – Burke had escorted him to his home where he was invited to inspect a body which he said, lay in the straw at the foot of the bed. Paterson declined, saying he should deal directly with Dr Knox. At 7 am on 2nd November the police had called and he had opened the tea chest for them - the woman within had, in his opinion, died of suffocation. John Broggan spoke of his leaving the chair by the bed in spite of being told to allow no-one near that part of the room; he also witnessed Burke throwing whisky around. James Gray and his wife Ann spoke of Mrs Docherty trying to leave the house but of her being detained by Helen McDougal. Sergeant Major Fisher gave evidence concerning the circumstances of the discovery of the body and the arrests of the four suspects.

There was a palpable stir in the courtroom, when the Clerk called the next witness:

'William Hare!'

Lord Justice Clerk Boyle told him he would not face a court of justice if he told the truth, and he was warned to speak only of Docherty's death.

'T'Ould woman, Sir?' he inquired.

He told of how he had come to know Burke and how Burke had arrived at *Rymer's* on the morning of 31st October saying he had a person to be murdered for the doctor. He said the old woman had left twice and McDougal twice brought her back.

He said when the old woman fell over, Burke had fallen on her and held her nose with one hand and placed the other under her chin for 15 minutes. He himself had sat passively in the chair watching, he said. The two women went out into the passage and waited until the job was done. After Paterson visited and declined to see the body, they had all gone to sleep.

Henry Cockburn cross-examined Hare but the result was disappointing. He asked:

'Have you been connected in supplying the doctors with subjects on other occasions?'

The Lord Advocate objected on the grounds it was an attempt to discredit the witness and after some discussion, the Lord Justice Clerk declared that the question could properly be asked, but that Hare was entitled not to answer if it would incriminate him. Hare answered saying he had never taken any bodies to any surgeon.

He was asked if this was the first murder in which he had been involved and he declined to answer. He admitted that he had known before noon on 31st October that the old woman was doomed.

Margaret Hare or Laird was next called. She appeared with an infant, with whooping cough, which interfered with her answering; more than once she declared she could not remember as she had a bad memory.

Dr Christison delivered the results of his post-mortem, indicating that the victim had no signs of disease, and her organs were healthy. He said her death was by violence but that this was merely his suspicion.

The prisoners' original statements were then read out to the court - and this ended the case for the prosecution. Dr Knox was not called to give evidence.

There were no witnesses called for the defence. And so the Lord Advocate addressed the jury. He spoke of events on the basis of the testimony of the witnesses and the circumstances of the woman's death; Burke's actions in seeking out Paterson before Docherty's death, and again immediately after it; his intention to murder, the murder itself, its motivation and aftermath. There were two essential points for the prosecution to prove, he said:

1 That the murder was done.
2 That it was done by the defendants.

The medical evidence, and the testimony of the Hares, all tended to this conclusion.

Concerning McDougal, he said she knew of Burke's intention, and not only did she not resist it but she assisted in luring and detaining Docherty to her place of execution. Her acts of concealment and to protect the murderer, by seeking to bribe the Grays, and her following the body to Surgeon's Square and then to Newington to collect payment implied her guilt. He demanded a guilty verdict against both prisoners.

It was 3 am on Christmas morning when James Moncrieff stood up to make the defence rebuttal of the prosecution case and 5 am when he resumed his seat. He complained of prejudice against the prisoners by the public, press and in handbills circulated. David Paterson proved, he said, that Burke was employed by Knox to procure bodies, so a body being discovered at his house was not an extraordinary thing. The fact of his being a resurrection man, a notorious and unlawful employment, made concealment natural, but it did not prove him to be a murderer. The Burkes and Hares and their neighbours were drinking morning, noon and night - this made accidental death more likely. The case of the Crown rested entirely on the testimony of the alleged accomplices - the Hares - could that testimony be trusted? If not, then there existed reasonable doubt.

The sum of the facts pointed to Burke having taken advantage of a situation to profit himself - no more. Even if murder had been done, there was no evidence - except Hare's testimony - to show that Burke rather than Hare was its perpetrator. And Hare's evidence was motivated by a desperate attempt to save himself.

Henry Cockburn, the defence counsel for Helen McDougal, made his address to the jury on her behalf at 5.30 in the morning. Even if there was a murder and Burke had committed it, he said, McDougal was as much under his influence as any wife would be. She was the wife of a professional resurrectionist and saw things few others would. If violence was done there was no suggestion it was done by her. She fled in horror; her concealment implied no guilt on her part. The evidence of the Hares was polluted - if the law admitted their evidence the jury should not. The idea of believing such malevolent witnesses as the Hares was shocking:

'The prosecution talked of their being sworn,' he exclaimed. 'What is perjury to a murderer?'

It was 6 am when Lord Justice Clerk David Boyle began his charge to the jury, which favoured the prosecution. He spoke of socius criminis - the status of the accomplice's evidence, and asserted of the Hares:

'The public faith has been pledged to these persons, wicked and criminal as they may be and certainly are, and it must at all hazards be kept sacred.'

At 8.30 am the jury retired to consider its verdict and 50 minutes later, almost 24 hours after the trial had commenced, it returned to deliver this to the court.

Its verdict against Burke in respect of the murder of Margaret Docherty was guilty. And the verdict in respect of the case against Helen McDougal, was not proven. Burke turned to his wife and said -

'Nelly, you are out of the scrape.'

It was Christmas morning. As people gathered for mass or kirk, as they exchanged Christmas greetings, and made preparations for the celebration, at the High Court of Justiciary, Lord Justice Clerk Boyle assumed the black cap and pronounced the sentence of death on William Burke. Furthermore, he ordained:

'Your body should be publicly dissected and anatomised. And I trust, that if it is ever customary to preserve skeletons, yours will be preserved, in order that posterity may keep in remembrance your atrocious crimes.'

On Friday 26th December, Helen McDougal was set free. She went to buy whisky in a tavern and was refused service. Word of her presence quickly spread, and the police had to rescue her from the mob intent on lynching her. She was smuggled out of Edinburgh and headed for Stirlingshire but was forced to flee the populace there and returned to Edinburgh. On Tuesday 30th December she attempted to visit Burke in Calton Jail and was refused. She went to Newcastle and was again rescued by police. Thereafter she disappeared and it was reported that she died in Australia in 1868 - though there is little evidence for this.

Mrs Hare was released from prison on 19th January 1829, was promptly recognised and chased - and taken by police to a police lock-up for her own safety and that of her child. She travelled to Glasgow but was recognised and again rescued by police. She then made several attempts to cross the Irish channel back to her native Ireland, before succeeding in this on 12th February - 12 months exactly after the first murder had been committed. She landed in Belfast later that day and was never heard of again.

Attempts to rescind Hare's immunity were, after much legal deliberation, quashed, and an attempt by Jamie Wilson's mother and sister to bring a private prosecution against him also failed. Hare was released from Calton Jail on Thursday 5th February wearing a cloak and with a hat pulled down over his eyes. He was taken by Hackney carriage to Newington and here awaited the south-bound mail coach. He rode on top of this to an inn on the Dumfries Road, where he was recognised and on his arrival in Dumfries a crowd of 6,000 people gathered at the *King's Arms* in Dumfries High Street. He was taken for his own safety to jail there. It was besieged by the mob and 100 special constables were deployed to defend it. At the crack of dawn Hare was smuggled out of the jail and escorted to the Annan Road south and set on his way for

England. He was last seen two miles south of Carlisle - and nothing but rumour was heard of him after this.

William Burke, the only person found guilty and sentenced to death in this business, spent his time in Calton Jail awaiting his execution, quite penitent; he renewed his religious faith - Catholic and Presbyterian, the duality of which he had long maintained, and was visited daily by a Father Reid and also by a Presbyterian minister. He made a confession to the Sheriff and Procurator Fiscal on 3rd January listing the 16 murders committed by the two men. This was the official confession, which seems primarily motivated by a desire to limit damage, to allay public fears that the medical community was responsible for all the missing people in Edinburgh. A second confession made on 21st January offers a fuller account of the murders but is clearly given in response to questions and parts of it are suspect in their determination to incriminate Hare and his wife and to exonerate Dr Knox and his assistants. It seems likely that some kind of deal had been done with Burke to protect the beleaguered medical profession in Edinburgh. A handwritten addendum to this, is clearly written at the request of one of Dr Knox's adherents.

At 4 am on Tuesday 27th January, Burke was removed from Calton Jail to the lock-up house in Liberton's Wynd. At noon that day work began to erect a scaffold and it was completed by midnight.

Rain fell in torrents all night long and at daybreak on Wednesday 28th January, as it cleared, crowds began to assemble. It was possibly as many as 25–30,000 in number - the largest crowd Edinburgh could remember. Windows had been hired out by people overlooking the execution place, for 5-20 shillings apiece - Sir Walter

Scott rented one.

Burke slept well that night and, in the morning, he was offered a glass of wine, which he took, and then spoke for several minutes with the magistrates while awaiting the hangman's pleasure. Father Reid had arrived at the lock-up after 6 am and joined Burke in prayer. At a little after 8 am the procession of magistrates, priest, Sheriff and the prisoner, William Burke, emerged from the lock-up - a huge roar went up from the crowd - 'where is Hare?' and 'hang Knox' were heard prominently amongst the cries.

Burke mounted the stairs to the scaffold with Father Reid, glanced once at the rope above and steadied himself. He was allowed to kneel a last time for prayer. Then he was led into position on the trap. A silk handkerchief was placed in his right hand, to drop as a signal of his readiness. Father Reid told him to say the creed as the hangman covered his head and the rope was placed around his neck. After the briefest of hesitations, he dropped the handkerchief, and the hangman released the trap, which killed Burke almost instantly.

Sir Walter Scott was surely right when he wrote of the event of Burke's execution in his diary:

'The mob, which was immense, demanded Knox and Hare, but...received with shouts the solitary wretch who found his way to the gallows out of five or six or seven not less guilty than he.'

There is no doubt at all that Hare was as guilty as Burke for the murders which occurred in that nine-month period in 1828, nor that both of their common law wives were also involved. There was in fact no moral or legal basis on which it could be argued that Hare was less culpable than his friend William Burke. But the law had to make a compromise as a matter of practical expediency, to ensure that justice could, at least partially, be served. The evidence to secure a conviction was simply not present. Thus the Lord Advocate had little choice in its absence but to allow two of the principal murderers to escape justice. The public was naturally outraged at the escape of Hare, and the two women - the justice system had settled for a single conviction where public and moral sentiment required the punishment of all four, and more.

But there was only one person hanged: William Burke was required to expiate all their crimes and in doing so the vengeance wreaked upon him was one of the most macabre and vindictive - and also one of the most unedifying spectacles - Edinburgh had ever seen. It could not be countenanced: the primitive brutality of the spectacle quickly led to changes in law and practice in hanging: the public dissection, a medieval holdover, an institutionalised drawn and quartered procedure, was quickly ended. Capital punishment was a state institution administered on behalf of the populace; it was not for their entertainment.

There was both a popular and widely held view that there was one other person outside of this gang of four, whose appearance on the scaffold was so earnestly desired and merited. That person was Dr Robert Knox.

A commission was established to inquire into Dr Knox's part in the 16 murders, but it was fatally flawed: Dr Knox was permitted to appoint those who would inquire into him; its evidence was not to be made public; only its outcome. Its chairman, the respected Marquess of Queensbury, resigned from its chair for unspecified reasons. It concluded in its report made on 21st March that Dr Knox had acted in a 'very incautious manner.'

Others were less generous: Professor Wilson, in Blackwood's Magazine, wrote of the stream of uninterred bodies coming into Knox's possession over a period of nine months, delivered to him by two wretches:

'Let him prove to all reasonable men that it was impossible he could suspect any evil!' he wrote.

And further:

'None but a base, blind, brutal beast can at the moment declare Dr Knox... free from suspicion of being an accessory to murder.'

Dr Christison, who conducted the post-mortem on Mrs Docherty said years later that he had put it to Knox that surely the bodies of certain victims had been delivered to him in such a condition of warmth and pliability that it must have caused the gravest of concerns? Knox's answer was wholly unsatisfactory. He called Knox 'deficient in principle and in heart.'

And public feeling ran high - twice the Doctor's house was besieged, and his figure burnt in effigy. One such effigy bore the sign:

'Knox, the associate of Hare.'

It was a widespread view that Knox's guilt was of omission, of being morally deficient and unprincipled in his actions. But this would not do for many - and it still will not do. Knox knew very well what was afoot. The corpses were warm, there was no sign that they had been murdered - but nor was there any sign of a natural death; he was a doctor and he knew this; their ages and dispositions made their deaths suspicious; the boy who was brought to him fresh and warm had surely been murdered; had a boy and an old woman coincidentally died on the same night and been happened upon by these two drunken and thoroughly rascally characters? Jaimie

Wilson was recognised by students and Dr Knox quickly denied that it was him - and when it became known that Jaimie was missing and being sought by his family, he quickly dissected the corpse - taking care in particular, to remove the head and feet by which he could be identified.

Knox may not have been alone in accepting illicit bodies from questionable sources - the practice had brought the medical community into wide disrepute - but he was a man who had suppressed his scruples to the point where he did not care by what means these corpses had been obtained. He had thoroughly objectified them by his immersal in his macabre profession. He expressed his delight when a corpse brought to him was still warm and supple - that they had lived and breathed a short time before, did not temper his delight; his thoughts did not stray to the families of these people, to their friends, but to the joy of dissection and the enhancement of his own knowledge and reputation. His disrespect of all human norms and taboos had turned him into something very inhuman. And the collective instinct of the mob knew this - for the unthinking mob which acts with one, subdued intellect, and by the sharing of responsibility without any moral intelligence, does not always err. Dr Robert Knox was guilty by his actions, of procuring the murders of a number of people.

Think of Lord Chief Justice Clerk Boyle's standard of proof in respect of Helen McDougal - *knowledge before an act, failure to act in prevention of such an act, knowledge after an act, and concealment of an act*: all of these conditions are met in Dr Knox's case.

The case of Dr Knox raises two issues - at what point does knowledge of an act and failure to prevent it become complicity in an act? And at what point does encouragement or the increasing demand of an illegal act become a commission of it? Dr Knox was an accessory before and after the fact and his actions surely amount to a commission of it. And if commission could not be proved in law, then in moral terms we may be quite certain of it.

And there is another element to this disregard, which must be alluded to: because those who were murdered, who were lured to their deaths, stripped and carted through the streets to be publicly dissected, were not the wives and husbands, sons or daughters of doctors or surgeons, magistrates or even shopkeepers or tradespeople: they were the detritus of society: many of them drunks, street sellers, mentally defective - people like Jaimie Wilson, obliged to live on the streets because of his deformed body and mind - the ill and impoverished: the forgotten ones. As Sir Walter Scott wrote, ironically:

'Our Irish importation...have cleared the streets of some of those miserable offcasts of society, whom nobody missed because nobody wished to see them again.'

Hated though Knox may have been, to prosecute him as an accessory to murder would be to expose much of the medical community of Edinburgh to criminal charges, so commonplace and general was the theft and illegal trade in corpses amongst them. The Lord Advocate met with medical chiefs after the trial - it was necessary to legislate. The reputation of the medical profession had never been lower; no-one was so reviled or distrusted as the medical practitioner in Edinburgh in 1829 - and far beyond. There were numerous cases of hospitals being attacked throughout Britain in the 1830s, and of mobs rescuing patients from hospitals because they feared they were going to be 'Burked' - killed for medical purposes. *The Anatomy Act* of 1832 was forced upon a reluctant medical community and upon Parliament by this collapse in trust; and it did at last bring an end to the business of the 'resurrectionists' - of which Burke and Hare were an extreme example.

The advent of Burke and Hare was a natural consequence of the tolerance of an illegal trade - they merely took the next logical step. And no-one cared because their victims were the poorest, the least valued in society - the utterly destitute, the deformed, and mentally incapable. The advent of Dr Knox was the next logical step in a medical community which turned a blind eye to unlawful, monstrous activities, which breached one of the greatest human taboos: respect of the dead. When medicine ceases to be practiced in the service of people alone; when its curiosity outweighs all else, and its self-regard bows to science alone, forgetting the art of healing in its favour, it becomes a monster in society. In the case of Dr Knox it becomes the murderous accomplice of men like Burke and Hare.

Dr Knox was ultimately deprived of his authority and positions; his reputation destroyed by necessity, by the needs of the self-preservation of the medical community, who in truth had been little better. He could find no chair at any university, despite his great learning and experience: his reputation was quite beyond resurrection. He finished his life as a doctor in Hackney in East London in 1862, which was nonetheless a better fate than that of William Burke.

After his execution, William Burke was cut down from the scaffold; an unseemly scramble for souvenirs of rope, of anything that could be salvaged from the scaffold began. His body lay overnight at the Liberton lock-up and in the morning it was taken to the college where Professor Monro publicly dissected it, lecturing on the brain, and even dipping a pen in his blood and writing with it - without the slightest grasp of the fact that his act was as inhuman and distasteful as that of the mob who bayed for Burke's blood; or that of the several miscreants whose appetite for corpses had caused the terrible events of 1828. Some portions of Burke's skin were taken, tanned to human leather, and used to bind some artifacts as curios - a card case and a few books.

And William Burke, affable as ever, was placed in a glass cabinet on permanent display in Edinburgh's Medical School - where he stands today, smiling the eternal rictus of the dead.

Messrs Burke and Hare.

Hare's Lodging house.

Supply and demand: the grisly business of the resurrectionists.

A mortsafe - to keep the dead safe from the living.

Surgeon's Square, Edinburgh.

Tanners Close, Edinburgh.

Daft Jamie.

There was little doubt that all four were guilty - but only one would pay the price.

'Deficient in heart and principle' - Dr Robert Knox. Many wished to see him hang.

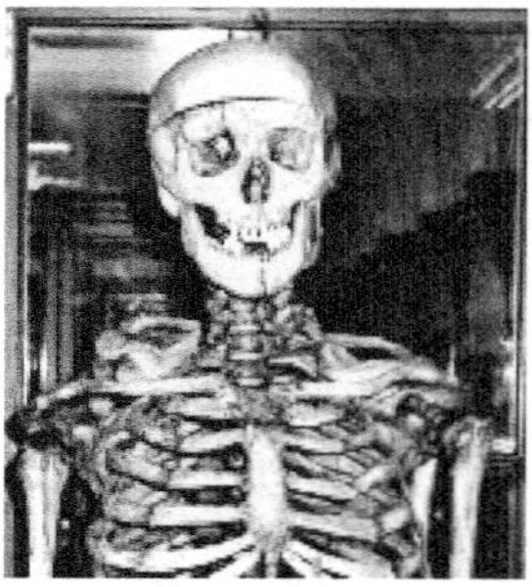

The Late William Burke Esq.

7. The Ardlamont Mystery: Alfred John Monson, 1893

It was a moonless night but not dark and Cecil Hambrough and his friend Alfred Monson had gone out fishing in a small rowing boat in Ardlamont Bay, in West Scotland. The boat unaccountably sank offshore. Hambrough was not able to swim, which made his situation that August evening in 1893 perilous - but fortunately he managed to get to shore and both men, now soaking wet, together with a third man called Scott who had remained on the shore, rescued the boat and gear, and then returned to Ardlamont House where they had a whisky in the smoking room.

Although thwarted in their fishing expedition, the three men decided to go hunting the following morning. They were up at 5.30 am for this purpose; Mrs Monson, Alfred's wife, left the house with their three elder children to visit Glasgow at around 6 am and the three men went out shooting at about 7 am. Alfred Monson and Cecil Hambrough took shotguns with them: while Scott, the third man, who did not shoot, went along to bag their catch in place of the usual gamekeeper.

As the morning mist cleared, the three men were seen by a holiday maker named Dunn striding out from the house, with Mr Scott in the middle and the two sporting men either side of him. The countryside echoed for a time with the sound of gunshots. A little time afterwards the guns fell silent, and Mr Scott and Alfred Monson were seen walking back towards Ardlamont House, where they informed the butler that Cecil Hambrough had accidentally shot himself. The butler and other servants of the estate hurried to the scene and found Cecil Hambrough dead near a dyke, with a gunshot wound to the back of his head. He was carried back to the house and here they washed his wound and sent for a Doctor Macmillan. The doctor arrived at noon and, upon being told by Monson and Scott that they had become separated from Hambrough and had found Cecil dead at the dyke, he decided it was a tragic accident and signed the death certificate accordingly.

The Procurator Fiscal, John Campbell McLullich, arrived in the afternoon and examined the scene. Monson said he had heard a shot and called out to Hambrough to inquire what he had got. Receiving no reply he and Scott had gone to the place and found him dead. He also told him, incidentally, that Hambrough had not completed an insurance on his life, which meant that Monson and his wife had lost out financially by his death. It seemed apparent to McLullich too, that Hambrough's death was an accident.

That same day, the third man, Edward Scott, who was apparently an engineer who had come to Ardlamont just two days before at Hambrough's request to examine a steam yacht he was purchasing, left the house. Alfred Monson sent a telegram informing Cecil's parents of the accident which had caused their son's death and they travelled up to Argyllshire from London and arrangements were made for Cecil's body to be interred in the family grave on the Isle of Wight.

Windsor Cecil Hambrough was born in 1873, the son of Major Dudley Hambrough and Marion Elers. The family was wealthy, but Major Hambrough was a spendthrift, had been broke for many years, and although there was considerable wealth in the family property still, he could not access any of this personally. This was because the family estates had been entailed, making him effectively a tenant for life, able to live on the income of the estates, but not the capital. His eldest son, Cecil, displayed neither prudence nor academic aptitude, and when he was 17 his father decided to appoint a tutor for him with a view to his getting a commission in the army. An acquaintance of his, a man called Beresford Tottenham, introduced him to a 30-year-old tutor who was duly appointed to instill in Cecil the necessary education required for an army commission. The tutor was Alfred John Monson.

Although well-connected, and to outward appearances wealthy, Alfred Monson was actually without any meaningful income. In fact, by 1892 he was himself broke. He was born in Ripley, Yorkshire in 1860 to the Reverend John Monson and Caroline Isabella Moncton-Arundell, a daughter of the Earl of Galway. He claimed he had attended Oxford University although there is no record of this, and in 1881 he married Agnes Maud Day, finding employment as a host and tutor to wealthy young men at Winchester for a time. By 1893 Mr and Mrs Monson had four children. But he aspired to greater things: he dabbled in numerous financial ventures as a means of elevating his fortunes, only succeeding in ruining himself - and by 1892, he was bankrupt, living on handouts from his friend Mr Tottenham - on credit he could never hope to repay, and by pawning the family's valuables. He and Cecil's father, Major Hambrough, fell out and the latter demanded his son's return home - but Monson was keen to hold on to his pupil, because he had not been paid by the father, and moreover, he knew the son would inherit £200,000 in a few months time when he reached the age of 21 - that's about £26 million in 2020 terms. Cecil Hambrough was more than a friend; he was a financial asset.

In spite of the state of his own finances, in April 1893, Monson, along with Cecil Hambrough, rented Ardlamont House in West Scotland, a Georgian mansion set in 600 acres. Here Cecil hunted and fished to his heart's content during the summer months until the shooting accident on 10th August which ended his life.

The funeral of Cecil Hambrough was held at Ventnor in the Isle of Wight on 17th August, and the matter seemed to be closed. But on 23rd August 1893, just 13 days after the terrible accident at Ardlamont House, two officials from the Mutual Life Insurance Company arrived at the Inveraray Office of the Procurator Fiscal. They had received a request for the payment of an insurance policy in respect of the life of Cecil Hambrough and they required details from the Procurator-Fiscal. It seems that Cecil Hambrough's life had, in spite of Monson's earlier declaration to the contrary, been insured just six days prior to his death, for the sum of £20,000 - more than £2.5 million in 2020 terms. *And the beneficiary was Alfred Monson's wife Agnes.*

The Procurator Fiscal, McLullich, was stunned, and he decided to look again at the shooting accident. He asked

Monson to submit the gun Hambrough had been using when he was shot, and Monson said he would dispatch both guns to the Procurator Fiscal in the morning. But the guns did not arrive, so the Procurator Fiscal travelled to Ardlamont and asked the gamekeeper, Lamont, to fetch the guns for him. Curiously, when Lamont returned with the guns he informed McLullich that Hambrough had been using Monson's gun and vice versa on the day in question. Thus Hambrough had been shot not with his own shotgun, but with Monson's gun...

From questioning workers at Ardlamont he learnt of the boating accident which occurred the day before the shooting. Although Hambrough had hired a boat for the summer, it seems that the man Scott and Monson had brought a second boat round from the Ferry on the afternoon of the boating accident and upon investigation a makeshift hole had been gouged in the hull of one. Efforts by the police to find the man called Scott, drew a blank: he seemed to have disappeared. Monson said he did not know the whereabouts of Scott - he believed he was from Greenock; he even placed adverts in the papers appealing for Scott to come forward - but Scott proved elusive. A nationwide manhunt began for Scott and it was soon discovered that far from his being a marine engineer summoned from Greenock by Cecil Hambrough, he was in fact a London bookie calling himself Edward Davis, whose real name was Edward Sweeney. He was also known to be an associate of Alfred Monson. The true state of Monson's financial woes were uncovered and it was clear that the insurance on Hambrough gave him a powerful motive for murder. Reports that Monson and Scott had been seen strolling back to the house after the shooting without any sense of urgency convinced police that Hambrough's death was not accidental.

On 30th August 1893, Alfred John Monson was arrested on suspicion of murdering Cecil Hambrough. Monson's story was that Hambrough himself had cut the hole in the boat with his knife; he said the boat had hit a rock 200-300 yards offshore and Hambrough had clung to the rock while he had swum to shore, returning with Scott in another boat to rescue his friend. He said the reason he had obtained another boat on 9th August was because he thought the usual boat used was 'unsafe.' Concerning the shooting, he said Hambrough and he had used each other's guns that day; that he had heard a shot and called out to Hambrough to ask what he had got - but receiving no reply, he and Scott had gone to investigate and found Hambrough lying in a ditch dead, from which they had carried him to higher ground. It was a self-inflicted accident, he said. But on being told that the man Scott, whom he had been advertising for, was in fact a man called Davis or Sweeney, who was an associate of his, Monson refused to answer further questions.

The body of Cecil Hambrough was exhumed on 4th September: a post-mortem was conducted by Dr Henry Littlejohn, of Edinburgh University and Dr Macmillan that same day. As a result, it was decided that Hambrough had been shot from behind by Monson's 12-gauge shotgun and had died from shock and blood loss - the sinus artery in the brain having been severed.

The trial of Alfred John Monson began on Tuesday 12th December 1893, at Edinburgh Court of Justiciary before Lord Justice Clerk Macdonald; the Solicitor General, Alexander Asher, prosecuted for the Crown and John Comrie Thomson appeared for the defence. Scott or

Davis/Sweeney had not been located, so Monson stood in the dock alone. The charge against him was that he had attempted to murder Cecil Hambrough on the evening of 9th August or in the early hours of 10th August by cutting a hole in the hull of the rowing boat, knowing Hambrough could not swim; and that this attempt having failed, on the morning of 10th August he and his accomplice, Scott, had murdered him by shooting him.

The Crown called 72 witnesses - including expert firearms, medical, and other witnesses to prove its case. A succession of accountancy clerks, agents and solicitors appeared in court to show the complex series of financial arrangements that linked Alfred Monson to the victim Hambrough and his father Major Dudley Hambrough. Although Major Hambrough was quite broke, living hand to mouth, his estates which he held in entailment, were considerable and both Tottenham and Monson had been involved in trying to squeeze more out of them.

A considerable amount of court evidence was devoted to establishing the nature of these arrangements. Monson had tried and failed to extend the value of Major Hambrough's life insurance and the two had fallen out because Hambrough distrusted Monson's motives. Monson, claimed the prosecution, sought to advance his own designs on the Hambrough estates: in 1894, the 20-year-old Cecil would come to the age of majority - 21 - and his interest in the entailed estates would fall to him.

Major Hambrough had paid nothing to Monson for his son's keep and education - his arrangements for doing so were all contingent upon the subsequent extension of his own life interest, which had fallen through. He could not pay Monson anything. Young Hambrough was not terribly interested in the finances of his prospective estate, it was doubtful he understood their complexity, and his sole interests in life appeared to be those of a 19th Century gentleman: shooting and fishing - which he did prodigiously almost every day. Moreover, Monson appeared to exert a strangely mesmeric influence over Cecil Hambrough.

The Crown attempted to show that Monson had tried to raise life insurance on Cecil Hambrough which would pay out to Mrs Monson - as a bankrupt he could not benefit himself. He had made attempts with different insurance companies to insure Cecil Hambrough's life, claiming he had incurred substantial liabilities in respect of the Hambrough estates to a value of £50,000. But the companies, naturally, wanted details of these liabilities - and Monson could provide none.

Then in July 1893, just weeks before the accident, he had changed tack: he sought insurance on Hambrough's life by another route: he applied for two policies of £10,000 each, with the Mutual Insurance Company of New York. The reason given for these was that Cecil wished to purchase Ardlamont House and Mrs Monson was going to lend him the deposit for this of £20,000 until his 21st birthday, when he would repay her on coming into his inheritance - she simply wished to cover this liability until she was repaid - in case Cecil Hambrough died... Confirmatory letters from Mrs Monson were now sufficient for the Mutual Insurance Company to issue the policies on Cecil Hambrough's life. These policies were issued and the first premium paid to activate them on 8th August 1893 - the day before the alleged first attempt on Hambrough's life.

Here then, was the motive for Monson's alleged murder of Cecil Hambrough according to the prosecution case.

The prosecution also produced witnesses to show that Monson, along with the man named Scott, had secured a second boat on the afternoon of 9th August; that he had pretended not to know Scott - although evidence showed that Scott was a London bookie called Sweeney, whom Monson was well acquainted with. Witnesses attested that there were no rocks 200-300 yards from shore, which Monson had claimed the boat had struck; it was shown that a hole had been made in the 4th plank from the keel with a knife, which had caused the boat to sink. And that when this plan failed, the following morning the three men had gone out shooting at 7 am and Hambrough was murdered; they sought to show that the body had fallen where it was found - not in a ditch as Monson claimed, because there were no signs of a body having lain in the ditch or of any blood traces anywhere but the place in which it was found. The gun used was Monson's, not Hambrough's, and they had both been using their own guns - which was confirmed by the fact that the cartridges found in Hambrough's pocket, were for his 20-bore gun, not for that which had killed him.

James McNaughton, an Edinburgh gunsmith, told the court he had fired shots into a cadaver at Edinburgh mortuary, to ascertain the effect of gunshots on it. Dr Henry Littlejohn, police surgeon and Professor of Medical Jurisprudence at Edinburgh, who had carried out the post-mortem, said it was 'impossible' for the injuries to have been self-inflicted. Dr Macdonald Brown, surgeon-anatomist, who had examined the skull of the victim, concluded that the shot which killed him had been fired from behind and at a horizontal point of entry. Dr Patrick Henry Watson declared:

'The wound...[was] fired by the hand of another; it could not have been fired by Mr Hambrough himself, either designedly or accidentally.'

Dr Joseph Bell, whose personailty and predilections for reason and the detection of crime, had inspired Conan Doyle in his creation of Sherlock Holmes, also told the court that the wound could not have been self-inflicted, and that the shot had been fired from a distance of between six and nine feet (2-3 metres) away. Pellet scars found in the trees at head height in line with the shot which killed Hambrough showed the position from which the shot was fired, according to the prosecution.

In addition, witnesses gave evidence relating to the disappearance of Scott in the early afternoon following the shooting. The fact Monson had advertised appealing for Scott to return, all the time being fully aware that Scott was a bookie called Davis or Sweeney without any association with engineering or marine surveys, pointed to his guilt. The gardener, Archibald Whyte, testified he had seen tracks in the grass which appeared to show the two men tracking and closing on Hambrough.

It was a good case, with strong circumstantial features, but the forensic evidence was its chief distinguishing feature. The expert witnesses Drs Joseph Bell, Littlejohn, Watson and the gunsmith McNaughton, placed considerable emphasis on the nature of the wound sustained, and on the direction and distance from which the shot had been fired. Dr Joseph Bell along with his colleague Dr Littlejohn, sought to establish the incontrovertible, scientific nature of their evidence. The prosecution felt confident that the forensics together with the strong insurance motive, would secure the case.

But the defence, led by John Comrie Thomson, met

the Crown on its own terms: in particular, evidence was heard from Professor Hay of Aberdeen University, which in almost every respect, contradicted that given by Drs Bell, Littlejohn et al - he stated that the shots in the three trees were at least two months old when examined, completely unrelated to the shot which killed Hambrough; that the experiments he had carried out himself on horses heads showed that the shot had been fired from two feet ten inches (less than a metre) at the most, and possibly from as near as two-three inches away. He denied that the ditch would necessarily have any blood in it or that there would be traces of blood on the ground if the body had been moved, saying that shattered bone fragments could have temporarily plugged the wound and rain washed away other traces on the ground.

The evidence given by Hay essentially cancelled out the expert testimony of the prosecution to the fury of doctors Bell and Littlejohn. It was rendered more damaging still, by the fact that the Crown had not been given precognoscence of the evidence - the content of Hay's evidence was not pre-disclosed to the prosecution - to ensure that its experts could be consulted. The Solicitor General had been completely blindsided. As his case had been based heavily on forensics, it was a serious blow. Solicitor General Asher did his best to shake Hay's testimony, but the body of Hay's evidence remained intact: and it stood as a bulwark against that of the prosecution.

The prosecution's summing up of such a complex case, was a substantial task for Asher: he had to simplify and clarify the matter for the 15-man jury. He did it very well, especially the part alluding to motive which involved the most complex financial arrangements put before a court at that time.

Comrie Thomson for the defence began his address to the jury to spine-tingling effect, referring to the case of Madeleine Smith in 1857, at which he had been present as a young man. He spoke of sitting in that same court 35 years earlier, at which Lord Advocate Inglis defended the life of Madeleine Smith; and he repeated the words spoken on that occasion:

'Gentlemen,' Lord Inglis had said, 'the charge against the prisoner is murder, and the punishment of murder is death; and that simple statement is sufficient to suggest to you the awful nature of the occasion which brings you and me face to face.'

Thomson said the prosecution case was based largely on motive. And motive, even if proved, was not sufficient, he said; it should not be used to eke out imperfect evidence. As regards motive, Tottenham was maintaining Monson, an arrangement which was dependent on Hambrough's life - to remove him was counter to Monson's interests. Concerning the insurances being sought on Cecil Hambrough's life by Monson, it was, he said, a necessary condition of the purchase of the Eagle company's interest in the Hambrough estates - that was its sole purpose. But the insurance policy was of no effect until Hambrough came of age in June 1894 - Monson knew this: it was Tottenham, he said, who had pressed the insurance claim, not Monson, as a bluff.

He said that the man Scott - if indeed he was Davis - had come to examine the boat Monson was purchasing for Hambrough; it was quite natural that he should leave without examining the boat because the sale of the boat would no longer go through. He was not required. Why, he asked, would Monson bring a third man - Scott - to witness him murder his friend?

Concerning the boat accident on the evening of 9th August, there was no evidence that it was anything other than an accident.

And regarding the death of Hambrough, it was known that Monson had got Hambrough's gun from Lamont that morning - there was no evidence he had given it to him. It was, indeed, his own contention that he had found Scott and Hambrough had already gone out, so he was obliged to use Hambrough's gun himself. There was nothing to disprove this.

Nor did the cartridges found in Hambrough's jacket pocket, relating to the 20-bore gun show it was a 20-bore gun Hambrough was using that day, as it was two weeks later when the jacket was examined, and many people had had access to it. The matter of the pellets in the trees was of no consequence because many trees in the wood were scarred in this way, as was quite natural in a wood used heavily for shooting. A cartridge had between 200-300 pellets in it - yet only 12 were found in the trees. It was quite clear that the prosecution's claim that the shot had been fired from nine feet distance away was wrong - the spread of pellets from the shotgun would have dispersed far more widely at such a distance. The shot had been fired from a distance of two-three feet at most - and possibly considerably closer.

Hambrough was walking on the wall - the high ground, naturally giving him the hunter's vantage point and he had tripped in one of the many holes in the rough, and slippery ground. The trails seen by Whyte, tracking eastwards apparently in pursuit of Hambrough, were actually old trails and had no bearing upon the incident. The reason the two men passed the stable returning to the house without alerting anyone to the accident, was that they did not see anyone there - they were seen but that did not imply their awareness of someone being present there.

In conclusion, all the evidence pointed to this being a tragic accident. There was no proof that it was otherwise. What a terrible regret it would be for them, he warned the jury, if they sent a man to his death and it was subsequently discovered by some means that he was quite innocent.

Lord Justice Clerk Macdonald's charge to the jury was exhaustive and detailed. Macdonald examined every substantive piece of Crown evidence and dismantled it: he referred to evidence unseen, to letters unheard in court and proposed his own theories to explain away instances detrimental to the prisoner.

The jury retired at 4 pm and was out for 73 minutes. When it returned, the foreman gave its verdict as one of 'not proven' on both charges. Alfred Monson was freed – but only just.

There were four reasons why the prosecution failed -

The first reason was the complexity of the case, particularly that of the financial evidence relating to motive: a bewildering number of witnesses were called to unravel the financial arrangements by which Monson hoped to gain control of the Hambrough estates - and ultimately the steps he took to insure the victim's life. The Solicitor General did his best to simplify this, but it was difficult to coalesce all of these strands into a single thread which pointed quite definitely in Monson's direction.

Secondly, the heavy reliance on the forensics was probably a mistake - certain aspects of this were brushed over lightly in the Solicitor General's address to the jury in recognition of their weakness: the assertion that the gun had been nine feet away when fired seemed doubtful; the testimony of Professor Hay suggested it was within three feet - possibly even inches away. The net effect of this gulf between the opinions of the experts was that for all their certainty and ability to conduct experiments on horse's heads, cardboard models and even cadavers, they might be wrong - one side certainly was. Perhaps even both.

The third reason for the failure of the prosecution case was the absence of the alleged accomplice. It was by no means certain that Scott was the man Davis or Sweeney. The absence of the man, his evidence and his explanation for appearing at Ardlamont the day before the alleged attempted murder was a weakness. Was he a marine engineer, as the defence counsel suggested - who had come to inspect the engines at Hambrough's request and had left after his death simply because he was not required? In his absence it was all merely speculation.

The fourth reason was the judge's charge to the jury - it was extraordinary. Macdonald took the defence line in nearly every point raised: the extensive lies and deceit of Monson should be given little if any weight by the jury, he told them. He dismissed the insurance claim as a motive. He declared the prosecution evidence concerning the rock which Monson claimed the boat had struck to be inadequate.

He accepted Monson's claim that he swam 200-300 yards on the night of the boat accident. He accepted the defence claim that if the two men knew Hambrough was dead there would be no need for them to hurry back - and he took the defence line concerning Scott, declaring that there was no advantage to the prisoner in his being present. He went further, suggesting that Scott may have come to Scotland to visit relatives - a claim not even made by the defence! And then said that it was 'perfectly natural' for Monson to conceal Scott's identity.

Evidence of Hay and Saunders, the defence experts, he said, 'confirm the theory of the body having been lifted from the place where it was...' - completely overturning evidence to the contrary. He even suggested to the jury that a 'whin bush may have caught the trigger...' of Hambrough's shotgun. And then with no sense of irony at all, he said:

'All I have said to you, however, is just suggested for your consideration.'

The points so decisively rejected by the judge and of such importance in the case, should have properly gone to the jury without the judge's predetermination of them. The choice they faced was a stark one: to accept the evidence that was so suggestive of Monson's guilt, in defiance of the judge's clear determination against this, or to free him. They knew very well that a guilty verdict could have only one outcome for the man whose eyes they looked into across the courtroom. As in the case of Madeleine Smith 35 years earlier, they quite understandably flinched from the consequences such a verdict would bring: they delivered a verdict of not proven. This verdict, peculiar to Scottish law, did not exonerate Monson, and it was not intended to: only a not guilty verdict, an absolute acquittal would render him innocent. The stain on his character should remain, in the jury's estimation: they believed him to be guilty but that the Crown evidence had not proved it to their complete satisfaction.

The evidence of the prosecution had been too

dependent on forensic deductions, and although intended to strengthen the case, its effect proved fatal to it. Sherlock Holmes was wrong. But from the safety of a historical perspective, it is, in my view, beyond a reasonable doubt that Monson was responsible for the murder of Cecil Hambrough, and that the man Scott/Davis/Sweeney was his accomplice in this. The chief reasons for this are:

First, the motive: in spite of the efforts of Thomson to characterise the insurance on Hambrough's life as a design on the Hambrough estates, it had changed in its purpose by the summer of 1893. It was no longer the means to securing the estate, it had become an end in itself. There was no need whatsoever, for a sane man to take out insurance at such high premiums, in the vain hope that it might assist him in procuring the interest in the Hambrough estates should its sale fall through. And yet he was so desperate to obtain this insurance on Hambrough's life he made unstinting multiple efforts, with several companies, in the weeks prior to the death; he had to commit numerous falsehoods in order to try to convince the insurance companies that he and his wife had such an interest in Cecil's life - because they didn't.

And then, when such hopes of gaining insurance by this means failed, he came up with an ingenious plan: to pretend to the insurance company that Hambrough sought to purchase the Ardlamont estate and needed to underpin a personal loan from Mrs Monson by insuring his life against accident. It worked. And the payment of the premium was obtained from Tottenham, £250, which Monson claimed - quite absurdly - was the deposit on the purchase of Ardlamont.

Here was the plain, unvarnished motive: it had

reduced unequivocally to a simple insurance claim on the life of Cecil Hambrough.

Second - Scott had no purpose for being at the estate, pretending to be a stranger to Monson, an engineer to inspect the boiler of a yacht Monson was buying on Hambrough's behalf. Scott made no attempt to examine the yacht during his three-day presence there. His sole actions were rowing a second boat round from the Ferry with Monson, bathing with him in the sea, being present when the boat capsized, and acting as gamekeeper on the morning of the death. His purpose was malign. Why did they want a second boat? Because it would be necessary to rescue Monson from deep water on a dark night, fully dressed.

Third - the gun which killed Hambrough was Monson's. Doubtless it was Hamborough's that was fetched from Lamont by Monson because Lamont confirmed this; but it was Monson's word alone, espoused only two weeks later when the Procurator Fiscal had become involved, that he did not, as would be expected at all other times, deliver this into its rightful hands and then fetch his own 12-bore gun, the gun which killed Hambrough. The cartridges found in Hambrough's pocket were indeed for a 20-bore shotgun, and if this was not conclusive, then it was surely highly suggestive.

Every circumstance and almost all the material evidence points to this conclusion.

That a shooting accident can occur accidentally and in the most improbable manner, the back of the head, is a rare thing - but rare things happen in the most improbable ways, as the judge was keen to point out. But the odds against such an accident occurring are long. And when such an accident occurs along with another unusual event - that the same man nearly drowned the previous evening, it becomes more difficult to dismiss such an accident simply to the long odds of nature. When the victim had been insured for a very large sum just six days earlier, and effect to this insurance was given just one day before the first accident; and further, the person in his company on both occasions was the beneficiary of this insurance, the odds become very long indeed. And when the alleged killer has brought a man down just one day prior to that accident, under false pretences, under a false name, feigning to be a boat engineer, and claiming not to know him; and all the accused man's attempts to secure a share of the victim's estates have failed in recent weeks; and he was bankrupt and pawning cutlery, and other items; was running up debts and defaulting on loans; and the victim was shot not with his own gun, but with the accused man's gun... When all of these improbable circumstances, each incurring its own inherent probability capable of being displaced, are placed in conjunction, they produce astronomical odds against their concurrence. They become as improbable as the universe.

But we do not require such a proof that is tested to the limits of the universe; we require only a conviction beyond a reasonable human doubt. And that conviction we surely have.

We can never know with certainty the exact events as they unfolded on those two days of 9th and 10th August 1893, because only three men witnessed them, one of whom was dead and the other two were his killers - but I believe that it was something along the following lines.

Monson was a man of greater ambition than wealth and he lived like a lord. Although he had undoubtedly been a tutor around 1881 at Winchester, he had found his association with richer and less bright men than himself to be a more profitable occupation. By early 1893 he was bankrupt and only the occasional payment from Tottenham kept the family afloat - on the expectation they both had of accessing Cecil's inheritance when he reached the majority age of 21. That was some months away and Monson took Ardlamont in April 1893. The rental cost was £450 per year, of which £225 was due on 1st August - only days before the death. The pressure on Monson was now enormous and by mid-July the last vestiges of hope Monson had of purchasing the interest in the Hambrough estates had gone.

Having failed to secure a policy for £50,000 on the life of Cecil Hamborugh based on liabilities he has incurred, he changes tack entirely; his fertile mind has conceived of a new plan to justify an insurance policy of such magnitude on the life of a man not related to him: he proposes the scheme to purchase Ardlamont estate - neither he, nor his wife, nor Cecil have a penny with which to do so, but it is only a device to justify an insurance policy. He approaches the Ardlamont agents so he can claim that the purchase is underway. It isn't - the cost of the house is £88,000 (approximately £11 million in 2020) and there is no prospect of any of them being able to pay even the cost of a 5% deposit of this.

But it fulfils his purpose: he can now go to the insurance company - the Mutual Insurance Company of New York - and take out two policies for £10,000 apiece, payable to Mrs Monson (as he is a bankrupt) on the basis that Hambrough is purchasing Ardlamont and cannot afford to pay for this for a few months until he comes of age; Mrs Monson will lend him £20,000, but to cover her loan to him in case of death, she wishes to take out insurance to that value. It is a perfectly sensible arrangement, and the insurance company accepts it. With Tottenham's help he pays the £250 premium on the policy.

The complex financial arrangements conducted over the years have now reduced to one of a simple insurance matter: Cecil Hamborugh's life is insured for £20,000; if he dies that money will be paid to Mrs Monson. In fact, he is now on familiar territory, because although it was not heard in court, he had been known for a number of fraudulent insurance claims associated with suspicious fires and other events in previous years. This plan is not a newly hatched plan, it has begun like all ideas, as a wish, a hope, and by July it has become a plan: the circumstances of his finances and the failure of all other prospects have made him all but destitute - a destitute living in a mansion, but that pretence is about to be cruelly exposed with the demand for rent due on 1st August. He cannot hope to pay the rent - and he doesn't have to: he has another means of taking care of all his financial woes.

He is seen many times in the company of a bookie called Davis in the weeks before; a man of dubious character, whose real name is Sweeney: the two discuss the matter - it is probable that Monson's idea is to hire Davis or Sweeney to murder his friend. What ideas were conjured by the two will never be known, but it is clear that the remote location of Ardlamont is the place designated for the murder and a boating accident as the means of accomplishing it. The matter is urgent by August, for two reasons: finances are desperate - first, the silverware is gone, so is Mrs Monson's jewellery; creditors are thumping on their door. And second, a lot of people have been invited and will come to stay at Ardlamont on 12th August - they will stay for the shooting season, until the late autumn. Any opportunity of killing Hambrough will be lost for the rest of the year. But he is unable to act until the insurance policy is settled: so he presses this with the greatest urgency and he finally collects this on 8th August. He sends a telegraph to his friend Davis/Sweeney in anticipation of this, covertly, calling him to Ardlamont to prosecute their plan. Davis packs immediately and takes the *Flying Scotsman* to Edinburgh, and from here makes for Ardlamont.

On his arrival, Monson and he greet each other as strangers - this has clearly been agreed: during Scott's three day stay there is no suggestion that Scott is a friend of Monson's - but that he is a marine engineer, called Scott, who has come down to inspect the boilers of a yacht Monson is purchasing for Hambrough. Scott is nervous; he has not Monson's self-assurance. Murder is a serious undertaking.

The following morning Scott and Monson go to fetch a second boat and bring it round to Ardlamont Bay, ostensibly because they require another boat because the usual one used by Hambrough is unsafe - but its real purpose is that they require two boats; one for fishing and one for the rescue of Monson by his accomplice. He also wants to show Scott the lie of the land, and to have a dry run at the plan. They row the boat round to Ardlamont Bay. As they enter the Bay they are seen by the governess Edith M Hiron and by the nursemaid, who are on the shore with the children - up above strolling on the clifftop Mrs Monson is seen walking with Cecil Hambrough. Monson walks up to the house alone, while Scott remains in the boat, for no reason anyone can discern. Scott is now engaged in sabotaging the boat by cutting a hole in it with his knife.

There follows a quiet evening meal at which the suggestion of some night fishing is made - by whom we do not know, and it hardly matters because Hambrough will certainly be enthusiastic to such a suggestion. It is arranged that Monson and Hambrough are to go out in the boat together and that Scott will sit on the shore. This is really rather peculiar, but Monson planned to row out to deep water; it is imperative that he be rescued in the dark night by a third man in a boat. To swim 300 yards or more at midnight fully dressed and in shoes would be hazardous for the best of swimmers. At 10 pm the 3 men went out.

We know the boat capsized at some point as a result of the hole in the boat taking in water - the story of the boat striking a rock 200-300 yards offshore is impossible: no such rocks exist. In fact, in the words of the Scottish national poet, *the best laid plans of mice and men*, often go awry. Scott cut the hole a little too large - presumably he plugged it with something - concealed under one of the crossboards: a plug to be removed when the boat was out in deep water. But it must have become dislodged, as the weight of the two men displaced the water and created pressure on the boat. The boat now began to take in water, prematurely... In fact, they will have been moving from shore rather slowly paying out the long 150-yard net for the fishing as they rowed - when it became clear the boat was foundering. It sank within easy reach of shore, both men being thoroughly soaked - but it was sufficiently shallow for Cecil to walk ashore.

One can easily imagine the grim darted looks exchanged between Scott and Monson under cover of the night as the three men gathered on the foreshore and surveyed the boat. Hambrough, sullen at the ruin of the night's plans, and Scott and Monson at the ruin of theirs. The plan had gone wrong; completely wrong. When they left Ardlamont at 10 pm Scott and Monson fully expected to be returning to the house in the early hours one man down: Monson soaked, possibly Scott also by this time, to report that Hambrough had been lost in the sea and in spite of their valiant efforts, they had been unable to find him. In the morning his body would be found, and in due course, the insurance would be claimed. It had seemed foolproof.

But it was three men who returned to the house, Monson's mind now working furiously. They sat in the smoking room and drank whisky; it was 1 am. At some point amongst the exchanges of looks between Monson and his accomplice, an opportunity was found to talk. It had failed: but Monson had an urgent, inventive mind, and something of the persistence of a terrier in all his dealings. He was determined that Hambrough must die, and time was short. He decides that a shooting accident must be arranged - it must be done as soon as possible - and the following day, his wife and children are absent - they go to Glasgow for haircuts and clothes, to prepare for the 12th, when visitors will arrive. The opportunity is too great to be denied. Perhaps Scott baulks at this - he is a nervous man - they are now making plans on the hoof. There has been no rehearsal, it has not been thought through at all - it is a serious mistake. But Monson is a man of considerable arrogance as all his enterprises before and later show. How it is arranged that the three men should go shooting at 7 am the following morning is unknown - but it was clearly done that night because the night later turned out thunder and lightning; rain fell heavily after 6 and the wind whipped in off the sea. It seems probable that Monson suggested it - possibly as a compensation for the ruined night's fishing.

Hambrough is up at 5.30 am to see Mrs Monson for some reason, which is not elucidated in the trial. And at 7 am the three men leave the house, Hambrough for the last time alive. Three abreast they go, to the East is Hambrough, oblivious as he hunts that he is himself the prey, stalked by his killers; glances are exchanged between the conspirators; soon they are out of sight of the house, and Dunn the holiday maker is the last man to see them as the fatal moment approaches. There is a mizzle of rain, it is an inclement August day, no day for shooting, but they will get some rabbits in the woods; perhaps the odd wood pigeon, thinks Hambrough. They move under cover of the woods - Monson looks anxiously about him, to ensure there is no unwanted witness to the events which are now closing fast upon them: no person illicit to his purpose, some poacher who may bag a bigger prize - but no, there is none.

He follows Hambrough, watches his unsuspecting back, perhaps only yards ahead, through the wet grass and bracken, checks for Scott close by, following silent in his footsteps. Perhaps Hambrough knows he is there, is careless of his youth, to have a man with a loaded gun behind him; perhaps his ears are plugged against the gunshots that rent the air, but he is apparently unaware as he rakes the ground ahead for signs of prey, that the hunt is truly on. He is unaware of the irony of his position: that he has only moments left to live. Perhaps he takes a rabbit or a wood pigeon in his sights: there is a breathless focus divided in its purpose. He reaches a broken wall and dyke, which affords him a good view; hears the bracken softly crack underfoot and some undistinguishable sound behind...and then from far off the open rush of an explosion thumps his head, the briefest sensation of the trees and sky and ground beneath him collapse inwards to a heavy, enduring silence.

The man behind him, his friend, trembling, adrenaline coursing within him, just three or four feet behind him, not nine, the hazard of such a miss could not be risked: he is close upon him, hears the sound of his gun singing in his ears like thunder, and he sees the body of his friend fold within, his life extinguished. They may have moved him, because they would certainly wish to be assured of his death - Scott looks at the fallen man - 'Is he...?' Monson cries hoarsely - Scott turns, shaken by this unanticipated violence, only nods, distrusting himself to words. They stand in silence a few moments, to gather their thoughts and calm their nerves; then forcing themselves to resolution, they collect the gun and leave the murdered man - a final hurried glance to check behind nothing is left undone and then slowly they walk back - without the urgency of accident to hurry them, but the steady claims of murder pressing upon them, required to still the panic now within, to order their thoughts for what will come. Their even pace to the house is noted as they pass the stables without a sign of what has passed; only the strange silence and the absence of their colleague looks amiss. Upon entering the house this same calmness prevails: they unload the guns, say nothing, and James Wright, the butler, comes to attend them:

'Where is Mr Hambrough?' he inquires.

'He has shot himself - he is dead,' is the reply.

It seems unreal - to the butler and both men too. They do not lead him to the site or put in place any actions - perhaps it is shock - certainly it must be; and yet there is a complicity in their actions, a guilt that speaks of their situation; of what has happened.

In time the doctor comes, the body is brought back to the house and washed and dressed, the doctor and others are taken to the scene of Hambrough's death, and the narrative unfolds. On her return to Ardlamont in the evening Mrs Monson is distraught when she hears the news and confines herself to her bedroom. But the plan was hasty, it was imperfect; there have been, inevitably, mistakes. All is well at first, the matter is an accident and the doctor and Procurator Fiscal are persuaded that those long odds of nature which sometimes intrude too brutally upon our lives are to blame for the death of the boy in the woods. There is nothing to investigate - and there is no motive to suggest that there should be anything more than an official account of the tragedy given. There is no insurance on the boy's life even and his friend and apparent benefactor, Monson, has only lost by the young man's death in friendship and fortune.

But when Monson two weeks later meets the Procurator Fiscal and tells him, as he walks to the office, that two insurance men are with him who wish to have a report from him that the death is purely accidental, he is naturally surprised -

'Why? There is no insurance,' he says, sharply.

Monson does not receive the quiet acquiescence he expected, and says -

'Apparently his father took out insurance on him without the boy's knowledge.'

It is a dangerous lie; not one that should have been dismissed by the judge, but it is one Monson must venture if he is to realise his fortune.

In time all is unpicked and he is charged with murder. And though there are no doubts on the part of the authorities, or Drs Bell or Littlejohn and many others, that Monson and the man Scott murdered Hambrough for the insurance money, the evidence does not satisfy the jury sufficient to find him guilty. They believe he did it but that the evidence has not proved the matter.

This may not be an exact account of what occured, but I believe it is close.

There is one final twist in this tale - in the summer of 1898, five years after the death of Cecil Hambrough, Monson entered a petition against his wife Agnes Monson for divorce. The grounds for the divorce were that she had committed adultery with an unknown person on 24th July 1891; and, that in October and November 1891 she had committed adultery at the *Hotel Metropole* in Whitehall, London, with *Cecil Hambrough*.

She did not contest the petition, but the specificity of the place - the *Hotel Metropole* - suggests he had proof; in addition, the presumption must be that such a terrible stain on a Victorian lady's character would only go unchallenged if there was such proof. This adds an intriguing dimension to the case, which is only obliquely caught in the murder proceedings. We know the Sheriff of Argyllshire admitted failing to take possession of

Mrs Monson's documents and in particular two letters referred to in court; we know too that Cecil Hambrough saw Mrs Monson on the morning of his death - for some purpose never disclosed in court; and we know also that Mrs Monson was seen walking on the cliffs with Hambrough at around 3 pm on the day of the boat accident; and that they were in plain view of the husband and Scott, bringing the boat in to shore.

What was the nature of this relationship? Was the fact that Mrs Monson confined herself to her room quite distraught on learning of Hambrough's death on her return from Glasgow something more than ordinary human grief at the tragic loss of a friend, or the pretence of it? It is difficult to judge at this distance - but Cecil Hambrough was a young man of 20 and young men of 20, even those passionate about shooting and fishing, have other needs that preoccupy them: is it possible that Cecil and Agnes Monson were involved in an affair? If so, Monson must have been aware of this; and furthermore, it is quite possible that he used his wife as bait, to keep the young Hambrough in his thrall - sufficient to resist his own father and mother's urgent requests for him to return home. The mesmeric effect and absolute control Monson exerted over Hambrough was a major part of the prosecution case - but no adequate explanation as to how he could achieve such control was given. Mrs Monson would certainly provide such an explanation for it. Monson was immoral enough to use his wife in such a way - and if he did so, it is also quite likely that, even in his complicity in his wife's adultery, he would have resented it. And it would have given him a just cause in his own mind when he considered the murder of his friend for the insurance.

There is one further persuasive incident, which gives credibility to this idea: when Monson met his wife on the evening of Hambrough's death, the manner of his telling her of the tragedy is interesting: he says that Hambrough has had an accident; she asks him is it serious? He says he is dead. It is a particularly cruel way of breaking such news: he meets her, looks in her eyes and tells her Hambrough has had an accident. This lessens the incident, tees her up for what is to come; her mind scans the possibilities: perhaps he has cut himself badly or fallen in some way. Is it serious, she inquires? One can almost sense the gloating anticipation behind the dramatic impact of his next words: *he is dead*. There is, of course, no easy way of delivering terrible news of this kind, but the time-honoured way of doing so is to say something along the lines of 'I have some bad news, I'm afraid - Cecil has had a terrible accident: he is dead.' In such a way one is led by a natural progression into the inescapable fact of what has happened. It would be usual as well on such an occasion to greet the recipient of such news with a face which foretells something of its gravity. But she seems to have had no hint of it - he seems to have greeted her in a quite normal fashion, judging by her reaction - as though nothing was amiss. And this led her into the inquiry, is it serious? Monson has had his revenge on them both.

And then there is that stubborn - and startlingly candid image we hear of from the governess and nursemaid in court: of the children playing on the beach, while on the cliffs Hambrough walks with Mrs Monson. Upon this fixed scene of innocence and evil on a summer's day, when clouds are gathering in the sky, there is all the intrigue and deception that an operatic quartet expresses so well but which is lost in a courtroom: a boat is in the bay with two men watching, who can hear the children's laughter murmuring across the waves - and they see the wife of one of them walking with a man whose murder they intend in hours. Young Cecil Hambrough and Mrs Monson serene and confidential upon the cliff, while the children play oblivious upon the sands.

No-one prospered from the death of Cecil Hambrough. The insurance money was not paid out. Monson was bankrupt still, exposed to all as a rogue and probably a murderer; Tottenham the money lender was thoroughly discredited and decidedly out of pocket as a result of his dubious enterprises - he subsequently tried to sue Monson for the £250 fraudulently obtained, but the matter was protracted, and Monson had no money. From frustration he took the matter into his own hands in late 1895 and broke into Monson's house removing the furniture and possessions - for which he received a three-month prison sentence with hard labour. He was eventually bankrupted, forced to live with his father and died in 1929.

The third man, Scott, who disappeared, was indeed a bookie calling himself Davis, whose real name was Edward Sweeney. He broke cover in early 1894, following Monson's inconclusive verdict, and applied to the High Court to have his 'outlawry' status revoked, which it duly was. Although it was claimed in court he was dying, in 1911, 18 years after the Ardlamont case, he was still working as a bookie - and living at 111 Brixton Road in London, with his brother and sister.

Alfred Monson wrote an account of the Ardlamont Mystery attempting to exonerate himself from suspicion, and to turn a profit - but it failed to convince anyone and in fact sold few copies. He was paid by *Madame Tussauds* to sit for a wax figure of himself - and then, when they placed the figure alongside those of known murderers, he sued. He won the case - and was awarded one farthing, a quarter of a penny, the smallest possible amount that could be paid and had to pay his own costs. But the case did establish the principle in English Law of 'libel by innuendo.' His dishonest life caught up with him in 1898 to the satisfaction of many: along with two other men he was charged with inveigling a young man into financial difficulties and then extorting money from his parents. He received a five-year prison sentence with hard labour, which he served at Parkhurst Prison on the Isle of Wight, just a few miles from the place where the man he murdered was buried. After his release from prison, he went to South Africa where he was last heard of in 1920 at the age of 60.

Cecil Hambrough's family had no doubts he had been murdered by Alfred Monson, and each year on the anniversary of his death, they placed a cryptic notice in the newspapers:

'In memory of Cecil Dudley Hambrough, shot in a wood near Ardlamont, on August 10th, 1893, in his 21st year: "Vengeance is mine; I will repay, saith the Lord."'

Ardlamont House.

Cecil Hambrough.

Alfred Monson.

Scott's real name was Sweeney - he was a bookie masquerading as a marine surveyor.

Agnes Monson.

Beresford Tottenham.

Drs Littlejohn (left) and Bell (right) believed logic would win the day.

Professor Hay spoiled the party.

Monson congratulated after his acquittal.

It seems everyone had their eye on Hambrough's fortune - except himself.

8. A Surfeit Of Cyanide: William Murfitt, 1938

William Murfitt, who had been up since 5.30 that morning and busy about the farm in the village of Risby, in Suffolk, came in to breakfast at his usual hour of 8 am on 17th May 1938. He sat down at the table in the dining room to read his newspaper while the maid went to get his breakfast. His wife, Gertrude, rose from the table to get him his Fynnon Salts which he took each morning for his health. Everything was quite normal, with one exception: he had less than an hour left to live.

Mrs Murfitt took the lid off the Fynnon Salts and noticed they looked brown, remarking to the farm secretary, Mollie Target, who was sitting at the dining table -

'Do you think there's anything the matter with these salts? They look brown.'

Mrs Murfitt took a teaspoon and removed most of the brownish crystals from the top of the tin and then made up a tumbler of the salts for her husband. William Murfitt drank off the glass of Fynnon's salts and pulled a face.

'Are you sure those are salts - they taste funny?' he said.

'Yes, of course,' she replied. 'Same as usual.'

She showed him the salts and he said:

'They are damp - you can see...'

A couple of minutes later William began to feel unwell, he stood up and clutched the table, and said -

'I feel ill. Fetch a doctor.'

He then collapsed to the floor, where some cushions were placed under his head, while Mollie Target, his secretary, called for Dr Hubert Ware. Meanwhile, Mrs Murfitt instructed the maids to tidy the dining room.

Murfitt was unconscious when the doctor arrived, but not for long - there had really been little need for urgency on the doctor's part. He said to Mrs Murfitt -

'I'm afraid your husband's dead.'

The doctor inquired about Mr Murfitt's recent health, but Mrs Murfitt said he had been well; he asked in particular what he had eaten for breakfast. Mrs Murfitt said he had not had breakfast and showed him the tin of Fynnon salts, which she said they both took each morning. The doctor inquired whether or not she had taken any that morning and she said that she had not, because 'she didn't fancy them,' because when she opened the tin they looked brown.

The doctor sniffed the tin, cautiously: the unmistakable aroma of bitter almonds came to him, the unique scent of potassium cyanide. The police were called and a Constable Ernest Carrington and Sergeant Clifford Bigmore cycled over to the house. Mrs Murfitt was very upset, at times hysterical, and said -

'I wish I had taken a dose as well!'

Sergeant Bigmore took a look around and inquired if anything in the dining room had been moved? Mrs Murfitt told him she had tidied it up, in anticipation of the doctor's arrival. Having noted the circumstances, Bigmore arranged for the body of William Murfitt to be taken to West Suffolk General Hospital; and then took possession of a glass tumbler, a teaspoon with powder on it and locked the door to the dining room.

A post-mortem was held that afternoon by Dr Ware at West Suffolk Hospital and various organs were removed. Along with the tin of Fynnon salts, these were sent to the leading authority on poisons, the Home Office Analyst Dr Gerald Roche Lynch at St Mary's Hospital, Paddington, for examination. Although William Murfitt was overweight, suffered from diabetes and had an enlarged liver indicating previous alcohol abuse, the post-mortem found he was in reasonable health, was a non-smoker and non-drinker. It was apparent, even without confirmation by Roche Lynch, that William Murfitt had been poisoned, and furthermore, the suspicion was he had been murdered.

William Murfitt was born in Wisbech in Cambridge, in 1882. His father was a farmer and William helped him on the farm as a young man - but he had an adventurous side to him: he joined the army and fought in the Boer War in 1901 and was promoted to sergeant. He married Gertrude Eleanor Green in 1903, who bore him a son, Joseph Leslie, in 1904, and afterwards he travelled widely, working for a time in Australia. Another son, Billy, was born in 1912, and during the First World War William Murfitt established a business in washing, and supplying vegetables to the London market, aided by the shortages created by wartime conditions. He prospered and by 1932 he was able to take the lease on the 1000-acre Quays Farm in the Suffolk village of Risby, which he shrewdly planted with crops best suited to the varying soil types there. Hard working and determined, by the late 1930s he had invested in the most modern farm machinery and he employed 80 workers. He paid good wages, and he himself worked hard, rising at 5.30 each morning; he played hard too. He was forthright, ebullient and sociable - a little too sociable with women apparently, rather like a prize bull amongst his heifers. Although not quite the country gentleman, he rode to hounds, hunted, and shot almost anything which moved. He was not a cerebral man - his loves were farming, expensive cars, horse racing and women. In no particular order.

The Chief Constable of Suffolk realised immediately that the investigation would require Scotland Yard's assistance and two experienced detectives from the CID were sent to lead the investigation: Detective Chief Inspector Leonard Burt and Detective Sergeant Reginald Spooner. They at once set about taking statements and making inquiries into the murder.

From their inquiries they learned that Mr Murfitt had spent most of the previous day at another of his farms in Norfolk, returning home sometime after 7 pm. He then went out shooting until 8 pm, when he returned and had supper with his wife. She retired at 9.30 and he a quarter of an hour later.

Dr Roche Lynch's tests confirmed that cyanide was indeed the poison which had killed William Murfitt, and from other tests, he discovered that when cyanide was added to Fynnon Salts it turned them brown over the course of a few hours - until they became virtually black after 12 hours. As those who had seen the salts on the morning of 17th May described their appearance as light brown, Roche Lynch calculated that even if the degree to which air was excluded from the tin had inhibited the discolouration of the crystals, the cyanide must have been added no more than 12 hours prior to their being taken. This appointed a 12-hour window in which someone had added the cyanide - between 8 pm and 8 am on 16th/17th May. It was also clear to Chief Inspector Leonard Burt that the person who had done this must have known of the salts and of the habit of their being taken by the Murfitts each morning. Furthermore, if Mrs Murfitt was not the killer, then she must also have been an intended victim. Mrs Murfitt told the detectives that only a few people knew of the habits of those in the house - including Mr Murfitt, herself, the secretary, the maid and the cook. There were also four friends and neighbours who might know of the salts and who were familiar with the house, she said.

Considering who might have a motive for wishing William Murfitt dead, the police discovered a gamekeeper who had quarrelled with him over gaming rights on the estate and a shepherd whom Murfitt had recently dismissed. But both were quickly exonerated from any involvement in the murder. The couple's two sons, Leslie and Billy, were both absent from home - one lived in London and the other was 4th engineer on a ship currently in the Mediterranean.

The inhabitants of the house itself knew of the Murfitts' habits, the salts and so forth, but the maid, who had been there seven years, the cook who had been there six years and the secretary for nine years had no motive at all that could be discerned.

Detectives made efforts to trace purchases of cyanide in the area and those in particular which had been made by any of the suspects. But this was no easy task, because it seemed at times as if everyone in Suffolk possessed cyanide as a means of destroying wasps' nests. In fact, in the 13 months prior to Murfitt's death, it was established that 425 purchases of cyanide had been made from five chemists' shops in Bury St. Edmunds. Police noted that less than 1 shilling could purchase enough cyanide to kill 100 people - thus the 425 purchases in Bury St Edmunds alone, was sufficient to kill something like 45,000 people - twice the town's entire population!

Regarding the death itself, detectives felt confident William Murfitt had not committed suicide - there was nothing in his life, nor in his behaviour the night before or on the morning of his death, to indicate that this was anything other than a normal day. To introduce cyanide into a tin for his wife to give to him would seem incredible as a means of suicide.

This left five possible suspects:

Mrs Murfitt and the four neighbours. These were: a local farmer at Moseley's Farm, Rippon Charles Browne, and Elaine Browne, his wife; and another farmer, James Walker, and his housekeeper, Mary Chandler.

All were in a position to know of the habits of the Murfitts, of the Fynnon salts being kept on the sideboard in the dining room and the means of access to the house. One of these five people had, in the view of Chief Inspector Burt, murdered William Murfitt.

Prima facie, there was a strong case against Gertrude Murfitt, who had put up with her husband's philandering for many years: and yet in spite of the apparent evidence for this, and after some initial suspicions, Burt and Spooner doubted she was her husband's murderer for several reasons:

1. To begin with she possessed a personal estate of £5,000 herself.
2. She had alluded to the strange colour of the salts quite

openly - to her husband, to the secretary, to the doctor and the police; she had not attempted to conceal this. She said she didn't fancy the salts herself because of their brown appearance, and she quite openly put them into the oven to dry them in the apparent belief that they were brown because they were damp.

3. She was distraught at her husband's death... In spite of the fact that Murfitt was serially unfaithful, she appeared to be genuinely devoted to him; she seemed to tolerate his affairs, forgave easily and held no grudges.

It was entirely possible though, the detectives thought, that one of the four friends and neighbours, might have gained entry to the house by some means. Detectives noted there were four doors to Quays Farm - three rear doors whose keys were kept in the locks on the inside, two of which were usually kept locked during the day, and a front door which was fitted with a Yale lock and an unused deadlock. The rear doors were observable from William Murfitt's office and also from other vantage points at the rear, business end of the house. To the right of the front door, however, immediately inside the hallway, was the door to the dining room, and here was a sideboard on which the Fynnon salts were kept. The front door therefore seemed the most likely means of entry: this had four keys - one which Murfitt kept on a chain about him, one which Mrs Murfitt kept in her handbag, one which their son who was away at sea kept in his bedroom, and a 4th key, that was missing...

Of the four friends, each had a motive:

Mrs Elaine Browne was a 41-year-old, tall, attractive woman, who owned a fashionable boutique in Bury St Edmunds and was a friend of Mrs Murfitt. She dressed stylishly and she had caught the eye of William Murfitt

- not necessarily a difficult task. Although married to a Suffolk farmer herself, Rippon Charles Browne, who was 17 years her senior, she and William Murfitt had engaged upon an affair two years before the murder. Elaine Browne had become pregnant by him and had an abortion.

Mrs Murfitt became suspicious of the two. She wrote in her diary, which she volunteered to police, that she had hired a private detective to follow her husband - and that he had obtained proofs that the two were engaged upon an affair. But she told detectives she had only done this so that her husband would read the diary and end the affair. At length she had confronted William and he denied it - so did Elaine. Then she made an alarming suggestion to them: she said she would divorce William so the two could be together.

They were aghast at her suggestion: Elaine had no desire to break up her own home, nor William his. They confessed all and agreed to end the affair, and Mrs Murfitt rather sportingly forgave her husband and remained good friends with Elaine.

Elaine's husband, Rippon Charles Browne, clearly had a strong motive for murdering Murfitt - but he was apparently unaware of his wife's infidelity until the police investigation obliged Elaine to inform him of it. In due course he was interviewed by Chief Inspector Burt, who asked him if he had never suspected his wife and William Murfitt of having an affair. Many people in the small village of Risby appeared to know of it - had he not known of it? He told Inspector Burt that he had heard rumours but did not believe them. Was it possible that Browne had known them and yet never challenged his wife over these stories? Browne said not. Did he know and choose not to confront the situation? Or did he know and choose to do something rather deadly about it? If he did, he was good at concealing his animosity towards William Murfitt, because he and Elaine spent most of the day with Murfitt and his wife on a motor yacht at Horning on the Norfolk Broads just two days prior to the murder and all had been well between them. In any case, Burt had difficulty in seeing Browne as being the kind of man who would sneak into the Murfitt's house at night and poison the salts as a way of exacting revenge. It seemed unlikely - and there was no evidence whatsoever of this, just a strong motive, which Browne claimed did not exist prior to Murfitt's death. It all seemed a little Sicilian rather than Suffolkonian.

The remaining suspects, James Walker of Hall Farm, 300-400 yards away, and his housekeeper, Mary Chandler, quickly came sharply into focus during the investigation. James Walker had moved to Hall Farm in 1926 and no sooner had he done so than his wife Minnie died. Somewhat lonely following her death, a short time afterwards, Mary Chandler arrived to keep house for him. Soon Walker was taking his housekeeper to social events, and to neighbours' houses for dinner - naturally this raised eyebrows in a small village like Risby. It was certainly an unusual thing for a well-to-do widower to consort so openly with his housekeeper. Rumours abounded - it was said that the housekeeper did not rise before lunchtime each day, that she dressed rather fancily for a housekeeper and had too much money, and that Mr Walker seemed far too happy for a recent widower...

When police went to interview Mr Walker following the death of William Murfitt, he said he would rather a solicitor was present for the interview. That struck police as being strange. However, he did make a statement to say he had known his housekeeper since 'before his wife died in 1926.' He also said he was born in Calcutta, and was aged 60 - in Leonard Burt's view, he was an educated and intelligent man.

Police learned that William Murfitt had, earlier that year, banished Mary Chandler from his house because he had discovered her cheating at cards. But what drew their greatest interest in Hall Farm was the affair of the fur coat. It seems that 41-year-old Mary Chandler had asked William Murfitt could she go to the Newmarket Races with him in September 1937 and he had agreed. She went with him and left with him. Apparently, she won a great deal of money there too, because a few days after her return she showed Gertrude Murfitt an expensive mink coat, which she said she was selling for a friend in Scotland. Mrs Murfitt suggested she sell it to her furrier in London's Regent Street. A couple of days afterwards Mary Chandler told her that she had bought the coat herself - but that she wished to sell it still. It was something of a surprise to her to find that a housekeeper could afford to buy such an expensive coat on a housekeepers' salary. Mary Chandler went to Regent Street in due course and sold the coat receiving £120 for it - £8,000 in 2020 terms.

Meanwhile, a few miles away in Newmarket, Mrs Edith Waugh, a haughty lady whose husband trained horses, and at whose house James Walker and Mary Chandler had been visitors on a number of occasions, found that she had a mink coat missing. She was greatly upset at this because she had bought the coat herself and it was her pride and joy: she called the police and demanded imperiously that they find her coat for her. They did. It was in an exclusive furrier's shop in Regent Street,

London. It had been sold to them by a Mrs Mary Chandler.

Police questioned Mrs Chandler, who now said that she bought the mink coat off a lady she met at Newmarket whilst there with William Murfitt. She had no receipt for the coat and said it had been paid for out of her winnings on that day. She had brought the coat back to Murfitt's car in his absence and placed it on the back seat. The police interviewed Murfitt and he said Mrs Chandler had had no coat with her and when they drove back from Newmarket she had not mentioned this in the car to him. He also said she could not have placed it on the back seat before his return to the car because it had been locked. He had, he said, dropped Mrs Chandler with his chauffeur in his other car, en route, and she had not had a second fur coat with her when she changed cars. The chauffeur also gave police a statement that Mrs Chandler had not had a coat with her when she got into the car from Murfitt's Buick. In fact, all she had in her hand was a racing card, he said.

Interestingly, a front door key to Mrs Edith Waugh's house was also missing after a visit by Mary Chandler and police believed she had used this to gain entry to steal the fur coat.

Mrs Chandler was charged with the theft of the fur coat, and William Murfitt and his wife informed James Walker that they intended to tell the truth to the police. Mrs Chandler fled to Scotland; she was in a bad position because it seems she had been bound over for the theft of a fur coat in October 1924 also - and that meant an inevitable prison sentence if convicted of this further theft.

Could this have been a motive for murder? To prevent the Murfitts from giving evidence which looked set to send her to prison? James Walker said he would stand by his housekeeper and dismissed the Murfitts' evidence to police. He said he had visited his housekeeper in Scotland on 2nd April and returned on 5th April. Mary Chandler returned to Hall Farm on 19th April.

Mary Chandler was interviewed by detectives and gave the same account as James Walker. Both said they did not know about the Fynnon salts. They also hinted that they knew a great secret about Murfitt, and when separately encouraged by officers to divulge this, intimated that Murfitt had committed suicide.

Further inquiries into her background revealed Mrs Chandler to be a fanciful woman: she told numerous people that her husband had been a doctor who had died on the polo field; her father was a barrister, and her grandfather was the Earl Marshall of Scotland - she herself had been presented at Court and owned property in India. But none of this was true.

Mary Chandler was, in fact, born Mary Fernie Elizabeth Higgins in 1897 in Pitlessie in Fife, Scotland, the daughter of a coal miner. When she left school at 14 she worked for a time in a colliery herself. But she soon went into domestic service for first one family, then just a few months later, for another family in Douglas Street, Kirkcaldy - she was dismissed from this employment when they caught her stealing from them. Two years later, Mary had used credit on their account to defraud them. They were about to prosecute her when she was taken on as a nurse to a 'Lord Beckenham.' They demurred at this apparent change in her fortunes and the police dropped charges.

Mary then travelled to India with 'Lord Beckenham' - he may have been a figment of her imagination as there seems to be no trace of such a person - but in any case here she married the Managing Director of Messrs JH Chandler & Co Ltd, Chemists of Naini Tal and Husrutgunge. He was a much older man, who had a daughter. For whatever reason, the marriage quickly foundered, and Mary left India in April 1924. From here she went to live at Kingston on Thames - she received sums of money from her husband at intervals, often inventing pretexts for these, which in due course he discovered to be false. It was then, in October 1924, she was charged over the theft of a fur musquash coat valued at £96, (approximately £6,000 in 2020) for which she was fined £50 (approximately £3,000) and bound over for two years. It was not known where she was between 1924 and 1926, but, according to Mr Walker, it was December 1926, six months after his wife's death, that she went to Hall Farm as his housekeeper.

The maid at Hall Farm said that Mrs Chandler had written to her from Scotland in the previous summer of 1937 and asked her to send a bottle from the left-hand corner of a bench in the cloakroom to her. When the maid went to look, she found a bottle marked 'poison - potassium cyanide,' there. It was the only bottle in the cloakroom. She decided it could not possibly be this she wanted and wrote back to the housekeeper saying she could not find it. Mrs Chandler sent a postcard saying she would ask Mr Walker to find it for her.

A farm worker said that on two occasions in the past two years, he had destroyed wasps' nests with Mr Walker, using the same bottle described by the maid. Both Walker and Mrs Chandler denied its existence - Mrs Chandler said the bottle she had requested the maid to send her was a lotion, and then, after consulting with a solicitor in private, that it was boracic crystals - which have the advantage of resembling potassium cyanide. But as these costed three pence per four ounces, the police thought it highly unlikely that it could be worthwhile to send this by post when it was such a commonly available commodity.

The police asked James Walker again about the cyanide in front of the worker who had told them about destroying wasps' nests with his employer - now Walker 'recalled' having purchased cyanide once in 1934, twice in 1936, and once in 1937... He had not, he said, 'as far as he could recall' sent his housekeeper any cyanide in Scotland!

Police also learned that Mary Chandler had taken a cake to Quays Farm the day after Murfitt's death - they asked her why she had done this, and she said she had made it from ingredients given her by Mrs Murfitt and had meant to take it over 'on 16th May but forgot.' But the maid at Hall Farm said she had made two cakes, neither of which were from Mrs Murfitt's ingredients.

Questioning both Walker and his housekeeper convinced police that both were compulsive liars: they changed their stories at will, Walker often said one thing and then claimed not to remember, then would alter his story again. Chief Inspector Burt's view of Mrs Chandler was she was an evil woman of unbridled cunning. The more he looked at Mary Chandler, the less he liked her.

Police were also informed of a local scandal involving a betting scam: Mary Chandler had apparently placed bets on a number of horses in a race, in the names of several women in the district - including that of Elaine Browne - collecting only on the winning ticket and leaving the payment of the losing tickets to the women. When these women received bills for the failed bets, they knew nothing of them and refused to pay the bookmaker. He became wary of taking any further bets by phone and when a woman with a Scottish accent rang to place a bet, he refused it - but minutes later a woman entered the betting shop and tried to place a bet. He recognised her voice and accused her of fraud. It was, of course, Mary Chandler. She denied the accusation. He was prepared to go to the police, but James Walker begged him not to and promised to pay him £40. The betting manager received only £15 of this.

There was another unusual and suggestive peccadillo Mary Chandler had: she seemed to have a habit of being discovered in places where she shouldn't be. Gertrude Murfitt told police that on one occasion she had discovered Mary Chandler in her bedroom, and when found, Mary had simply said -

'Sorry, I rang the bell and couldn't make the maids hear. I've got a car outside and wondered if you would like to come up town with me...'

Gertrude said that this could not have been true because the doorbell battery had recently been changed. On another occasion Mrs Chandler had been at Quays Farm for supper, she excused herself at some point and was gone for a long time - so Mrs Murfitt went to find her. She found Mary Chandler in her bedroom standing beside a wardrobe... Mary Chandler said she had rung a maid for assistance, but the maid had not heard the bell. Mrs Murfitt did not believe her.

Another time Mrs Murfitt discovered some bedsheets were missing from the house following a visit from the housekeeper. Her sister, Mrs Kate Ruston, entertained James Walker and Mary Chandler - Mrs Chandler excused herself at some point and was subsequently found by Mrs

Ruston in an upstairs bedroom. Mrs Chandler said she was looking for a needle and thread to mend a ladder in her stocking. Afterwards, a nightdress was found to be missing. Another time Mrs Ruston discovered £5 was missing from her handbag after Mrs Chandler had been alone with it in the dining room.

Numerous other thefts were associated with Mary Chandler, too - including an ermine coat from the Farmers' Benevolent Ball in February 1937, which a maid at Hall Farm said she had subsequently seen in Mrs Chandler's wardrobe. A lady's handbag had gone missing from a cafe in Bury St Edmunds during a visit by Mary Chandler; the daughter of a couple Mary Chandler had visited found money missing from her handbag, and the husband had, disconcertingly, discovered Mary Chandler at his desk during her visit, which she accounted for by saying that she 'wanted to write a letter.' Mrs Elaine Browne had lost an evening dress; Mrs Murfitt a gold lighter, and subsequently saw Mary Chandler with an identical one - and a local Golf Club suspected her of several thefts: there seemed to be no end to Mary Chandler's larcenous activities. But there was an even more suggestive incident - that of the fire at Hall Farm.

Every year, James Walker's wealthy mother came to stay with her son for three months. Mary Chandler did not get on with her and there was clearly a mutual dislike between the two women. Mary left on the occasion of one of these visits, refusing to be in the same house as her employer's mother. Mrs Walker was in the habit of buying her son a new car every couple of years or so and on one such occasion Mary had refused to accompany mother and son when they went to buy a car. James returned from this shopping trip with a brand-new

Triumph sports car. Mary Chandler told a neighbouring couple that she hated the car; that she loathed everything about it. They then reported to James Walker and his mother that they had seen the housekeeper slashing the tyres with a pair of scissors. The next day the car had mechanical problems and had, according to the garage, been tampered with; the nuts on the wheels were also found to have been loosened. After this, the car was left in the garage at Hall Farm.

Then one evening the fire brigade was called to Hall Farm - it seems the garage had caught fire and destroyed the garage and the new Triumph car it housed. On being told of the fault with the car on a previous occasion, the fire brigade determined that it had been caused by 'faulty wiring' in the car. The insurance company paid out £200 to James Walker for his loss, but insurance officials told police there was disquiet over this.

Concerning the murder at Quays Farm, detectives Burt and Spooner learned that Mary Chandler was seen by two witnesses - the chauffeur and a maid - outside the Farm four days before the murder on the evening of 12th May. When asked about this, she denied it.

The inquest into the death of William Murfitt under the Bury St Edmunds Coroner Thomas Wilson, was opened and adjourned the day after Murfitt's death, and his funeral took place on 20th May. The inquest was tricky for Thomas Wilson, because the trial concerning the theft of the fur coat was impending. The outcome of this case would clearly impact on any case against Chandler in respect of the murder of William Murfitt, because it would furnish motive. If she was acquitted, then a mainstay of the prosecution case against Mary Chandler for the murder would disappear. The inquest was thus delayed to allow the fur coat case to run to completion.

In this regard, Mary Chandler appeared before the justices at Newmarket Petty Sessions on 16th June 1938.

There were two charges against her: the first was of theft of the fur coat from the home of Mrs Waugh; the second was of receiving stolen goods. There was sufficient evidence for the theft of the mink coat - Mary Chandler had, quite obviously stolen it and her story of buying it from an unknown lady at Newmarket races, was clearly a fabrication, rebutted by Murfitt's evidence that he had locked the car at Newmarket so she could not have put the coat in there as she claimed; and by the fact she had neither spoken of it to him on the return journey; nor removed it from the car when she changed cars. But with Murfitt's death his evidence could not now be heard: the larceny charge was dismissed, but Mary Chandler was committed for trial for receiving stolen goods. The receiving charge still stood, and although weakened by the absence of Murfitt's evidence, the prosecution looked likely to succeed because it could be proved that she was in possession of a stolen coat and could offer no reasonable account of how this was so. But it wasn't enough: Mary Chandler was acquitted on this charge also. Police were surprised, especially as both James Walker and his housekeeper had performed badly under cross-examination. It was a blow not just to the detectives who had brought the case of the theft against Mary Chandler - but to Burt and Spooner. A major plank of their case against Mary Chandler, by which they were hoping to establish motive at the inquest, was swept aside. Police noted that had Mrs Murfitt also died, no prosecution would have been attempted in respect of the fur coat at all. As it was, the absence of Murfitt's testimony had caused the prosecution to fail.

The Inquest into Murfitt's death resumed on 24th June. A carefully briefed coroner did his best to place the facts of the murder and the suspected role of Mary Chandler in this under maximum scrutiny:

Coroner: Were you in Mrs Murfitt's house or on his premises...between 8 o'clock in the Monday morning and 9 o'clock on the Tuesday morning 17th May 1938 when Mr Murfitt died?

Mary Chandler: Never.

Coroner: Was the Hall Farm farmer, so far as you know?

Mary Chandler: No.

Coroner: Can you say he could not have been there without your knowledge?

Mary Chandler: He could have been there.

Coroner: Could you have been there without his knowledge?

Mary Chandler: No, because I was in bed.

Coroner: I don't understand. Why does the fact you were in bed make it impossible for you to be out without the farmer's knowledge?

Mary Chandler: He knew I was in bed when he went out and I was still in bed at lunch time.

Coroner: Well...could you have got up and gone out, or he got up and gone out, without each other's knowledge?

Mary Chandler: No.

Coroner: Why not?

Mary Chandler: Because we were in each other's rooms.

Coroner: 'We were in each other's rooms'?

Mary Chandler: I mean he was in my room.

Eventually:

Coroner: So it really comes to this, neither the farmer can say what you were doing on Monday morning, nor can you say what the farmer was doing...Is that right?

Mary Chandler: Yes.

Coroner: And the same applies to the afternoon?

Mary Chandler: Yes.

And concerning the night:

Coroner: Were you sleeping in the same bed?

Mary Chandler: Yes.

Mary Chandler was keen to establish an alibi for the night, not the previous morning or afternoon - the police believed this was because she knew that was when the poison had been introduced to the salts.

The inquest was adjourned until 21st July 1938 to give police more time to carry out inquiries.

Under apparent great mental strain, James Walker went to see Chief Inspector Leonard Burt on 7th July. He had split up with Mary Chandler he told them, he had been a fool and wanted to be open and frank - but he told detectives nothing further, and remained obscure concerning the cyanide and other matters pertaining to the murder. He was careful to tell them he had asked the housekeeper to leave the house, was concerned she might take her own life... He seemed to be hedging his bets.

Mary Chandler saw her solicitor and then went into a nursing home in Cambridge that same day.

The police went to see Walker five days later, on 12th July, hoping that now Chandler had gone he might be more forthcoming - he said he was a fool and had been blind, but he gave no further useful intelligence on anything at all. Police began to treat him rather cautiously - they knew him to be a very intelligent man, and an unmitigated liar. The police thought it incredible that a man of the farmer's intelligence could be deceived by the woman. They simply did not believe him.

On 21st July the inquest resumed: the coroner noted Walker and Mary Chandler had been unreliable witnesses, and also noted Chandler's acquittal over the fur coat. It was all somewhat disappointing. The jury was absent for 30 minutes before giving its verdict of 'murder by a person or persons unknown.'

Mary Chandler was not named. It was a victory of sorts for her.

Burt did everything he could to find new evidence: he even walked from Hall Farm to Quays Farm at night to see if it could be done without being seen. He recorded that it had taken him 10 minutes round trip, and that he was seen by no-one. He interviewed Walker and re-interviewed him, but he said nothing which incriminated Mary Chandler. Throughout, Walker's main interest seemed to be in ensuring that he did not himself go to prison by proving an accessory after the fact.

For Chief Inspector Burt there was nowhere left to go. The investigation had failed and he and Sergeant Spooner returned to London.

The case failed for three reasons: 1) lack of evidence: there was nothing to prove that Mary Chandler had been at Quays Farm between 8 pm and 8 am on 16th and 17th May - the crucial window of opportunity at which the killer must have entered the house and added cyanide to the salts. There was a great deal of anecdotal evidence to support the theory, but without a proof of her being there, it amounted to nothing more than a reasonable suspicion.

2) There were a number of other people who had motive sufficient to murder William Murfitt: Mrs Murfitt resented her husband's affairs, and therefore might wish to exact her revenge on him. In addition, she had given him the cyanide in the salts, abstaining from taking any herself. Mr Browne surely must have known of his wife's affair with Murfitt - if the whole village knew and he admitted to having heard such rumours - had he really not taken steps to verify them? If he did know, his

own motive was a powerful one indeed - and he knew the habits of the Murfitts, could easily have taken steps to procure the missing key. Elaine Browne too, jilted by Murfitt, jealous of his other affairs, may have wished to prevent her husband from finding out about Murfitt - the fact that he learned of this as a consequence of Murfitt's death could have been an unforeseen consequence. And there were surely other men, whose wives had succumbed to Murfitt's ebullient charm: too many suspects had the effect of removing the focus from the most probable one. A jury would very quickly be distracted by such possibilities by an adept lawyer.

3) The third reason for the failure of the case was the support given by Walker to the chief suspect Mary Chandler. Much of the anecdotal evidence could have been supported by him, had he so wished; he tacked in the course of his evidence outrageously, and yet its effect was to undermine the case against Mary Chandler.

It was surely Mary Chandler who killed William Murfitt. She was a cunning and spiteful woman. She was a woman who would slash the tyres of her lover, and sabotage the car rendering it dangerous to drive; and ultimately was prepared to burn the garage and car to the ground to remove the object of her annoyance. Although the motive for Mary Chandler to commit murder was lightweight, for her it was sufficient motive. She was slighted by the cheating accusation. She feared the testimony of the Murfitts concerning the fur coat, which would probably have sent her to jail; and moreover, she resented their willingness to give such testimony against her, additional to their previous offence of accusing her of cheating and ostracising her.

She was an ingenious woman; endlessly inventive

and drawn to criminality in all its manifestations, often merely for the sake of it. And more than this she had astonishing nerve. She had what Burt characterised as 'effrontery.'

When police spoke to Mary Chandler's mother in Scotland during the course of their investigations, she told them that Mary had fallen on her head as a child and was 'not right again' afterwards. Perhaps this may offer an explanation for her behaviour.

James Walker was a weak man; in thrall to her and an accessory after the fact. He found Mary Chandler exciting - he thrilled to her ingenuity, her lack of fear; and the complete absence of anything moral in her make-up. He lacked her nerve, her criminal resolution - and he had the natural fear all normal people have when confronted by the police. He was stressed to the point of collapse when interviewed; on one occasion, prostrate, according to Burt, eyes closed, under great mental strain. They were soul mates of a kind. Perhaps the two fell out because he could not stand the stress he was under as a result of the inquiry. He did what he could to extricate himself from police pressure - distancing himself from Mary Chandler - but he could bring himself to go no further; he did not incriminate her and it may be that the split between them was contrived. Walker visited police ostensibly to come clean, but the sole information he imparted was that he had split up with Mary Chandler and she was suicidal; she consulted solicitors and promptly entered a nursing home that same day. They were such a devious pair nothing can be ruled out in their case.

Mary Chandler had had enough of the Murfitts by May 1938. and she needed to remove them just as she had the Triumph sports car. She had the missing key; just as she had almost certainly stolen the key of Mrs Waugh's house for the purpose of stealing her fur coat. She probably stole the key from the Murfitts' at an earlier date simply with the intention of perpetrating a robbery in the future. It is simply a likelihood based on her previous form, and on the congruity of events which suggest this. She walked under cover of the darkness that evening from Hall Farm: she was seen by two people four days earlier: on that occasion it may have been, as Burt suspected, a reconnaissance mission - or it could have been that she intended to poison Murffitt and his wife on that occasion but was thwarted by being seen. She would prefer the twilight as there would be some visibility to make her way down the unlit lane or across the adjacent field; the morning light would not be her friend for the journey, because farmers rise early. She did it with her customary nerve - that effrontery which had served her so well over the years, and which had brought her to the verge of ruin, had now brought her to murder.

This enterprise was one requiring the greatest nerve of all. She had an excuse at the ready, she always did; when she was caught somewhere she shouldn't be, caught almost in the very act of theft, she explained it with the most trifling, the most improbable of excuses - it didn't matter that she was not believed only that she had an explanation which could not be disproved. She had such effrontery. Her lies were preposterous; only a fool would believe them. She did not flounder or stammer as she delivered the improbable excuse to Mrs Murfitt's sister, 'I was looking for a needle and thread,' her eyes were not darkened with guilt, averting those of her inquisitor. She greeted them with the supreme confidence of the conman, of the magician, of the pathological liar, her gaze unfaltering: 'I was looking for a needle and thread; I seem to have a ladder in my stocking.'

On the occasion of the murder she was ready too - perhaps she had a cake with her or something she wanted to drop off with her neighbour. Perhaps it was a make-peace on account of the soured relations of late. Whatever it was, she was prepared. She went to the house on 12th May but she was seen by two people, the maid and chauffeur separately. She had no reason for being there. But she needed only to deny it. It was sufficient. It was merely suggestive to the police, it didn't amount to evidence. Of course, it meant she could not go through with her plan.

Mary had in her possession that night the bottle of cyanide - probably the one seen in the cloakroom by the maid. But it didn't have to be because there was a surfeit of cyanide in Suffolk in 1938. Her purpose was clear: she was going to kill the Murfitts. And she would do it by the same means by which she undertook all her dishonest undertakings: by stealth and by casual effrontery. She walked the 300-400 yards to Quays Farm on the evening of 16th May 1938. The sun set at 8.46 pm; after 9 pm Risby was dark and deserted. Had she been observed it would have been necessary to abort the enterprise a second time. But this time she arrived at the front door unseen, and she unlocked the door and entered.

It would seem to a normal person to be dangerous and incriminating to be caught inside a locked house and in the evening at twilight, after being banished from the house: it was reckless, but that was the secret of her success. Like a magician, only hesitation and guilt would betray her, and she did not possess these adversaries to enterprise. Mary Chandler would have been ready with an unfaltering explanation: *the key was in the door she had thought it odd and came in to check...she found it lying in the road outside and she thought not to disturb anyone - here is a lovely cake I made for you.*

Only Mary Chandler knew what was in her mind: if caught before the salts were laced with cyanide she could always abandon it - she had abandoned thefts on many occasions when almost caught. If Mrs Murfitt or anyone else were uncomfortable, disconcerted by her presence, what did their suspicion amount to? Could they call the police and tell them that their neighbour had entered the property and left a cake with them? The sheer nerve of Mary Chandler outwitted normal people because it defied normal behaviour.

In any case, Mary Chandler was not seen entering the house and she turned right into the dining room and without any difficulty located the salts on the sideboard where they always were, and she poured in the grains of cyanide, and left the house by the same means. She returned to Hall Farm.

What did Walker know of this? He knew of it. Mrs Chandler revelled in all things illicit - she was a most thrilling companion for Mr Walker. She dared what others would not; to do the things with equanimity that caused them to falter.

Walker knew that she had murdered Murfitt - if he had not known of it beforehand then he certainly did after its commission: he was an accessory after the fact but quite probably before it also. He was with her during countless thefts - when fur coats, ermine, no less, materialised magically in her possession; gold lighters, money, jewels; she requested a bottle of cyanide of him. He knew better than anyone her inexplicable, but timely absences during dinner at other houses, he knew she had slashed the tyres of the car he drove his mother in, knew she had interfered with the mechanics, and of course, knew she had burnt the garage to the ground and the car with it. He had no qualms about claiming the insurance on this and other property. He knew she had stolen Mrs Waugh's fur coat, and he knew a great deal more than the police and others ever discovered. And before William Murfitt's murder, when being questioned about the fur coat, he said to detectives:

'Mark my words, both of you. Before this case is over there will be another strange coincidence and there won't be any collusion.'

He had known there would be a murder: Mary Chandler was already aggrieved over the cheating accusation and her banishment from the Murfitts', from all other society in the area as a result; from the rumours now spreading openly about her. She was a spiteful and vindictive woman: there would be a reckoning. He knew this because he knew Mary Chandler, as no-one else did. And he had something dark in his own character - a deep dishonesty at least - and probably much more. 'Remember,' he said to a startled Mrs Murfitt, tapping her on the shoulder significantly, the day of her husband's death, 'We never let our friends down...'

As for Mary, she had no such difficulty with detectives - she lied with confidence and ease; the practised liar does not blink to an honest man. At the inquest her solicitor asked the coroner if Mary Chandler might be excused due to her incapacitation in a nursing home. The coroner remarked acidly, that she had been known to have left the hospital in the past few days and so she could remain for the inquest. In the event she was not called.

The police pinned their hopes on Walker - they thought he might have feared being himself exposed by his involvement in her 'other depredations.' It was a reasonable supposition that he had been involved in Mary's thefts in some capacity - he was not merely her defender, he was her confederate.

Of course, none of this could ever be used in evidence against Mary Chandler, it was merely anecdotal evidence which the police could use privately to obtain a full picture of their suspect. And therein lay a problem for the police: Mary Chandler had motive, she fitted the bill perfectly from several points of view, but there was no proof at all - and certainly nothing which could be brought before a court of law in a murder case. She may have had a grudge against the Murfitts; she may have obtained a key; she may have obtained cyanide from Hall Farm; she may have known of the Murfitts' habits of taking Fynnon salts each morning - and she may have entered the house on 16th of May and added cyanide to the salts. But there was no proof whatsoever that this is what occurred. And the proof required by a court of law is not of reasonable suspicion; but of conviction beyond a reasonable doubt. That standard of proof was not met. All that was required to pull these threads together was for Mary Chandler to have been seen entering Quays Farm - but no-one had seen her.

There is a final possibility which might explain the curious relationship existing between Walker and Chandler: this concerns the matter of his wife Minnie Walker's death in June 1926. Mary Chandler's arrival as housekeeper occurred six months after this event. The police looked at this because Walker's first wife's family had grave suspicions concerning her death. She died of cerebral haemorrhage and Raynaud's disease. The symptoms were vague and ambiguous. The local doctor wrote out a death certificate and gave Minnie's cause of death on the descriptions of symptoms given by her husband. There was no post-mortem and no inquest. Minnie was 47 years old at the time and in good health. The way in which the death had been dealt with was clearly unsatisfactory. But it was now 12 years on - there was no prospect of finding poison in a body in 1938 after such a lapse of time - and the doctor concerned was now dead.

Police could find no evidence of Mary Chandler's whereabouts during 1926, nor could they find any evidence that she had been at the farm prior to December 1926. The only reason for demurring was that Walker in his various accounts of his relationship with Mrs Chandler, had said he had known Mary Chandler 20 years, 15 years and 10 years respectively before settling on the convenient date of December 1926. There was nothing to contradict this. In spite of the family's misgivings concerning Minnie's death, there was nothing that could be done about it.

It gives rise to a surmise, and if it is a wild one, then that is because the circumstances invite it, that Mary Chandler or James Walker, or both, killed Minnie Walker in June 1926. The vague symptoms, the untimeliness, the after events and the character of those involved suggest it merely. There is little else to recommend it without further proofs. Its advantage to me is that it offers a psychological affirmative of the candid and amoral relationship that subsisted in this pair. A relationship founded on a kind of anti-social glee: a united front against society, founded in its breach of taboos.

When the inquest returned a verdict of murder against an unknown person it was as good as an acquittal for Mary Chandler. The police still had a murder on its hands, albeit one which they had already investigated to exhaustion. Without fresh evidence, the suspicion of police - and the public - would remain fixed on Mary Chandler, but beyond that there really was nothing further that could be done. War was coming, resources were required elsewhere; the police force would be pared to the bone by the need for manpower resources in countering the subversions that become a society's priority during time of war.

Mrs Murfitt, distraught initially at her husband's death, seemed quickly to arrive at a point of apathy, perhaps it was depression - he was in truth no saint. Murfitt left his wife £23,000 in his will (£1.5 million in 2020). A sale of the farm livestock and machinery realised £1,600 on 10th June: Mrs Murfitt was certainly a wealthy woman afterwards but she chose to live modestly. She went to live with her sister, Kate Ruston, at 10 North Brink, Wisbech for a while, and then lived at 13 All Saints Road, Ipswich, and it was here she lived until 1973 when she died. Mrs Elaine Brown, Murfitt's paramour, whose affair caused Mrs Murfitt and her husband Rippon Browne such distress in 1938, and brought titillation and disapprobation in equal measure to the residents of Risby, never really recovered from the scandal. She aged quickly and died in 1947 at the age of 51.

James Walker was finished in Risby. He sold up and left Hall Farm. But within a few months, he had reunited quietly with Mary Chandler, now calling herself Fernie and the two set up home together in Horley in Surrey, as

Mr and Mrs Laing-Walker. They ran the *Cambridge Hotel* in Gatwick for a time, and then retired in the 1960s to a house at St Leonard-on-sea near Hastings, Sussex. James Walker died at the age of 91 in 1971 and Mary Laing-Walker continued in the house, still fond of baking cakes, unknown in her community, except for being a rather eccentric elderly woman and a teller of tall-tales involving herself and her elevated status. She died here on August 19th, 1994, at the age of 97 leaving £660,000 to her niece. She was cremated at Hastings Cemetery a few days later on 2nd September.

William Murfitt.

Mrs Murfitt.

Elaine Browne.

Quay's Farm.

Elaine Browne, Murfitt and his wife (right).

Mrs Mary Chandler.

Inspector Leonard Burt.

Ripon Browne - did he know he was a cuckold?

The murderer was one of five: Mrs Murfitt, Ripon Browne, Elaine Brown, Walker, and Mrs Chandler - but which one?

Edith Waugh - her fur coat seems to have been at the core of the mystery.

Printed in Great Britain
by Amazon

48045310R00165